I. Joseph Kellerman

a novel by
Debra Lauman

I. Joseph Kellerman
Copyright © 2003 by Debra Lauman

Fiction

ISBN trade paperback: 0-9729304-9-3

All rights reserved. No part of this book may be reproduced or transmitted in any form or by any means, electronic or mechanical, including photocopying, recording, or by any information storage and retrieval system, without the written permission of the publisher, except in the case of brief quotations embodied in critical articles or book reviews.

This book was printed in the United States.

For inquiries or to order additional copies of this book, contact:

Gardenia Press
P. O. Box 18601
Milwaukee, WI 53218-0601USA
1-866-861-9443 www.gardeniapress.com
orders@gardeniapress.com

To Steve, for welcoming these characters into our home.

Chapter 1

Once upon a time, there was a boy named Isaac in a cattle car. The moans of the sick and the stench were making his stomach hurt, almost as much as the question lodged in his mind.

Is it *my* fault we're here?

Yesterday, as he walked on the street with Lila Stein and her daughter, Ellie, Isaac stuck his tongue out at a soldier. The same soldier who, with a rifle, pushed Papa onto this train. At first, the boy had smiled at the uniformed man, but hostile eyes glared back, sending a chill up Isaac's spine. Then and now.

Yes, he decided, as the pain tore into his middle. This is my fault, too!

Isaac's whole body began to tremble, harder and faster than the train. He felt Lila's arm slip through his, and his trembling stopped. Turning his head, he nuzzled Ellie's mama's hair, as the two Steins and two Kellermanns huddled silently, together. Waiting.

***

Forty-nine years later, there was a man in a chair in a building, with a name and occupation on a shingle next to the front door. The door was heavy and gray, the shingle, brass. Engraved on the shingle was "I. Joseph Kellerman," and he was a psychiatrist. The chair was in Dr. Kellerman's office on the first floor of the building, a row house on Hopewell Street in Boston. This was an old chair, its yellow Jacquard fabric worn thin on the seat, with armrests soiled from years of use by thousands of people. A few feet in front of the dingy armchair was the doctor's large desk and, on a corner of the desk, an alarm clock radio. At 12:12 on a Monday afternoon, the numbers on the clock faded with cigarette smoke as a vision faded in. Today, the midday session had taken twelve minutes to begin. Two minutes earlier than on Friday.

The man sitting in the yellow chair knew he was about to watch a series of familiar scenes from long ago, yet they always felt so *now*. At times confusing and disjointed, these scenes were more real to the reluctant observer than most anything in the present. He could see and hear them so clearly. He could smell them, and feel them on his skin, and sometimes taste them. Though they were someone else's memories.

At least, it was much easier for him to think of them that way.

So, through the cigarette smoke, there appeared a familiar boy. As usual, the boy didn't move straight off. He just stood there in the midst of nothing, expressionless and silent, staring back at the stranger in the armchair. The man knew the boy was ten, born in Austria on February 21, 1934. The man knew the boy so well, he could read his mind as if it were his own.

Next, from nothing, a room appeared around the boy. A dreary room. No pictures, no frills, and not much else. The man in the yellow chair was also in that room, and suddenly he heard a familiar voice. The words were in German.

"*Geht's dir gut, Isaac?*"

The boy turned to look up at his father, and the first scene began.

Isaac shakes his head. No, he's not okay, he's still terribly hungry. "Erzaehl mir nochmal das Rapunzel *Maerchen," he pleads, clasping his hands and dropping to his knees, right onto Papa's feet. But the boy's eyes alone convey the urgency to the man with his chin to chest, staring into them.*

Mama and Rosa set down the bowls and rags. Cleaning can wait; the girls need a fairy tale as much as Isaac does. And no one

I. Joseph Kellerman

tells a story better than Papa.

Jakob Kellermann was a protective and affectionate father, not the least bit aloof or apathetic. He had a gift for making troubled people laugh and the worst circumstances bearable. And there was Anna, elegant and graceful no matter how crude the conditions. Her touch was the ultimate comfort to the two children and adoring man, who called her Mama. Rosa Mari was a compassionate sister, always a willing playmate to her younger sibling, Mama's helper and Papa's pretty girl. She was tenacious and spunky.

That's how the man in the yellow chair pictured them. Papa, Mama and Rosa were Isaac's family, his entire world. As long as they were together, his world was intact and secure.

"Alles für das Geburtstagskind," Papa replies, grinning through his beard. Anything for the birthday boy. With an exaggerated groan, he lifts his son, swinging him in a circle before sitting and placing Isaac on his knee.

The child slips a gentle hand behind his father's neck, tugging on one of Papa's earlobes with the other. Mama rests her head on Rosa's as they sit arm-in-arm beside Papa at the end of the bed. The last fragments of the bench are smoldering in the stove, having been sacrificed to boil potatoes — the main and only course—warming numbed fingers and feet in the process.

"Bist du bereit?" Papa asks with a light nudge.

Rosa responds with a sideways glance of grownup irritation.

What a rascal he is, of course she's ready.

"Auch bereit, Mama?"

"Erzaehl mal!

Mama always looks at Papa like that, with an affectionate gleam in her eyes, even when she scolds him. But her unconvincing frown only makes the storyteller more wonderfully aggravating. All eyebrows rise in anticipation as Papa inhales. With wide eyes and puffed cheeks, he holds his breath.

"Pa-p-a-a-a," *the impatient trio harmonizes as they often do.*

The words that follow the long exhale sound like poetry. "Es war einmal ein Mann und eine Frau." The tale begins with husband and wife as it always does. Where the story will go from there, however, none of them knows for sure. Not even Papa. The plot changes with each retelling, but the theme remains constant.

Mama closes her eyes and listens. Such long lashes she has, and a tiny mole below the left corner of her mouth. A subtle indentation at the tip of her nose. Lips, slightly smiling.

Rosa closes her eyes. She too has long lashes and a mole below the left corner of her mouth. Rosa is a smaller version of Mama, except for her hair.

Isaac concentrates on his father's words of fantasy and each of those three familiar faces. Yes, he thinks, this is how it's supposed to be.

Although, that wasn't exactly how it had been. That was a snapshot taken by an eight year-old boy's eyes, capturing only what he needed to hold onto. Once again, the man in the yellow chair filled in the gap and missing pieces. Two years and two faces. But despite the harsh reality beyond what Isaac, the ten year-old and the now fifty-nine year-old man, chose to see, that had not been an uncommon scene in the Kellermann home, wherever the family might have been at any given time. "Home" no longer had a connection to anything but each other.

When Papa's body shakes with laughter at his own silliness, Isaac throws back his head and howls. The girls laugh too, and tears wet Mama's cheeks.

Jakob Kellermann always diluted a fairy tale's sober events with humor and new details from his own imagination, adlibbing with comic voices and facial twists, creating continual surprises and breaks for *ein paar Gekicher,* a few giggles, as

I. Joseph Kellerman

Anna would say.

But those stories were more than fun, they were also temporary distractions. The Kellermanns' hunger was often most severe just after they finished their rations. Despite the food smuggled into the ghetto, there was never enough to eat. Especially for a big, tall man or a growing boy.

At one time, Jakob had been a successful and substantial baker who sampled many of his own creations. That is, until the Third Reich took his livelihood, along with most of his worldly possessions and a considerable amount of his weight. What they were unable to rob him of, though, was his dignity, his stubborn optimism and, without a doubt, his wit.

Those were the qualities Anna Schmitz was attracted to when she met the strapping, six-foot-four gentleman at his shop in Vienna. Jakob's heart had been likewise captured by the fair-haired beauty the moment he looked up from the dough he was poking fun at and saw her watching him — hands on her hips, her head shaking, and an expression of tender amusement she couldn't conceal, no matter how she frowned and contorted her lips.

Several months later, Anna accepted Jakob's proposal on the condition that she receive a free lifetime supply of his strudel. She loved him more than she could say, and the feeling was mutual. They married in the summer of 1929.

Jakob and Anna Kellermann were best friends and passionate souls. Not a day went by that they didn't make each other smile in spite of the callous world closing in around them. Together, they remained happy and hopeful through the births of their two children. Together, they remained cheerful and enthusiastic, though they lost their business, their home and their country. And they remained together until hatred and evil finally succeeded in tearing the Kellermanns apart. That happened on February 21, 1944. Isaac Josef's tenth birthday.

Such was how the man in the yellow chair thought of it nearly half a century later. He shifted in his seat, tapped the ashes from his cigarette, and prepared to observe Isaac relive the rest of a somewhat altered version of that day yet again. As much as he would have preferred to, there was nothing he could do to avoid the memories. And he knew he shouldn't. That's why he was sitting in the yellow chair instead of the one on other side of the desk.

After a quick inhale and puff of cigarette smoke, the next scene began.

More of a bang than a knock, a hard object rapped against the door, brings the storytelling to a stop. The youngest Kellermann can't see who's outside. He sees only the worry on Mama's face when she closes the door seconds after opening it barely a hand's width.

The boy on his father's knee was not oblivious to the other world beyond that room, but he comprehended little of it. What he did understand and could never ignore were the emotions of his family. He could sometimes see fear on those three familiar faces or hear it in the inflection of simple words. And he could always feel the fear deep inside, even when they were laughing.

"What is it, Mama?" Papa asks.
The boy studies his mother's eyes. She doesn't blink and seems to be looking through Papa and him. That's not like Mama.
"We're to join the next transport," she says.
Mama's unhappy.
"Immediately," she adds, clenching her teeth.

That wasn't the first time such an order had come by way of a rap on the door, nor was it a surprise. During the last few weeks, people had been taken away in large numbers. They hadn't returned.

Papa's body stiffens. Isaac turns to look at his father's face, inches

I. Joseph Kellerman

from his own.
Papa's covered with blood!

The man in the yellow chair caught his breath. Time occasionally folded back on itself in these scenes, sometimes forward, like double exposures. He blinked hard to rewind.

Papa's body stiffens. Isaac turns to look at his father, but the rage in Papa's eyes makes the boy very uneasy. He stares instead at ...the waltzing couple.

The man in the yellow chair shook his head. No, he told himself, stay focused. Concentrate on your work.

Isaac stares at the glowing coals in the open stove, as Papa sets him on his feet and Mama puts him into his coat, one wilted arm then the other. Three Kellermanns rush around the fourth and the room, grabbing what they can of what little they have left.
Minutes later, a soothing mother holds a bag and her protesting daughter's hand as they leave the building. A reassuring father with a suitcase guides his bewildered son, a big hand on a drooped shoulder, into the cold chaos.

The man in the yellow armchair followed.

Engulfed by the mass of exiles, the Kellermanns move closer to the line of cattle cars. The air is filled with loud pops and bangs, barking, shouting, and the hiss of a steam engine. People not bound for the train taunt the innocent and defenseless, who stare at a figure in an impeccable uniform. Shiny boots on stiff, spread legs. A slanted smile on a wicked face as the monster watches their removal with pleasure.
Papa is shoved from behind, and Isaac looks back, along the barrel of a gun, up shiny buttons on another military coat and through

thick lenses into the hostile eyes of a little man. He knows where he's seen those eyes before.

Two big hands lift the stunned child onto the train.

Despite years of forced labor, Jakob Kellermann was still quite strong compared to most other malnourished men, especially when it came to his family. And though tall for a ten year-old, Isaac wasn't as heavy as he should have been. But his height had been an asset. That's why they'd believed Anna when she told them her son was eleven, when he was only eight. That's why Isaac hadn't been taken from his family, while so many other children had been separated from theirs. Too young or too old, unfit to work. Gone.

Isaac Josef worked very hard.

Inside the car, the sound of misery overwhelms the boy. Then he sees Mama. Her back is pressed to the corner, her arms around Rosa, whose face is buried in Mama's coat. But Mama isn't crying. There's not a hint of emotion amongst her features, not even in those intense blue eyes. Isaac has never seen his mother so unresponsive, but he can feel her fear as if it were his own. Then he too is afraid. He and Papa maneuver closer to the girls, as the compartment fills beyond any possibility of comfort.

Swoosh-bang! The door is closed.

Bang! The bolt is thrown.

More swoosh-bangs and bangs down the line, as they stand and wait.

Day is like dusk in the windowless compartment. The openings are cracks between boards, and barred slots only very tall adults are able to reach. In this car, that means only Papa. The air inside is thick with the smell of breath and bodies, and the bodily functions of those who came and went before, the latter soaked into the straw the current captives are standing on.

Isaac looks up at the underside of his father's beard, breathing in time with the body he's leaning against. Inhale and hold ... exhale, as Papa does. Inhale and hold ... exhale. Thirty-eight controlled

I. Joseph Kellerman

breaths through his mouth until a steamy whistle sounds. The train lurches and the clacking begins.

Soon the cramped cell shakes the resolve from even the most resistant hostages. The Kellermanns lower themselves as Papa's broad back slides down the wall, his knees to his shoulders, his feet on either side of his wife and son. Isaac bends his arm to touch Mama's hair. There isn't another person in this car with hair like hers. Rosa's is wavy, the color of gingerbread like her brother's. Papa's is a mass of curls almost as coarse as his beard and black as molasses.

"Keine Angst, Mama," Isaac reassures her. "Es ist alles nicht echt." This isn't real.

As night seeps in, he watches the light fade on Mama's face, but her expression never changes, her eyes fixed on some other place and time.

Rosa had lifted her head out of Mama's coat to settle with difficulty on the straw. Flanked by maternal legs, she'd twisted this way and that, then turned to the side wall, her head tipped almost horizontal as she put her face to a sliver of cold daylight. She hasn't moved since.

The man in the yellow chair extended his legs, his arms and fingers, his neck. His body was aching all over. He exchanged his exhausted cigarette for a fresh one, then sat back to observe the next scene. He couldn't see a thing but knew what was happening.

When the sun is replaced by stars and a three-quarter moon, Isaac can see the glow and glitter only when he presses his palms against his eyelids. Outside, the air is crisp and clear, but the boy in the cattle car can scarcely breathe. The moans of the sick and the stench are making his stomach hurt, almost as much as the question lodged in his mind.

Is it my fault we're here?

Yesterday, as he walked on the street with Mama and Rosa, Isaac stuck his tongue out at a soldier. The same soldier who, with a rifle, pushed Papa onto this train. At first, the boy had smiled at the uniformed little man, but hostile eyes glared back through thick lenses, sending a chill up Isaac's spine. Then and now.

The man in the yellow chair shivered.

Isaac's whole body begins to tremble, harder and faster than the train. He feels Mama's arm slip through his, and his trembling stops. Turning his head, Isaac nuzzles his mother's hair, as the Kellermanns huddle silently, together. Waiting.

The man in the armchair nodded off. When he opened his eyes, the next scene began.

Some time during a night that may be their third on the train, Isaac awakens when the rhythmic clacking slows to an eerie stillness. Light pierces the railway coffin, illuminating grayish-white slices of face, body and baggage. Those able to stand push and pull themselves to their feet, while others don't move at all.
Again, they wait.
"Please, we need air!" shouts a woman somewhere inside the car.
And they stand, and sit, and lie, and wait.
"Give us water!" shouts another.
And they wait and wait.
Papa speaks to someone outside the car only he can see. "Will the transport go somewhere from here?"
"Of course," the Kellermanns and many others hear a man reply. "Up and away, through the chimneys!" Laughter shoots through the cracks.
Without warning, the body Isaac has been leaning against gives way, as the desperate man unbuttons his trousers and squats. The child feels miserable and helpless at the sight of his father humiliated in front of all these people. Papa puts his head in his hands, and Isaac closes his eyes. He tries to believe, as he's told Mama many times before, this isn't real at all. Nothing is real but each other. The rest is another

I. Joseph Kellerman

sad part of the fairy tale.

This time, the car has been shaken but never moved forward. Or the train made a big circle and they can go back to their room. Or maybe, just maybe, they're returning to where the Kellermanns lived until Isaac was six. He doesn't remember much about the place, but he knows it must have been beautiful. Yes, that's where they've gone. Now he, Papa, Mama and Rosa can sit by a cozy fire and finish the story. There's always the same happy ending, whatever the path taken to get there. That's how it's supposed to be.

Isaac smiles and opens his eyes.

Bang! Swoosh-bang! The bolt is pulled and the door is thrown open.

More bangs and swoosh-bangs down the line.

"Raus! Raus!" shout menacing voices, and Isaac is pulled to the ground, onto raw, burning knees. He stands and stumbles, then stands up again. There's barking and snarling, sharp teeth bearing down in the darkness. He feels Mama's hand take his, as the blinding searchlights immobilize every sore muscle in his body.

So much noise, so much confusion, orders flying. "Leave all belongings on the train! Men here! Women there!" There's music, slapping, shoving. What's going on? Isaac feels Papa's hand take his arm, but Mama's hand is gone.

In the cold, they stand and wait, stand and wait. Isaac's pants are wet. His nose is running.

The smell of the chimney smoke is strong and sweet, nothing like crackling stove fires. No, this is a peculiar odor that makes Isaac feel ill. He doesn't understand why.

The man in the yellow chair didn't want to remember that smell. Bodies burning. He gagged, then sucked deeply on his cigarette.

The line is moving now. Who's that whistling man up ahead? And why is he smiling? He's groomed and handsome. Is he a nice man?

"Right," or "left," he says, directing with a flick of his riding crop.

Where's his horse?

"How old?" the man asks.

"Eleven," replies a father for a son who doesn't answer.

"Right," the handsome man replies, then flicks and smiles. He continues to whistle.

Isaac is getting closer to right or left.

Where's Mama? And Rosa?

"How old?" asks the man.

"Forty," replies another.

"Occupation?"

"Mason."

He's sent to the left.

"Fifty-eight, accountant," the next man answers.

He's directed to the right, with a flick and a smile.

More and more lefts and rights. The oldest ones, the youngest, the weakest—they're all going right. The whistling man smiles every time he flicks to the right.

"You're fourteen," Papa whispers to Isaac. "Stand up tall."

Whatever Papa says. Isaac pushes his shoulders back, his chest forward, and copies his father's expression. Forehead, eyebrows and lids relaxed, chin up. Eyes blank. When the boy again looks ahead, the whistling man is staring at him. He stops whistling as Isaac stops moving.

"How old?"

Isaac's mouth is dry. He's dizzy with thirst, and the sound almost doesn't come out. "Fourteen?" he says, his voice cracking.

Would anyone believe such a thing?

Up and down the man looks the boy over, hesitates, then flicks and says, "Left." Then immediately to Papa, "Left."

Is this good? The man didn't smile.

Isaac and Papa stand in another line, watching while listening

I. Joseph Kellerman   19

to dozens of questions and answers and lefts and rights.
    They're herded into a large, empty room. There are others with them, but only a fraction of those who'd been on the platform. There were many more rights than lefts. Where are all the women and girls?
    This must be some stupid game, Isaac decides. The Kellermanns will be together again soon.

    The boy and his family had lived in the one dreary room, sometimes with as many as eight other people, since being transported to the ghetto almost four years earlier in another cattle car. But that didn't matter to Isaac Josef. If he and Papa, Mama and Rosa were together, he was where he was supposed to be.

    "Remove your clothing!" a guard commands, pacing before the rows of men and boys. "Wool to the left!"
    The rest is muffled. Isaac can close his ears without using his hands. He's practiced this trick many times before. He does what the other naked people are doing, dividing and bundling his clothes, while watching the piles of shoes and spectacles swept away.
    He searches the room with his eyes. So many strangers. Where are all the other young boys? There were some on the train. Where are all the old men?
    And where's Papa?

    For a moment, the memories didn't seem like someone else's, but the man in the yellow chair corrected that.

    The gaunt shell of a human male approaches Isaac. A hand of tendons and bones beneath translucent skin grabs the boy's head, and another hand begins to shave. The new arrivals old enough to have body hair—all but Isaac—are removed of that as well, by identical ghosts in blue-and-gray-striped prison garb.
    "Dies ist alles nicht echt, dies ist alles nicht echt," Isaac repeats, clamping his eyes, then opening them as wide as he can. He doesn't

want to cry. If this is all part of a fairy tale, it's taking much too long to get to the happy ending.

Then he sees him. Like the others, Papa stands, hairless and naked, but, unlike the man and the teenager on either side of him, his chin is up. Isaac raises his own chin, and father and son look into each other's eyes from opposite ends of the room. Isaac shivers violently but keeps watching Papa. As long as he can see him, everything will be all right.

Now they're in a different room. The sheared men and boys stand for another long stretch. Locked in, ankle-deep in cold water, forbidden to speak. Waiting. At least Isaac can stand next to Papa.

If only he could hold Mama's hand.

At the sound of a bell, scalding water falls from the ceiling. As the heat pours over him, Isaac closes his eyes again and imagines himself, Papa, Mama and Rosa somewhere beautiful and peaceful. Anywhere far from this horrible place. Isaac concentrates on the scene beneath his lids and the feeling of Mama's hand in his until, once more, father and son are separated and Mama is ripped away.

A rough, tattered coat that should be worn by someone as tall as Papa and a pair of broken-down boots at least a size too small are all that Isaac is given. He's forced into the icy, blue dawn, with no chance to cover himself. Each naked body clutches a small bundle of clothing.

Yet another room, another line. Isaac watches Papa, only Papa, as they dress. Papa's blue-and-gray-striped pants are much too short. His striped shirt is missing buttons. Isaac continues watching his father, as the needles sting his left forearm.

Many days would pass before the boy first looked at the six numbers tattooed in his tender skin.

The man in the yellow chair refused to look at them.

Isaac watches as Papa is branded, too. As long as he can see him.

Once more they're driven outside, where a blow to Isaac's lower back propels him forward. He trips in those awkward boots but regains

I. Joseph Kellerman

his footing. Must keep up, keep going. Must stay strong and fit to work. Must be a man, not a boy.

But where's Papa?

Isaac panics. Frantic, he looks from one bald head and beardless face to the next. He wants to be brave, but—

"Go!" shouts one of the monsters.

Isaac turns to see his father shoved toward a group of blue-and-gray-striped forms moving in a different direction. This time, the elder Kellermann stumbles onto one knee when he's pushed.

"Papa!"

The boy didn't mean to yell like that. It just ... came out!

If only the man in the yellow chair could have reached into the past and slapped a hand over that boy's mouth. If only he could have changed places with Papa.

A father hears his child's frightened voice. "Isaac!" he shouts back.

The boy stares as the guard aims his rifle at Papa's head.

"Get up!" the monster bellows.

Papa doesn't move.

"I said, get up!"

But Papa won't obey. Again, he calls to his son, who starts towards him. Papa yells, "Come, Isaac!" and the child begins to run. Then, a mere step from the safety of his father's arms, there's a brilliant flash.

And for a second, everything stops.

What had occurred in an instant now replayed in extreme slow motion.

Isaac!

The blast combines with that final, repulsive, reprehensible word. At the same eternal moment begins a slow burst of flesh and blood. That's all the boy sees. He feels the warm flesh and blood on his hands and face. That's what he tastes in his open mouth.

Isaac!

As the boy falls into the snow, so too does Papa. One last time they stare, their faces again just inches apart. The son's eyes are suddenly almost as lifeless as the father's.

Isaac!

Papa's voice echoes, as does the crack of that gunshot.

Isaac.

The boy wants never to hear anyone call him that ever again.

But the man he'd become couldn't help but hear it, over and over, no matter how hard he tried not to.

***

At 12:58, the numbers on the clock radio faded back in. I. Joseph Kellerman sat motionless in the yellow chair and stared through the cigarette smoke, as a father's shout through almost half a century's time became the buzzing of the alarm. That sound didn't even make the grown son jump anymore.

The dazed observer looked towards the calendar on the far side of his desk. Though the light shining in his eyes and the distance prevented him from seeing the date, he'd stared at "Monday, April 12, 1993" off and on throughout the morning, while doodling faceless heads with various hairstyles all over the page. Dr. Kellerman now just needed to remind himself where he was. And when.

Instead of shutting off the alarm, the despondent man who'd once been the laughing boy on Jakob Kellermann's knee closed his eyes and leaned his head against the seatback. Seconds later, he felt her pass by, and the buzzing stopped. He heard the click-click of the floor lamp as the light dimmed beneath his lids. The smoldering cigarette was slipped from his hand, and, after the routine pause, his name,

Joseph, was spoken softly. He felt that very familiar, comforting touch on his shoulder and opened his lifeless eyes.

Chapter 2

A long puff of smoke streamed over the desk, gathered into a disorganized swirl, then dissipated, revealing the profile of the speaking man's upper half. A light pink oxford much too big for the pubescent-like body it covered. An Adam's apple about to poke a hole through a straining neck supporting a constantly moving head. What the face was lacking in chin was overcompensated for with an ample forehead and a thick lower lip. A familiar face and a nasal voice, repeating the same basic story as last Tuesday and so many Tuesdays before that. The details changed, but the plot and theme did not. Weeks had turned into months, months to years, and years into more than two decades, and still the man came. He flopped back in the yellow chair, clenched his fists, and continued in his usual, agitated tone. He spoke quickly and stumbled over his tongue.

"I know he said plac — plastic, that's what he always says. So then the guy, he says, 'I *said* I wanted paper,' and so I says, 'No, I heard you, you said plac-stic.'" The man uncrossed his skinny legs and slid further down in the chair. The typical change in his demeanor had begun. "And then he says a nasty thing to me. Can you believe that crap?"

There was no reply from the man seated eight feet away on the other side of the big desk. Just another puff of smoke.

"So I says, 'Fine! There's no need to be raisin' your voice, sir!'" the one in the yellow chair scolded, wagging a finger at a person only he could presently see. "And so I was unbaggin' all those groceries, right. Three things of Cheese Whiz, if you can believe

I. Joseph Kellerman

that crap. Pickled beets, frozen peas. All kindsa crap he prob'ly didn't even need. I mean, I seen him the day before buyin' all kindsa other crap."

The speaker's eyes narrowed as he thrust his face towards the reluctant listener and lowered his voice. "An then I dumped out the condoms. Four boxes, if you can believe that. So he gets all pissed off, right. But, I mean, who *wouldn't* laugh? I mean, *four boxes?* Man oh man. So then he says to me, he says, 'F you!'" The speaker spread his knees wider and belched. "Mother woulda washed his mouth out with bleach," he said.

At the mention of Mother, two vertical grooves appeared between the little man's eyebrows and he squeezed the arms of the chair. He was feeling angry. Very angry, as usual.

The other, much larger man could hardly stand to hear it anymore, and most of the time he managed not to. He closed his ears without using his hands, raised the cigarette to his lips, and inhaled.

Yet another puff of smoke obscured the scene.

***

There was a hole in a wall at 4991 Hopewell Street, hidden on one side by the lower right-hand corner of a painting behind the front desk. The woman sitting at that desk had simply to turn around, nudge the painting to the left, and lean forward to peer through the eye-sized opening. The man who usually sat behind the desk on the other side of the wall was oblivious to the existence of that small but sufficient portal.

So, it seemed, were all those thousands of people who'd occupied the yellow armchair during the twenty-five years that hole had existed. There were too many other things to look at and think about when sitting in the back office, on either side of the desk. And who would have noticed such an insignificant hole in that dark-paneled wall, a quarter inch above two dozen books piled next to one of three jam-packed bookcases in that extremely cluttered room? Perhaps someone in a state of mind to examine such details, but not the patients. Surely not Dr. Kellerman. If anyone *had* noticed it, that person must not have considered there might be a corresponding hole on the opposite side of the wall, in the very next room. Either that or no one who had seen it cared.

For the past twenty-three years, Constance Fairhart had been the woman who'd often watched and listened through that small hole to what was happening in the back office. She'd discovered it two years after someone else had drilled through paneling on both sides and plaster in between.

The motive behind the making and initial use of the hole was much different than the reasons for its continued service, once the former peeping secretary had deserted both that front desk and the man who, by now, had occupied the back office and lived upstairs for thirty years. While the hole was created from jealously and distrust, it was used throughout most of its existence because of interest and genuine kindness — though not without guilt where Constance Fairhart was concerned.

***

Hostile eyes glared through thick lenses and across the big desk. The doctor shivered and looked away.

"That *bitch*," spat the very nearsighted man in the yellow chair, kicking its mahogany legs with the heels of his black, ladies size six sneakers. His tale of woe had reached its vile climax. "I should chop 'er to pieces," he snarled with his end-of-the-hour, evil smirk. "And there'd be a lot of 'em, cuz Mother ain't a *skinny* whore."

Dr. Kellerman was as disgusted as ever. A wave of nausea swelled from his stomach to his throat. No! he yelled inside his head. Not now!

So many things grabbed at those unwelcome visions, not the least of which were the tirades of this disturbed little man who fantasized about revenge. The doctor rushed a Tums to his mouth, followed by the cigarette.

"Then you know what I'd do?" As the speaker drew his breath in preparation for a loud and well-timed finish, Dr. Kellerman closed his ears again. He cleared his throat at length as the man exhaled, "I'd flush her down the toilet, where she belongs!"

Those hateful words gave way to the obnoxious buzz of the alarm clock, and another puff of smoke streamed into Constance's view. Seconds later, a little man with very big troubles emerged from the back office in a much different state than when he'd entered an hour ago.

"Ay, girl," he drawled, leering at Constance. "See ya next week." He adjusted his undersized self with one hand, while roughly turning a doorknob with the other. He left the room and headed down the dim hallway. Back out to the cruel world to try to behave until next Tuesday at eleven, sharp.

Constance shook her head. How sad, she thought, as she had for so many years, each time she'd watched Bernie Babbish come and go. Maybe there *is* no hope for this one.

On the other side of the wall, Dr. Kellerman was shaking his head, too. Is there no hope, he wondered when he heard Bernie Babbish slam the waiting room door.

There was a time when Bernie, along with the rest of the hourly occupants of the yellow armchair, had seemed to Joseph more real than anyone else. But, over the years, that had changed. Now they were mere projections from the world beyond that narrow tunnel and distant front door, as through a zoom lens but warped in the process. Most of all Bernie Babbish.

No, Dr. Kellerman decided when he heard the final door slam. There's no hope.

But he wasn't thinking about Bernie.

Constance walked to the middle of the room. No, she reconsidered as she once again saw Bernie's uppermost curls pass the window. There's always hope.

***

Constance Fairhart had been Dr. I. Joseph Kellerman's secretary, although assistant was more accurate, since April 13, 1970. She was twenty-seven at the time. At fifty, she was still as loyal and committed as ever to the man she'd long respected and worked for. Yet even assistant was an inadequate description of Constance and her many years of devotion to the man whose shingle on the row house at 4991 Hopewell Street, a location he'd chosen in part because of the street name, read, "I. Joseph Kellerman, MD, Ph.D." with "PSYCHIATRIST" displayed beneath. For twenty-three years, Constance had kept the books and paid the bills, answered the phone and entertained clients — most, including the doctor, preferred that label to patient — as they sat, stood or paced in the front office, awaiting their turns to occupy the yellow chair. And that only scratched the surface of what Constance Fairhart had done for the man she sometimes called Joseph and most everyone else called just Dr. Kellerman.

Chapter 3

Marta Von Schlossberg wasn't considered pretty exactly, with an ever-present shroud of bitterness over her long face, but heads did turn when she paraded through a room. At five-eleven, her streamlined figure, accented by slick, black hair, made quite an impression. To augment her presence, Marta dressed in bold colors with makeup and high heels to match. Her presence was noticed, loud and clear.

The air of indifference and conceit surrounding Marta kept most of the eyes that followed her at a distance. With few exceptions, that's what she preferred, but the exceptions were relentlessly pursued. Daughter of a Harvard department chairman and practicing psychiatrist, Marta fixated on Daddy's "bests and brightests." *They* were her exceptions, and one of those men was a thirty-three year-old Dr. I. Joseph Kellerman.

***

"Marta, dear, come meet the guest of honor!" Wilhelm Von Schlossberg publicly insisted one late February evening in 1967, at a reception following a lecture series on behavioral and biochemical studies of lithium treatment.

Marta wanted to visit the powder room, she told her father, but Daddy had had enough of her nagging.

"Let's just get this over with," he grumbled under his breath, as they headed for the latest object of Marta's desire. With one hand gripping his only child's arm, Dr. Von Schlossberg walked up to

Joseph, who was in the midst of a private thought, and grabbed the back of his neck. "Dr. Joseph Kellerman, meet my favorite daughter, Marta."

"Oh, Daddy," she replied, conspicuously demure.

These preplanned introductions were the only occasions Marta received such attention from her father. The fact that she'd insisted on this meeting had been disregarded on the approach and, in effect, forgotten by Marta the moment the event began. As usual.

The back of a limp hand was presented to the straight-faced and startled young doctor. His head immobilized, Joseph lowered just his eyes. He looked at that hand with the deep-red, half-inch nails and figured the proper thing to do was give it a firm shake.

Marta grimaced and pulled away.

There was a considerable pause while father, daughter and unwitting suitor stared at Marta's polished claws.

She is *not* real, Joseph was thinking.

"The pleasure is mine," he said.

Dr. Von Schlossberg released the arm and neck he'd been constricting and hoisted his trousers. Beaming at Joseph, he informed anyone within earshot that "Dr. Kellerman here was and always will be my absolute best and brightest student. And now look at him, shooting right to the top of the field!"

A nearby group of doctors, professors and spouses stopped talking and turned to look. A number of others had been watching the scene from the start.

"This here's my proudest accomplishment!"

Dr. Von Schlossberg slapped his protégé on the back and puffed himself up. Standing next to him, Dr. Kellerman appeared almost frail by comparison. Which he wasn't.

Joseph looked at his feet, while Marta glared at them.

If she heard "best and brightest" once more, she'd retch. All over those scuffed black shoes.

Joseph felt the same.

I. Joseph Kellerman

Maybe this isn't such a great idea after all, Marta thought. The others had turned out to be total disappointments, and if this was Daddy's *absolute* best, well —

Although, this Doctor *Kellman* isn't bad looking, she now decided for the third time that evening as she reexamined him. Marta concluded that Daddy had at last realized what was good enough for her and, then and there, determined that, yes, she must have *this* upwardly mobile doctor for herself.

So began a very unhealthy relationship.

***

Joseph could no better have explained how he'd become involved with the daughter of his one-time professor than a complete stranger might have. Even a stranger could see Marta Von Schlossberg was nothing like Dr. Kellerman, that she couldn't have cared less about psychiatry or, for that matter, helping anyone but herself. Spectators would often witness the doctor engaged in conversation, while his mask-faced dinner companion, with her hair yanked into a knot, picked lint from her haute couture or studied her glossy fingernails. Dr. Kellerman would associate the topic of his discourse with a particular unnamed or renamed client, but only an eavesdropper would listen to determine if the monologue might be about something he or she could relate to. Marta had nothing to do with therapy and even less with anyone who needed it.

So she thought.

Joseph and Marta had soon adapted to their unspoken arrangement. She was a conditioned social climber, and he was to continue ascending the professional ranks. Marta knew that with herself at the helm, guiding the doctor's career, his status would improve. Joseph was not a man with the strength to resist such a determined woman.

Dr. Kellerman did make a comfortable living, but Marta

was dismayed to find how low his rates were. A respectable psychiatrist should charge his patients at least twice as much for the opportunity, the *honor*, of having his undivided attention for an hour. But no more than an hour during a single week. Such was the gist of Marta's vocal opinion on the matter.

She also told her mother that the doctor was far too accommodating. Dr. Kellerman would schedule an appointment for any hour, even on a weekend or holiday, often ignoring the clock on his office wall when the minute hand reached XII. And he'd always reserve time to consult with other, what Marta by and large considered lesser, doctors. For that reason as much as his lack of ego and most of all his ability, Dr. Kellerman was well-liked amongst his colleagues, though none could, in truth, claim to know him as a friend. Least of all Wilhelm Von Schlossberg.

All of Joseph's public interactions could have been categorized as professional, academic, or both. He didn't attend purely social gatherings. He declined numerous invitations to weddings, anniversary dinners and other events, which would involve a more demanding atmosphere, sending generous gifts in his place. And there was never an occasion that should have been called a date.

Which isn't to say Joseph didn't have a sex life before Marta entered the picture. As a participant, he enjoyed sex in the corporal sense, but it had always been followed by intimate desires on the parts of the females involved. Those kinds of requirements Dr. Kellerman felt incapable of fulfilling. With Marta, that seemed a non-issue.

Though affection was glaringly absent between the two of them, intercourse was not. Their frequent coital sessions were devoid of conversation, quite rough, and carried out in complete darkness. They never kissed, and, like foreplay, eye contact was impossible. Even in daylight and fully clothed. But Marta and Dr. Kellerman did look rather impressive together, and appearances had become crucial to her.

The soft-spoken psychiatrist was indeed pleasant to behold.

I. Joseph Kellerman

Six-foot-two, lean but not skinny, with distinct dark eyes and darker mustache and goatee. While the doctor didn't appear joyous at any time, his unpretentious demeanor gave the impression that he was approachable. And he was. He was an amiable, thoughtful man who never talked about himself. The mystery of I. Joseph Kellerman rendered him even more alluring to a number of women, and he had been, on many occasions, successfully tempted. That was a fact well known amongst the Harvard psychiatric community, and Marta Von Schlossberg had ears fine-tuned to gossip.

Not three months after being introduced, she and the doctor were betrothed, but that development had nothing to do with any sudden influx of fondness or friendship.

Marta was a very jealous woman and often acted on that emotion. And she had been suspicious of Dr. Kellerman from the day they'd been dragged together by her father, the man Marta trusted least of all.

Unlike Wilhelm Von Schlossberg, however, Joseph was not one to have multiple sex partners during a single period of time. Infidelity would have been far too much for the young man or his busy schedule to handle.

But Marta didn't see it like that. How could she? She'd never known anything different. She'd known Daddy, and he had been the first to break her heart.

Nearly every woman who entered Dr. Kellerman's office was a potential and probable affair as far as Marta was concerned, and she was forever accusing him of such acts of betrayal. Though his honest denials ceased weeks before their engagement, her charges continued to be unfounded. Dr. Kellerman had nothing but ethical intentions during those early years of his practice, and, over the years that followed, his intentions were not what changed.

There wasn't a more dedicated psychiatrist. The young Dr. Kellerman was consumed by his work, and he consumed it. After all, when one spends most of his waking hours listening to and thinking about other people's issues and many nights having punishing, dispassionate sex, little time remains to contend with one's own demons.

When Joseph's thoughts did drift from matters discussed within hospital, lecture hall and office walls, it was not to romance that his mind wandered. No, far from it. The images that would occasionally flash in front of his vacant stare were too horrific for him to accept as having been real. They were from a client's past. Many clients' pasts. That was the only way he could deal with those disturbing visions: they had nothing to do with him. Joseph had been almost as successful at persuading himself that he was just fine as he had others. Even other psychiatrists. To the rest of the world, Dr. Kellerman was as stable as could be.

Regardless how far from the truth Marta's assumptions were about what went on in the doctor's office or his mind, she resolved to take much tighter hold of what was supposed to be hers.

And that's how the engagement of Joseph Kellerman and Marta Von Schlossberg came to be. With a little help, that is.

***

"I have something to tell you," Marta whispered to her father, as he was speaking to a colleague at yet another professional function. "Daddy."

"Not now," Dr. Von Schlossberg replied, grinning at his audience.

"Daddy, I need to talk to you. This is important."

The occasion's keynote speaker closed his eyes and conceded with a sigh. "Harold, would you excuse me for a moment? Mrs. Lutz."

Dr. Von Schlossberg turned to his overdressed daughter. Marta had taken an extra long time primping and preparing earlier that evening. The crimson gown, which exposed the wide expanse between her barely-there breasts and her right leg from foot to thigh, was quite inappropriate for the occasion. Yet another embarrassment for Daddy.

"What *is* it?" he asked, then checked his tone and facial expression lest he upset his little girl. She made enough of a fuss when she got her way. "Is everything all right, sweetheart?"

Marta reached for her father's hands, but he was quick to stuff them into his trouser pockets. "It's about Joseph," she said, taking hold of an anchored arm.

Marta almost never referred to "the doctor" even by last name anymore, but it was vital Daddy be on her side. The absolute best and brightest had ignored all of Marta's veiled attempts to raise the subject with him. But this had nothing to do with the doctor *or* the man, whose name was painted and already fading on a small wooden sign next to the door at 4991 Hopewell Street. This was all about Marta, whose desperation now warranted desperate measures. The lone product of Wilhelm and Myra Von Schlossberg's union was determined to live up to and beyond their status. Maybe then, Daddy would be proud of *her* too.

Daddy said nothing.

"He keeps bringing it up," Marta continued, while her father gazed into the mingling crowd. "He says he's never wanted anything more in his entire life. But he's concerned you'll think he wants special favors. You know, *to be on the faculty.*"

Still no response. Though Wilhelm Von Schlossberg turned his head in his child's direction, he looked past her crimson-contoured cheek.

"I keep trying to tell him," she said, "when it's meant to be, there's no reason to waste time. I'm sure you agree. And I know he'd prefer to come to you himself, but...." Marta's voice trailed off as she dropped her eyes to the floor.

"But what?" Wilhelm asked when his daughter stood her ground.

Marta moved in closer, her crimson lips a hair's breadth from his ear. "He wants to marry me," she said scarcely loud enough for her father to hear above the noise. "But he's worried how you'll feel about him asking for your daughter's hand so soon. But I told him, I said, 'Joseph, Daddy loves you as much as I do. Of course he'll be thrilled.' Isn't that right?"

This response required careful deliberation. Dr. Von Schlossberg removed his arm from Marta's grip and stepped back to digest this most unexpected news and analyze the situation. Rapid double blinks, a slight pout, one hand to sternum, the other to stomach. Yes, classic scheming Marta. Dr. Von Schlossberg was well schooled in her shenanigans, he'd known her for almost thirty-two years. To further support his current hypothesis was the fact that none of the others had even wanted to date her.

On the other hand, Dr. Kellerman was a fine young man. The kind of man he would have been proud to have as a son. And Marta wasn't getting any younger either. *Or* cheaper. The thought of his daughter being provided for by someone else was all Wilhelm Von Schlossberg needed to take action, no matter what the guy may or may not have said.

"Of course, sweetheart, of course! Joseph has no reason for concern. In fact," he scanned the room, "I'll tell him so myself."

"Oh, but Daddy!" Again, Marta grabbed her father's arm. "You *won't* tell the doctor I spoke to you. Any decent man would want this to be completely of his own doing."

Dr. Von Schlossberg swallowed a laugh as Marta went on babbling.

"It would be a blow to any man's ego or ... or pride," she said, "for his chosen bride to have paved the way for his future father-in-law's blessing."

A crease formed in her brow, leaving a similar crack in Marta's foundation when her frown gave way to a tight-lipped smile.

Daddy patted her cheeks with a sly grin of his own. "I'll say nothing of the sort," he assured his little girl.

***

Joseph had no idea what hit him, nor time to reflect on it until hours later. Then he tried his damnedest not to.

"Kellerman!" a jovial father exclaimed and whacked a very distracted man between the shoulder blades. Joseph had been staring through sheets of rain when Dr. Von Schlossberg's arrival sent the wine in his glass streaming down the window.

Joseph turned to face a large mouth full of extra-large teeth, and flared nostrils packed with hair. Avoiding the man's bag-laden eyes, he said, "Yes, sir?"

Von Schlossberg caught a passing victim by the back of his white jacket. Indicating Joseph with a jerk of his head, he told the young man with the tray, "We're practically related and he's *still* calling me sir. Yes sir, no sir, I love your daughter so, sir. That's respect for you, though, and that's a rarity these days. Yes sir, this here's my best and brightest."

The waiter looked down over his shoulder. "Hey, man, that's cool, but this here's a *rented* jacket."

He was set free in exchange for two crackers and a hefty lump of caviar.

Joseph declined the unburdened cracker with the palm of his hand, so Dr. Von Schlossberg ate what was, for him, a one-bite fish egg sandwich, as the waiter made a beeline for somewhere else.

"Oh, come on, Kellerman," Von Schlossberg said after wiping his mouth and nose with a single swipe of his hand. "You and I can skip the formalities, can we not?"

"Formalities?" said Joseph.

"Sure! Things are different nowadays. It's not like the dark ages when I was courting Myra. Why, everyone can see how close you two are."

"Myra?" said Joseph.

"No, *inseparable* is the word they're using. And they're right, you two were made for each other."

Joseph's mouth opened again, but the faint "Uh" that dropped out was overpowered.

"Yes, my boy, I'm thrilled to give you my daughter's hand. Hell, you can have all of her!" With that, Wilhelm Von Schlossberg produced a guttural "Ha!" which turned many heads that hadn't already been turned the second before by his announcement to the impending groom.

Joseph's chin sagged to its lower limit.

"Well, congratulations, son, you and Marta will make a gold medal team. And your children will be way ahead of the game." Von Schlossberg guffawed and added, "Not to mention tall!"

The thought of creating children with Marta made Joseph's stomach revolt. Many things had that effect on him, and he nearly vomited when Wilhelm grabbed his shoulders, pulling him in for a strong-arm, headlock sort of hug.

Just at that moment, an enthusiastic Mrs. Von Schlossberg rushed up and threw her jiggling arms around the waists of the embracing and embraced. "Oh, Joseph, we're so happy!"

Wilhelm and Myra released the frozen psychiatrist, who gaped from one to the other and back again.

"Ooh, and look what I have!" Myra exclaimed as she held something in front of Joseph's nose.

He had to angle his head back and a bit to the side in order to see what that something was.

"This was my mother's and her mother's before that, and now it will be Marta's!" Myra squealed. She lowered her voice to say, "There's no need to spend all that money for a decent ring, when we have this perfectly adequate one," then proclaimed, "Two carats!"

Myra pressed the heirloom into Joseph's free hand — he was still gripping the empty wine glass with the other — and closed his fingers around the diamond ring. Had Joseph been in a more lucid state and only a fraction as suspicious as his apparent fiancé, he might have wondered how much of a coincidence it was that Marta's mother happened to have that piece of jewelry on her person.

Myra Von Schlossberg had an even larger rock on her own left ring finger than the one she was so intent on passing along and currently embedding in the doctor's skin. Her other fingers had been likewise adorned by her devoted husband. Little did she know those gems also were genuine fakes.

Like the star of a well-rehearsed performance, Marta wasn't long in making her own grand entrance. Right on cue she appeared, seized the doctor's white-knuckled hand, and pried open his fingers. She gasped, covered her mouth in utter shock, and, after a very brief intermission, snatched the ring from his clammy palm. "Oh, Joseph!"

The sound of his name emanating from those thin, dark lips was enough to make him blink. Twice.

Marta threw her forearms around the doctor's neck, then instantly let go to hug Mum, then moved on to Daddy. That last unreciprocated squeeze was the longest, before she held the ring to the light.

"It's beautiful!" she screeched. Marta turned to bat false eyelashes at her beau. "How sweet it is to share this moment with my friends and family. This is the happiest day of my *life*."

Alas, that turned out to be true.

And off Marta went, making her rounds throughout the room, as did the sparkling gem.

One after another, more hands were slapped on Joseph Kellerman's back. Strange women kissed his face, until the patchwork of multicolored lip prints covered his ashen cheeks. Blurry people talked at him, teeth from ear to ear to ear, as the room spun around a nearly comatose man.

Chapter 4

Not that Joseph fell in love with his fiancé. On the contrary, he liked her less — or rather disliked her more — as time crept by. And he felt guilty about that. But he did grow accustomed to the idea that, despite his massive shortcomings, he was wanted. A sense of security accompanied the theory there was someone even for him, and that was enough to sustain Joseph Kellerman. At least, for a while.

Just twelve hours after the future husband of Marta Von Schlossberg was declared, he and Marta began spending much more time together. She appointed herself Dr. I. Joseph Kellerman's office manager, leaving the same position in Daddy's office once again to Mum. A lucrative psychiatrist and distinguished author would not be answering his own telephone or handling an appointment book. Or checkbook, for that matter. Marta was the only suitable candidate for the post, as she knew the doctor's needs better than anyone else. Including the doctor.

That was *her* version of reality, of course.

So it came to be that Marta replaced a modest wooden sign disclosing nothing but a first initial and a middle and last name, with a larger brass shingle displaying credentials and a capitalized occupation, then positioned herself between the front door of 4991 Hopewell Street and Dr. Kellerman's office. Not to mention the doctor.

The tasks of everyday business now handled for him, Joseph had much more idle time. Taking up cigarettes and mastering smoke rings wasn't near enough to fill the void, so doodling geometric patterns on his desk calendar became another source of distraction. As did the daily paper. He read every printed word, not excluding advertisements and classifieds, and wouldn't quit a crossword puzzle until each and every square was filled with the proper letter. And Dr. Kellerman asked his manager to schedule more clients. If they didn't call or come in on their own, he told her, he would find them himself. Joseph hoped he wouldn't have to.

But he need not have worried. Marta wouldn't tolerate that. *She* had to be in control of who was permitted to pass her desk. Marta was pleased that, while his appointment book filled beyond capacity, the doctor didn't seem to notice that the number of female patients dropped precipitously.

Joseph did notice and he cared, but at the same time it made things easier. Just by being there, many of the women who'd sat in the yellow chair had often reminded him he was lonely. Especially since he'd met Marta.

As Dr. Kellerman became ever more immersed in the minds and hearts of his clients, sex occupied less and less of his time and energy, until he had no physical contact with his fiancé at all. Somehow, though, he was *still* wanted, regardless of the fact he couldn't stand to be alone in the same room with the woman anymore.

So why force himself? That wasn't a conscious determination on Joseph's part; that simply was how it became, which was fine with him.

Marta, however, was far from satisfied.

"He's going nowhere," she complained over a cup of lemon with tea, two and a half years after she had placed the hand-me-down ring on her own left hand. She counted off the grievances, finger by red-nailed finger, raising each in succession in front of her mother's wide-eyed face. "He sees patients who can't pay. He's accepting far fewer invitations to lecture. He dresses like a bum. Won't even put on a tie, for God's sake. And he spends way too much time with all those pathetic people." Marta made as much of a fist as she could without damaging herself and told Mum, "He should stop being so damn selfless and do something for *me* for a change."

Ask me something about me for a change, she almost added.

Myra Von Schlossberg sympathized with her daughter, but she was afraid Marta might do something she and her husband would both regret. "Oh, honey, it's just a phase, he'll snap out of it. He was your father's — "

"And always will be," Marta scoffed, glaring into her cup.

She'd stopped wanting to cry about that sort of thing a long time ago.

"You know how men can be before their own weddings," Myra continued in earnest. "Now that we've made all the important decisions, I'm sure he knows the time's come to choose the day."

Marta's searing glare rose from her cup to her mother, and she started in with the fingers again. "My dress is more than two years old and completely out of style, that caterer is out of business, the photographer died, and now the damn church is booked for the next year!"

"I know, dear. And we'll find you new and better ones."

Myra reached across the teapoy and touched her daughter's hand, which was whisked away.

"Oh, right, and *then what?* Wait another two years until the doctor wakes up?"

"Of course not," Myra assured her. "We'll go ahead and choose the date ourselves, and make the arrangements. That's what women have to do sometimes. Joseph is scared. Excited, of course, but — "

"Scared!" said Marta. "Oh, pshh."

"Yes, dear, afraid of failure, that's how men are. But you'll see, once you're married and living under the same roof, it'll be perfect. Your father and me, for instance. Why, it took *him six* years to come around. And look at us now."

Hardly an appropriate example, Marta knew for a fact. Myra

Von Schlossberg was much better at pulling the wool over her own eyes than her daughter's. Marta's eyes had seen far too much.

The thought of living under the same roof as the doctor, in particular the grossly inadequate roof over 4991 Hopewell Street, repulsed Marta. It was bad enough that's where they'd always ... upstairs in that hard, unforgiving bed. She squeezed yet another lemon into her tea. And squeezed and squeezed and said, "He doesn't even touch me anymore."

Myra squirmed at the reference to sexual contact. That was not a topic she discussed with her spouse, let alone her daughter. "Now, honey, I don't think — "

"It's all those whimpering floozies in dime store dresses, who come running to our office, pleading to see the doctor."

Just like Daddy, Marta thought but didn't say. She wasn't sure why she'd never said anything about what Daddy had done on a number of occasions. The money he could withhold from her? The public shame, which would undoubtedly reflect on her as well? Yes, but she'd been much more concerned about earning Daddy's love.

"Little cunts," she hissed.

Myra Von Schlossberg balked.

"Woe is me," Marta mocked in a high-pitched whine. "I'm so sad, Doctor, make me all better. Tickle here, lick there! Oh, *Doctor!*"

"That's *e*-nough!" ordered Myra, who realized she too was shouting. She whispered, "My goodness, Marta, I'm sure Joseph's doing nothing of the sort. Why would he? He's got *you.*"

"Ugh" was Marta's final word on the matter. For the moment. She dumped her tea into a fake poinsettia, then sulked and plucked lint from her Laurent skirt.

***

Four months later, a still unmarried Marta had had all she could take. She'd done everything within her power to help the impotent doctor, but he was a lost cause. And he couldn't seem to keep his hands off other women. That's what Marta told people. What she did not disclose was that, for two years, she had been spying on the man through a self-made hole in the wall behind her self-appointed desk and the bottom-right corner of a self-made painting. She also didn't tell anyone that she'd seen and heard nothing but pure doctor-patient dialogue and genuine emotion shared on the other side of that wall. No one believed her accusations anyway. Least of all Daddy. But that wasn't all that important to Marta anymore. What did matter was that Dr. Kellerman had stalled, with no hint of continuing up the escalade of success. He'd stalled, period. But *so what?* Daddy would have new bests and brightests for her to choose from. He always had before, and next time he would get it right. Marta never had known what exactly she'd wanted from Dr. I. Joseph Kellerman, but she knew she didn't want *him* anymore.

So it came to be that, twenty-three years ago, Marta Von Schlossberg screamed, "I don't want to hear your damn apology! It's too late!" Then she stormed out the front door of 4991 Hopewell Street and Joseph Kellerman's life forever.

And so it came to be that, twenty-three years ago, Joseph again suffered a loss. Loved or not, and she never had been by Joseph Kellerman, Marta Von Schlossberg had reopened a large and painful wound in Joseph's soul that would leave him on the verge of bleeding to death.

But then there was Constance Fairhart.

Chapter 5

Constance wasn't a connoisseur of art, but, by age twenty-seven, she'd already acquired an ample collection. She enjoyed the process of buying the creative works from their often struggling creators as much as the works themselves. No matter how blasé an artist would sometimes act as she gushed over a piece, Constance always noticed pleasure in the actor's eyes. Eyes were something she took great care in studying. The windows to the soul.

Constance allowed instinct, interest and, above all, emotion to carry out most of the navigation through her life, and she employed the same guides for choosing art. If a piece made her smile or laugh, sigh, or blink away a tear perhaps, she would consider taking it home. And Constance was often considering; she was a woman of deep emotion.

Price was of concern, because Constance was not far above the level of financially insecure. Aside from putting something away each payday for later years and unforeseen emergencies, she added however many dollars she could spare to her stash in the bottom drawer of her bureau. The cash in her mother's old needlepoint purse, which Constance tucked away behind the sweaters more from her own hands than anyone else's, was for her one true indulgence. She'd feel her pulse begin to race when opening that certain drawer —a twinge of guilt, excitement about a decision made, and a bit of nervous doubt that, after all that consideration, the chosen art might be gone when she'd return with money from that treasured purse.

From her collection, Constance selected several pieces to transfer to her new workplace. The art to move had to be particularly special, as she was sure she'd be spending more time at the office than her own apartment.

Before her first day of employment, Constance had seen the room where her new desk was located. She'd been there once already and knew the place needed considerable cheering up. Despite the fact her previous visit had been brief and unsatisfying, she hadn't failed to take in her surroundings.

"M. Von Schlossberg," as the secretary's gold nameplate on the desk had indicated, had brusquely turned Constance away several months earlier.

***

"No, there isn't any way you might speak with the doctor," Marta replied, mimicking the polite query without looking up from her work. She'd been facing the wall behind her desk until seconds before the waiting room door had opened and wasn't at all involved in her bookkeeping. "He's with a patient," she said, "and you don't have an appointment."

Constance leaned forward for an overview of the upside down schedule. "May I make one, then?" she inquired. "I'd love to talk to him about his work."

"The doctor doesn't have time to give free lessons, miss."

"Oh, no, I would pay."

"Lessons, period."

Constance couldn't believe this woman's nerve. M, she thought. As in Mad about something? Definitely Mean.

She took a deep breath and exhaled through her nose. Constance was an extremely patient person, but she'd been wanting to do this for more than a year and had, at long last, gathered the courage to speak to him. She'd lost her nerve on three previous occasions and, feeling out of place amongst that sophisticated, erudite crowd, left the lecture hall as soon as Dr. Kellerman had concluded his talks.

Still maintaining a slight smile, she now asked the familiar-looking secretary, "You don't have any openings whatsoever? Morning, afternoon, any time. It doesn't matter."

Marta closed the appointment book as the threat again leaned over the desk. "We're booked to the end of the year," she said.

That was true.

"Oh. Well, next year then."

Constance could wait a month or so. She'd waited this long.

Marta tilted her head and lowered her eyes further to admire her stiletto. "I meant the *next* New Year's."

That was *almost* true.

"He has no openings for an entire year?"

This time, there was no response. Dr. Kellerman had openings.

"Not even a half hour?"

Constance Fairhart could be very persistent when she wanted something badly enough, and this was one of those things.

M. Von Schlossberg raised the penciled-on arcs above her charcoal-gray eyelids and plucked something off her sleeve. "Not even a half hour."

"Okay, so give me your first available in 1971. I'll check in for cancellations."

"Can't do that," said M.

"What do you mean you can't do that?"

"Don't have an appointment book for '71."

Constance's frustration was building and seeping through. She compressed her pocketbook and said, "But I need to see the doctor."

Marta still hadn't looked up. She'd seen all *she* needed to the instant the blonde had come through the door.

During that same moment, Constance had been looking past the top of the secretary's head.

Marta opened a magazine. "If you have a problem, miss, you should find a doctor who's available. There are plenty of other psychiatrists in the city."

"I don't want to see another psychiatrist!" Constance snapped. Finally. She said, "I want *Dr. Kellerman.*"

And Dr. I. Joseph Kellerman's self-appointed keeper finally faced the irritating woman in front of her desk. Marta pressed her ruby lips into a petulant smile. "Well, we can't always have what we want, now can we."

The moment Constance looked into those outlined eyes, she knew for certain she'd seen this infuriating woman before. Somewhere.

One didn't need psychiatric training to recognize there was no getting past the hag in designer clothing, so Constance gave up the effort. "Fine," she said, feeling defeated. "I guess I'll speak to him at the next lecture."

No comment from M, whose eyes returned to her magazine.

Constance took her time leaving the building, but not to make a statement. Since she'd first seen Dr. Kellerman step up to a podium just over a year ago, she had been wondering what it might be like within these walls. Despite the usual jargon, Dr. Kellerman's written words had struck her as much less affected than those of most other doctors she'd read. In person, he'd been downright captivating. As unwavering as his prosaic tone and expression had been, Constance could feel how much Joseph Kellerman cared, all the way from the back of the auditorium. Without a doubt his office would reflect such profound emotion, she'd thought each time she later passed his gray door and looked up at the name on the shingle. To Constance, "I. Joseph Kellerman" brought to mind cozy rooms with soft lights and cushy couches, potted plants and fluttering curtains, pictures of peaceful scenes, soothing music.

Boy, was I wrong, she now thought, beginning a slow, stationery turn.

There wasn't much to see besides the rigid woman behind the desk and an unsettling painting behind her. Cold hardwood floors and stark walls, an L-shaped staircase rising to another closed door, a bare wooden bench, a file cabinet and a silent cuckoo clock that had stalled not a minute before three on some morning or afternoon. She'd seen only the hall and front office, but Constance could feel the entire building, its internal spaces removed from one another like submarine holds, like opaque bubble wrap packaged around people.

Are the other rooms as barren as this? She lifted her purse strap onto her shoulder and her gaze to the ceiling.

Having made a half rotation, Constance began to move towards the door to the narrow passage where she'd tripped over a newspaper on her way in. And the hall, it felt like a decompression chamber. Do you get the bends if you exit too quickly?

"Who's this?" she said, stepping up to the photograph hanging near the door. In black-and-white was the full-body profile of a large-bodied man in a suit, his back against a statue. The man and the statue were holding cigars. Constance read the engraved plate on the ornate, gilded frame: Dr. Wilhelm Ludwig Von Schlossberg, 1965.

When she saw the name, Constance recognized the real man, as well as the one in bronze. She'd once slipped into a class at Harvard, of all places. There was no forgetting *that* daring feat, though the name of the professor had escaped her consciousness soon after she'd sat down at the end of the last row. Constance had been distracted by all those students, wondering about them and how they'd come to study at that grand institution. She'd also wondered how they must be different than herself. With that lecture hall filled with scribbling people, Constance had felt almost certain no one who mattered would notice she wasn't a member of the class.

Maybe Dr. Kellerman *is* booked for the next thirteen months, she now accepted. Her anger having already evaporated, Constance looked kindly at M's reflection in the glass over the photograph. "Is this your husband?"

"That's my *father*."

"Your dad! Oh, he was great."

When Constance glanced over her shoulder, she met with a suspicious glare. And that's when she realized where she'd seen M. The expression in those severe eyes had been the same when Constance had observed them several months earlier, on her way to an exit right after Dr. Kellerman's talk.

Marta now stood up, looked down, and said, "What do you mean by *that*?"

Not another one of Daddy's little whores.

In a show of camaraderie, Constance smiled and said, "I mean, I know your dad. Or, well, sort of. He's helped a lot of people."

She realized this woman had an unpleasant disposition, but Constance did not expect the acidity that would spew forth from those red-hot lips.

"Look, why don't you take your issues elsewhere and leave the doctor and my father *alone*."

Constance shuddered as M's stare ate right through her. "What are you so upset about?"

"Goodbye," said Marta.

And that was almost the end of that.

For a brief moment, both women contemplated apologizing, though neither of them had the foggiest idea for what. Both made the same decision.

Constance turned back to the door and, as she did, again noted the statue in the photograph. Further conflict could be avoided by leaving, so why not make the final statement. It wasn't something that happened often, but her next words had come to mind without effort. With one hand on the knob of the reopened door, Constance squinted at the thought. "Wasn't it Freud who said some girls desire sexual relations with their fathers and have that ... Now, what did your dad call it? *Penis envy*?" She smiled at the glaring reflection.

If M. had been short for Medusa, Constance would have been

I. Joseph Kellerman

turned to stone.

She shut the door behind her, then made her way to the street. Constance felt a twinge of guilt when the voice in her head said, maybe it's Miserable.

She sure wasn't wrong about that.

Constance had no idea at the time, as she greeted the woman in the turquoise apron on the steps next door to 4991 Hopewell Street, that, four and half months later, M. Von Schlossberg's desk would be her own.

Chapter 6

"Excuse me, Dr. Kellerman?"

He was standing by the side exit near the lectern when the first of them approached. Unbeknownst to anyone in the room, he'd been contemplating a swift escape. The presentation was over, and now this would be more personal. What if someone asked about Marta?

Though she'd always been missing throughout the lecture portions of these ordeals, for three years and one month Marta had been materializing at Dr. Kellerman's side when he finished his talks. Now there would be no one standing next to him. No one to intervene. Joseph wished he'd never agreed to come.

The audience had formed clusters among the seat rows and engaged in dozens of simultaneous conversations, most about the topic just presented by the well-known, thirty-six year-old psychiatrist. However, none of those conversations included the doctor. He appeared very unapproachable tonight.

But Constance didn't see him that way. She had waited four months for this opportunity and was more than ready to try again. To her relief, M was nowhere in sight.

The moment the applause had begun, Constance had excused herself along the second to last row. She'd descended the steps and crossed the floor of the already chatter-filled room.

"Dr. Kellerman?" she repeated.

He'd been stroking his goatee, staring at the exit sign. When he turned his head in her direction, his arms dropped to his sides.

Joseph began to focus on a vision so familiar it hurt. The build,

I. Joseph Kellerman

the mouth, those blue eyes. And the golden hair captured his attention and held on tight. Mama had been gone for such a long time, but not many more years than her image had been missing from Joseph's mind. Now, in an instant, he could see her again, as though she were standing there in front of him.

"Hi," the young woman said with an engaging smile.

Joseph couldn't seem to form a thought that could be translated into appropriate words.

"I'm Constance," she told him. "Constance Fairhart?"

He managed to nod.

"I just wanted to tell you, I think you're great. Your work is great, I mean. *Really great.*"

She had the urge to hug him. Constance often embraced people she hardly knew, and Dr. I. Joseph Kellerman she felt she already knew intimately. But she wrapped her arms around her own waist and said, "It's so nice to meet you."

All the questions Constance wanted to ask had vanished from her mind somewhere between the first "Dr. Kellerman?" and the third "great." Standing only a few feet away, he was even more appealing than she'd realized, and the hint of cologne was delicious. She had never been closer than the thirteenth row.

Constance took another step forward.

"The pleasure is mine," Joseph said and meant that statement more than ever before.

Constance swooned over the doctor's diction, the way he meticulously pronounced his words. And, for the first time, those eloquent words were directed at her. She had to concentrate to continue speaking, as a flock of winged creatures took flight in her stomach.

"I've been wanting to talk to you," she told Dr. Kellerman. "I tried to make an appointment, but you're booked solid."

"Oh, well I, uh...." Joseph cleared his throat. "Is there something you need help with?"

Constance detected concern in his eyes. Suddenly overcome

by acute insecurity, she said to the doctor's chest, "Well, I'd really like to do the kind of work *you* do. Not that I could ever be in your league at all, but I'm studying, and I've read everything you've written. And that woman you call Mary? Her story's fascinating, and I'm curious about what's happened. So I was wondering if we might —"

Just then a much more dominant voice interrupted. To Constance's surprise, when she stopped talking and once more looked up to the doctor's face, he was staring at *her*, not the man in the tweed jacket. She took two steps back to make way for the intruder, and a second man stepped in.

"Absolutely," Joseph replied.

Constance read his moist, sensuous lips, framed by that trim mustache and noble beard. Internal wings began flapping wildly again.

More and more people were drifting down from their seats, gathering around.

This was neither the place nor time to continue a conversation, Constance decided. Not the kind she wanted to have with Dr. Kellerman. What to do?

On impulse, Constance opened her pocketbook and removed a pen and small spiral pad chockfull of her notes from the lecture and a sketch of the lecturer. She tore off half the back cover, printed her name and phone number, then held it out to him.

The two men between Constance and Joseph were arguing a point with one another, but still he was looking at her. The debating duo didn't seem to notice that Dr. Kellerman extended his hand between them and accepted the cardboard from the young woman he couldn't take his eyes off of, his fingertips contacting hers in the process.

She felt fire blast into her cheeks and said, "If you ever have some time to speak with me, I would be so —"

Joseph lip-read "grateful," as a third man slipped in to occupy his attention. The newcomer was not very successful either.

I. Joseph Kellerman

The choreography was flawless as Constance rotated her way through the crowd that had congregated on the floor of the auditorium. Joseph would look at her the moment she would turn to apologize to each person she bumped into. Constance would glance at the doctor the instant his eyes were diverted by one handshaking member of his audience after another. Only in passing did their gazes reconnect, as Constance pirouetted out the door. The bashful smile she caught as the door closed between them melted her idealistic heart.

***

With one hand stabilizing the slapdash turban, Constance hurried to the phone. The trail in the carpet progressed from saturated footprints at the bathroom door to faint, damp impressions on the far side of the living room.

She thought she might have heard ringing before, but the water cascading over her head had drowned out the sound. Constance had figured whoever it might have been would call back if it were important. She disliked cutting her showers short a tad more than missing a phone call. Several minutes later, when she'd turned off the water, the telephone was ringing again. Constance was sure this was a different call than the one she may have heard earlier.

The ringing had never stopped.

"Hello," she said, but there was silence. "Hello?"

After several more empty seconds, Constance began to move the receiver away from her head.

That's when the man began to speak. His voice was fuzzy. "Yes, uh, Mrs. Fairhart, please?"

Not another telemarketer, she thought.

Constance pushed the towel over her ear and told the caller, "This is *Miss* Fairhart."

Pressing the phone to her head with a shoulder, she bent one knee and put her hands on her hips, prepared to suffer a few minutes of forced politeness. Just hang up? No, not Constance Fairhart. Not even when she was naked and covered with goose bumps.

The man cleared his throat, and Constance stopped breathing.

He spoke into the mouthpiece. "This is Dr. Kellerman. We met at the, uh, the amphitheater last week? You gave me this number?"

Constance yanked the towel off her head and wrapped it around herself, as the man she couldn't see rubbed the perspiration off his free hand onto his pant leg and the receiver slid off her bare shoulder.

"Dr. Kellerman!" she said after a quick catch-and-lift. "How *are* you?" The question just came out. She often asked people that and almost always wanted to know.

Again, there was no immediate reply. Constance thought she heard paper rustling on the other end of the line. She was about to fill the gap with "I'm so glad you called" and "It's great to hear from you!" and whatever else she could think of on the spot that hopefully wouldn't sound asinine, but he said, "There's something I'd like to ask you."

"Of course," said Constance, thinking, I'll tell you anything.

"Well, you, uh, you mentioned you were interested in the psychiatric field."

"Oh, yes, very!"

Dr. Kellerman closed his eyes. "So I wondering if ... uh."

For a quiet moment, Constance thought she was about to receive an invitation, to lunch or dinner perhaps, and began nodding.

Then the doctor jabbed a letter opener into the seat cushion he was sitting on and blurted out, "Miss Fairhart, I'm calling to inquire as to your possible interest in a job."

Her nodding stopped. "Oh," she said. "A *job?*"

"Well, yes, actually. My, uh, my secretary has been made a better offer, and so I'm left ... or that is to say—"

Constance heard paper being crumpled.

Dr. Kellerman picked up speed as he said, "There's a position available in my office," then slowed again. "I apologize if this is insulting to you, my calling about secretarial employment."

Constance's next gesture was a rapid head shake.

"Although, it's rather more of a managerial position," the doctor continued. "And it might ... well, for the time being it might provide an opportunity for further discussion and insight into the field?"

A heavy exhale went from his mouthpiece to her ear when Dr. Kellerman finished his poorly executed speech.

The eager listener hadn't been critiquing.

Constance did have a job. For the past eighteen months, she'd been working the six p.m. to two a.m. shift, Wednesday through Sunday, at the Blue Moon All-Night Cafe. The hours made it possible for her to take a class or two at Boston University as funds allowed, as well as slip in on others and attend lectures, there and elsewhere. Constance had hopes of one day earning a degree of some sort and following, at least at a distance, in Dr. I. Joseph Kellerman's footsteps.

"No!" she exclaimed, startling both herself and the man struggling on the receiving end. "I mean, not at *all* insulting. Oh gosh, no."

She could hardly keep the words "I love you, I love you!" to herself.

But Constance didn't try to quell her excitement. She let the towel drop to the floor and bounced on her toes. The phone was pulled off the table and spun in the air, dangling at the end of the cord. This wasn't even close to what she'd hoped for and not at all what she had expected. Not that she'd expected anything. She was shocked and thrilled he'd called in the first place.

Constance stopped bouncing and tried to sound a tiny bit sophisticated. "When may I come by to speak with you, Dr. Kellerman?"

***

Two hours later, a dynamic young woman was seated at the edge of a yellow armchair, her leg muscles as tense as the rest.

Constance had figured it out back at her apartment, between the moment she'd hung up the phone and shouted, "Y-y-e-s-s-s!" and when she'd pulled on the sage-green skirt with the white daylily print, and white cotton sweater, having gone through every suitable outfit before making a selection from the pile of rejected clothing. She would give her notice at the Blue Moon and work both jobs until those two weeks were through. Hopefully, Dr. Kellerman wouldn't mind if she left a little early until then, so she could get to the cafe on time. And this opportunity to learn from, not to mention be close to, *Dr. I. Joseph Kellerman.* Well, this was far more important than taking or slipping into classes.

As Constance had been changing clothes and figuring and changing again, a mile away Joseph had been agonizing. What if she didn't *want* the job? As if fighting off a boa constrictor, he'd wrangled the tie that was choking him and flung it to the floor, then unfastened the top three buttons of his shirt. Maybe Constance Fairhart didn't want to be around *him*, he'd worried while rebuttoning. He wouldn't blame her, but he hoped she would change her mind. Although Joseph could barely make it through a day without someone there to handle many things for him, he didn't want just anyone between himself and the rest of the world. He wanted *her.*

As Constance had hurried to Hopewell Street, she too had begun to worry. What if he changed his mind? That is, if he'd made up his mind at all. What if she'd misunderstood? What if, after talking with her, he decided she didn't have enough experience and she didn't get the job? Not that Constance knew what it was she'd be doing if she did get it. She'd wondered if she should have worn the navy dress. It made her look older, more professional. Then a cool updraft against her satin panties had informed Constance that she'd forgotten nylons. She felt so naked! Maybe she should have worn lip gloss. A number of worries, maybes and what-ifs had streamed through Constance's mind on the way to that yellow chair.

The stiff-backed psychiatrist in a buttoned-up oxford, balanced on the edge of his own chair, catty-corner to hers. His left knee and her right were an inch apart.

Following a bit of throat clearing after a likewise unnecessary sniff and scalp scratch, all on his part, Dr. Kellerman said, "So."

And that was about it for the next ten seconds, until Constance opened her mouth. The words she'd rehearsed between the corner of Hopewell Street and the steps of 4991 spilled out as fast as she could form them and not as smoothly as she'd hoped. "I'm sorry, since this was so sudden that it came up, that I don't have a resume, but I have references I can give you. Whatever I need to, I'm sure I can learn very quickly, and I'm a very independent worker and a team player, and I have lots of experience with people. I have great organizational skills."

Joseph realized his jaw had dropped. He snapped it up, as Constance did the same with hers.

It's your turn, he told himself. Speak, you idiot!

"Oh, well, good," he said. "That's wonderful."

Was it her turn yet?

Apparently not. She leaned forward and stared with those huge blue eyes.

Joseph addressed a daylily. "I really need you," he said. "Uh, to start very soon, if you could. Please, I'm so busy I can't seem to keep up with everything. So I would be most grateful if you could." He raised his eyes. "Would you, Miss Fairhart?"

She'd been nodding since the word need.

***

By the end of that same day, Constance had polished the desk in the front office and wiped out the drawers. She had measured for curtains, bench cushions and throw rugs. She'd wound that cuckoo clock in the room where she would sit and clients would wait, and had begun to mentally decorate, with much attention paid to those dark-paneled walls. It had been no surprise to Constance to find that the photograph of Dr. Wilhelm Ludwig Von Schlossberg leaning against the mirror image statue of Sigmund Freud was no longer there.

Chapter 7

Aside from the revived cuckoo clock hanging above the three-fronded fern Constance added to the decor on her first full day as Dr. Kellerman's assistant, there was only one other object on the waiting room walls. The large, abstract painting behind her new desk. It was the first thing Constance had noticed when she'd entered the office and met the belligerent daughter of the illustrious Dr. Wilhelm Ludwig Von Schlossberg. The painting was again the first thing she'd seen when she rushed in four and a half months later, expecting an interview but receiving instead more of a plea. And it was the last thing she had regarded before leaving for home that evening with a momentarily diminished smile.

That piece of art gave Constance the creeps. She thought the red slashes on a black, blue and somewhat skin-toned background looked too much like bleeding gouges. A painful image. When, the very next morning after placing the fern in its new and dimmer home, she took a longer and more thorough look, Constance discovered the main reason the painting disturbed her. The last name resembled a series of lies on a polygraph, but she knew whose signature that was on the bottom right-hand corner. The M was large and clear.

On the morning of her second full day as Dr. Kellerman's assistant, following what felt like a weeklong weekend, Constance made a beeline for that painting as soon as she entered the office. Off the wall it came, never to hang on any wall again, she vowed with a triumphant nod. She ignored the twinge of guilt.

Back out through the hallway and front door went Constance,

I. Joseph Kellerman

then down to the sidewalk where she had left her cart. She retrieved two more packages, as the little girl with the freckled nose ran up the steps, dropped her doll, and heaved open the door with both hands and a grunt.

"Well, thank you again. Such a helpful young lady you are."

The woman in the turquoise apron stopped sweeping the steps next door to listen to the stranger who was talking to her four year-old daughter.

The child said nothing.

For the third time in ten minutes, that same unknown person directed what seemed to be her permanent smile at the cautious parent with the broom, then went back inside.

Upstairs, Joseph heard the front door close for the third time in ten minutes.

Mother and child stood on different stoops, waiting for the sunny vision in the light yellow dress to reappear. Not a minute later, the gray door next to the shingle above the little girl's auburn head opened again, and the young woman emerged singing *Hello, Dolly!*

Joseph heard the front door clunk a fourth time. What's going on down there, he wondered while brushing his teeth.

On her way back up the steps with the folded cart in hand and final package under her arm, the singer ended her song with another melodious "Hello."

Then, "I'm Constance," she told the child, loud enough for her mother to hear. "What's *your* name?" The result was an uncertain stare, so Constance tried a different question. "What's your doll's name?"

The girl checked behind her for permission, which was granted with a dip of the chin and simultaneous raise of the broomstick. This time, there was a somewhat audible reply. "Gretel," the girl mumbled, her eyes on the rag doll she retrieved by a handful of yarn.

"Greta. Oh, that's a lovely name. I'm sure it's almost as pretty as yours."

The shyer the child, the harder Constance tried and more animated she became. The younger the child, the more often the effort succeeded. Constance loved children.

"Gretel" was repeated a bit louder.

"Gretel! Well, it's wonderful to meet you." Constance propped the cart and package against her legs, bent, and held out her right hand.

But the girl shook the doll in her face. "That's *her* name, and it's way prettier than mine."

"Oh, I doubt that. Such a pretty girl must have a *very* pretty name."

The two boys on the sidewalk snickered, then whacked at each other with plastic hockey sticks, as the little actress looked from her dirty Winnie the Pooh sneakers to untarnished white pumps.

The child's head remained hanging, so Constance repositioned the cart and package against the building, crouched, and told her, "I'll be coming here almost every day."

"Boys!" scolded the woman in the turquoise apron, pointing straw bristles at the hockey players, who'd started acting like morons.

At the same moment, a mix of fear and disapproval appeared on the little girl's face, so Constance added, "I work here now."

"O-o-o-h. I'm Delilah."

Constance was satisfied. "Now, *that* is a beautiful name. Well, it's a pleasure to meet you, Miss Delilah. And Gretchen too." She shook the doll's fingerless hand and stood.

"Greh-tlll."

Constance nodded and picked up her things. "You both have a lovely day."

"Okay," Delilah agreed. She once more dropped the doll and assisted her new friend.

As the door creaked on its hinges behind her and the hallway darkened, Constance smiled even wider when she heard a little voice singing, "Well, hel-*lo* Cons-tents. Yes, hel-*lo* Cons— "

For the fifth time in sixteen minutes, Joseph heard the door clunk.

***

Back in the front office, Constance set to work. First, she removed the brown wrapping paper from the five pieces of art— two oil paintings, a pastel, a collage and a paper cutting.

The paintings she had carted with her for a mile were by Roxbury artist Tobias Edwards, an eccentric but genuine man with revealing hazel eyes and extraordinary talent. Toby, as Constance called him, was among her favorite artists and now a close friend. She looked forward to their Saturday morning treks downtown to Faneuil Hall, where she would sit on the bench and watch him paint, as she'd been doing each week for almost a year. During that time, she'd gotten to know Toby well.

Constance had a knack for putting people at ease. Many acquaintances and even some near strangers had confided their most private thoughts and feelings, without her asking. Constance rarely asked anything specific of a very personal nature. Forward or aggressive she was not in most situations, but she did seem to have an instinct for knowing just what and how much to say in reply. That's how others perceived her.

What most were unable to detect was that Constance often struggled to find the words. She wanted so much to say the right thing. But it was the soft vitality in her voice, how she looked at people, and the way she often touched them when she spoke that made her simple and sometimes awkward or melodramatic responses so comforting. And Constance listened with care and tolerance, trying her best not to judge. "More than two sides to most everything," she often said. "Especially people."

Thanks in large part to those Saturday walks and talks with Constance, combined with the therapeutic process of painting and a very good therapist, who was not Dr. Kellerman, Toby had come a long way from the gloomy, frustrated young man he once had been. His eyes and recent paintings exhibited the changes that had taken place in his mood and outlook.

Little thought was required for Constance to choose the piece that would occupy the wall behind her new desk, the antithesis of the one she'd removed. "*The Dance*, by Tobias Edwards, III" was signed at the bottom-right corner of the canvas. The painting was made just for her, Toby had explained as he'd handed it to Constance a month earlier. He would accept not a penny. This was a gift, as had been several other moving scenes she'd watched him create.

Constance admired *The Dance*. The face of the painted woman was turned away from the viewer, as she gazed up into the eyes of the man whose one hand guided her at the waist, while his other held hers in the air. The woman's free hand rested on the gentleman's breast. They were surrounded by cobalt-blue, while the sun shined on them from outside the picture frame. This was a simple piece, but Constance could stare at it at length, and, as she did, the painting would always come to life. She could see the woman's long, yellow hair sway, as the dashing man in a black tuxedo led his new bride around and around, her white dress flowing. She could hear the melody, a romantic ballad or a spirited instrumental, often something she'd recently heard. And when Constance listened to music, she would often see *The Dance*, whether she was looking at the painting or not. *Till There Was You* now faded into her ears, as the ticking of the cuckoo clock faded out and the painted couple began to move.

When Toby Edwards had touched brush to canvas one autumn morning while Constance Fairhart sat by his side, watching with anticipation and listening to his thoughts — with a significant exception — he knew well the pretty face seen only by him and the painted man who held her. Constance could see just the edge of the man's face, but she had completed the image time and again. He was not the same man Toby saw when he'd painted what was in his heart.

The music ended when the phone rang.

Constance's smile remained as she spoke, which was heard along with her voice by the person on the other end of the line. "Good morning, Dr. Kellerman's office, Constance speaking." She'd been practicing that greeting for two days, but it came out much faster than intended.

The tempo of the response was much the same. At first, Constance couldn't tell if the rather meek stutter belonged to a man or a woman.

"Yes, good — good morning. This is Bern — Bernice Babbish?"

"Hello, Bernice. How may I help you?"

"I *said Bernie*," the caller insisted. There was a pause, then an anxious, "Who — who's this?"

"I'm Constance. I'm new here."

Following another brief silence, breathy whispering crescendoed into an "I don't know!" that made Constance pull the phone away from her ear.

"What happened to the other lady?" Bernie asked, but he didn't wait for an answer. "*Dr. Kellerman's still there, right?*"

Constance responded as soothingly as possible. "Oh, y-e-e-e-s, absolutely. Would you like to make an appointment?"

There was muffled arguing on Bernie's end.

Constance heard the receiver uncovered and then a snuffle. He said nothing, so she repeated the question. "Do you need an appointment, sir?"

"What'd you say your name was?"

"Constance. Constance Fairhart."

"Oh. Well, okay," he said. "Welcome aboard."

"Thank you. Is there something we can help you with?"

"Yeah, the name's Babbish. That's B, as in *boy*, a-b-b-i-s-h."

Constance inhaled through her nose. Her first phone call was turning out to be quite a challenge. But this *is* a psychiatrist's office, she thought. Best not upset him.

She exhaled away from the mouthpiece, then smiled again and said, "Yes, Mr. Babbish. And what may I help you with, sir?"

Again, there was poorly concealed squabbling, followed by Bernie rambling into the phone. "Yeah, well, I gotta cancel Tuesday. I'm real sorry, but I gotta fill in for another girl from eight till eleven. She has an appointment somewhere, and my boss don't care that I got one, too. He says I gotta cover cuz nobody else can, and I got in a fight with this customer, so I'm kinda on my boss's shit list. Ow! Oh ... excuse me, ma'am."

Constance said, "That's quite all right," as Bernie halted only for a refill of air.

"So I should cover for that girl," he said, "or else my boss's gonna can me. The next girl's gonna come in at quarter to eleven, and I can't get off till she gets there, so I'd be late for my appointment. So I guess I should reschedule it maybe. Maybe I could come like, Wednesday or Thursday maybe? Or maybe tonight. Yeah, what about tonight?"

Constance had opened the appointment book and begun turning pages. So far, they were all very much the same, with a first initial and last name in every slot, every hour on the hour until five p.m., and some written in the bottom margins for six and seven. She kept turning and found that today, tomorrow and the next two days were no exceptions. Nor, to her surprise, was the weekend.

"Well, I'm afraid this week's schedule is full," she told Bernie as she turned another page. "But you're down for next week."

"*Next* week? No, no, I have to see Doc this week *and* next week. I always get an appointment. I see Doc every week. He wouldn't want me to miss a week."

Constance flipped the appointment book over and turned more pages, back to front. "B. Babbish" was written in at eleven on the last Tuesday of the year.

"Yes, sir. Well, let's see, how late do you think you might be tomorrow? Perhaps you could still see Dr. Kellerman then ... if you wouldn't *too too* late."

Constance cringed. She had never done this kind of work before and wasn't sure how to handle much of anything. But neither had the doctor given her any direction other than "If they want to make an appointment, give them one, no matter what" and "Whatever you think is best." So that's what she did.

"Oh, y — yes, Miss Fairhart." Bernie sounded much like he had at the beginning of the conversation. He said, "Tuesday then. At eleven. That'd be good."

Constance heard someone say something she couldn't make out, then Bernie's feeble, "Yes, Mother."

"Well, I might be five or ten after eleven," he told Constance. "But if that's too late, well, Doc is real busy. I shouldn't be late. The other lady told me never be late. So maybe I *should* cancel."

For God's sake, thought Constance.

"Oh, no, no!" she said. "That's not a problem at all. The doctor will be very happy to see you."

"Oh, well thank you, ma'am. Thank you very much. I'm glad *you're* there for Doc now."

"That's sweet, Mr. Babbish, thank *you*. We'll see you tomorrow then."

"Oh. Well, okay. Well, bye then."

"Goodbye, Mr. Babbish."

Constance listened for a moment, but he didn't hang up. All she heard was breathing, two people breathing, until she pressed the button and returned receiver to base with great relief. Would it always be that hard?

***

Back to prettifying the room and *Till There Was You.*

Constance hummed as she picked up *The Dance* with care and proceeded to hang it in its new location. She walked around to the front of the desk to examine her favorite painting from a distance and make sure it was straight. But as she did, something caught her eye and the humming stopped.

Is that a hole?

She hadn't seen it before. Constance stepped back around for closer inspection. She slid a finger into the opening, then pulled it out. She turned her chair and sat down, now a few inches below eye-level with that strange little hole. A glance back at the stairway confirmed she was still alone, so Constance half stood and leaned forward.

Part of the yellow armchair came into view. That was the chair she'd sat in four days earlier, uncertain but hopeful, and the one that would be occupied by today's first client in less than an hour. The light of the floor lamp that had perhaps been left on all night illuminated the empty seat.

Constance sat back. Hmm, she thought. And that was the last thing that went through her mind before a door opened above her left shoulder.

Constance was on her feet and facing front in an instant. The chair remained facing the wall.

"Dr. Kellerman, good morning!" The greeting echoed off the bare walls, as the bleary-eyed man descended the stairs from his apartment, leaning on the handrail.

Constance smiled again, wider than ever. She hadn't seem him in three nights and two whole days. An eternity, more like.

But what happened to that sexy mustache and goatee? Now he looked so ... *young*.

"Morning," he said. "It's good to —"

The doctor stopped mid-stride on the next to last step and stared past the top of Constance's head.

The rest of her smile vanished, as his expression hardened.

"What have you *done*?"

During the past several days, Constance had often felt her heart race a bit, but now she thought it may have just stopped altogether. Her eyes were cemented to his, though she wanted to look anywhere else.

"No, I didn't do that," she told the doctor, reaching around her neck to point over her shoulder. "I just noticed it."

"Where's my painting!"

As Joseph approached the side of the desk and the shaken young woman behind it, the sudden rush of adrenaline turning his ordinarily calm, almost deadpan face into something fearsome, he noticed Marta's tantrum in oil paint leaning against the wall. He grabbed it and shoved it at Constance. "Put this back up."

"Dr. Kellerman, I'm sorry. I didn't mean to offend you, I just … I'm sorry."

As she stood there holding the painting at arm's length, Constance looked to the floor, where her stomach had already fallen. This was not *at all* how it was supposed to be.

Joseph too stared at the floor in silence. *What have I done? I'm so sorry, I never meant to hurt you. Please, please don't leave.*

When Dr. Kellerman began to speak again, Constance heard the familiar voice of the gentle man she worshipped.

"It's all right," he sighed. "Really. It's just, that painting was … a gift. It wouldn't be right to take it down. Not just yet." And that was all the explanation Joseph was able to give.

He said, "I apologize, Miss Fairhart," and reached out to touch the side of her head.

Dr. Kellerman drew back his hand. Without another word between them, he walked around to the other side of the desk and disappeared into his office, as Constance lowered herself into her chair.

When the shock subsided a bit and she was able to think again, she didn't know *what* to think. M and Dr. Kellerman? Could they have been a couple?

Constance shook her head.

Then she reconsidered.

Well, M *was* the daughter of a great man, and he was a psychiatrist, too, and Dr. Kellerman had gone to Harvard, so obviously he and Dr. Von Schlossberg were friends. So that did make sense enough. Maybe M had been having a terrible day. After all, there are more than two sides to most everything. *Especially people.*

Okay, so they'd been a couple. But what had happened? Dr. Kellerman said she'd been made a better offer.

Aaah, thought Constance. But wouldn't he rather get rid of the painting, then? Or at least put it away maybe. He'd acted more like M had died.

Constance gasped. Oh, that poor woman. And poor, bereaved Dr. Kellerman!

Still, though, what a hideous painting.

Minutes later, Constance was steady enough to stand. She removed *The Dance* from the wall and reluctantly hung M's painting where it had been. And as she did, Constance noticed that curious little hole was no longer visible. Not unless one gave that bad excuse for a piece of art a nudge to the left.

Chapter 8

Joseph studied his companion while she puttered around the room. He found comfort in watching her. That sweet mouth, slightly smiling. The thin lines of happy years at the corners of those luminous eyes. Her relaxed, trouble-free expression. He couldn't help but smile a little himself when he looked at the subtle indentation at the tip of her nose or the tiny, dark mole below the left corner of her mouth.

Joseph was in awe of Constance Fairhart and had been since the moment he'd first seen her. And now there was even more depth and over twenty-three years of history to that emotion. This incredible woman's presence in his life and the unconditional friendship was a gift Joseph had never understood and felt he did not in the least deserve. Nonetheless, he was profoundly grateful.

The two o'clock client had called to say he was running late, so Constance had taken the opportunity to spend a few minutes with Joseph. Perhaps make him laugh. It had been such a long time.

"Let's see what goodies we'll find today!" she announced with overstated cheer.

The more depressed the person, the harder Constance tried to be upbeat. She now began the day's fourth rendition of *You Are My Sunshine*, while picking up various this-and-thats to dust, setting each back down precisely where and how it had been.

To Joseph, Constance was ageless and full of grace, the embodiment of tranquility. The way her hair was drawn into a loose French braid that often lay in front of her shoulder. Her smoc cream-colored neck. How each part of her petite figure flowed like liquid into the next. He felt with his eyes the soft roundness of her cheeks, their hint of rosy pink matching the color of her lips.

Unpainted pink lips that had never spoken a harsh or angry word. Not to him, anyway, which was all he knew for sure. Nothing more than lighthearted sarcasm, banter was what it was. He could always see the gleam in her eyes and the upward twitch of her mouth when Constance tried to look annoyed with him. And when she wrinkled her brow and gritted her teeth to enhance censure of his intentionally childish behavior, Joseph delighted in the play even more. That was the closest he could get, the most he could manage.

He leaned back in the creaky desk chair, took a drag from his fifth cigarette since breakfast, and watched her glide about the room in what little open space there was.

So much like Mama.

Constance stopped moving and singing, and stared at the floor with determination. Then she dove into action.

"There are dust bunnies as big as bears under here," she said, now on her knees and forearms, peering under the yellow chair. "We've *got* to get a new vacuum."

The other chair let out a mournful screech as the occupant leaned forward and craned his neck. From his vantage point, Joseph could see the back of Constance's head, the arc of her back, and the underside of her shoes. How perfect she is, he thought, watching the lilac fabric of her dress stretch across her body, though it wasn't in a sexual way that he stared. At least, not the way he'd ever looked at any other woman and with an emotion he experienced only with Constance. This was, to Joseph Kellerman, a complex sensation with the power to penetrate all of his defenses. He could never seem to block the feeling, no matter how hard he tried. At times, it was almost too painful to bear.

Constance groaned as she fished around beneath the chair with the feather duster. "I'm too old for this," she said.

I. Joseph Kellerman

You're too *good* for this, thought Joseph, tapping his cigarette into one of four ashtrays in the room. He wanted to touch her hair.

Joseph had often imagined what it might feel like to be close to Constance, to put his arms around her. To feel her arms around him. But he knew the brief connections between her hand and his shoulder, and the light brushes of her waist across his arm as she reached for his mug or extinguished a cigarette in front of a sometimes dozing and frequently distracted doctor would have to suffice. Yet those fleeting moments meant everything to him. From those moments and so many others over more than twenty-three years' time, he'd created a safe and tranquil castle in the sky, into which he'd escape as often as possible.

"I could fill a mattress with all this!" Constance stretched an arm to display the evidence, while propping herself up with the other.

"Could use a new one," Joseph replied, squinting through the cloud of smoke exhaled with those words. He'd been silent for the six minutes she had been in the room. "And while you're at it," he told his assistant, "why don't you make me a new pillow." He tried to appear playfully smug, but knew his eyes didn't sparkle like hers.

Constance pushed herself upright with another dramatic groan and blew an errant wisp of hair off her face. "As humorous as ever, you are," she said, and the hair settled back where it had been.

The desk chair complained in shrill pitch as Joseph bent sideways over the wooden arm and plucked a flake of dust and cat fuzz off the floor. He had watched it stir earlier that morning while he'd generated a bit of a current with the shaking of his foot, then quite a bit more with a manila folder while the ten o'clock client was fretting about the spies in her neighborhood. Somehow, though, the flake wouldn't leave. Joseph now placed it on his open palm, leaned forward and blew.

"There you go," he said with a lopsided grin. "For my mattress." Again, as was most often the case, his eyes didn't coordinate with his mouth.

Joseph sat back in his chair and Constance on her heels, with only her head and neck visible to him. They watched the dust drift between them as it rode confined drafts from ducts and lungs, and landed on the desk calendar. A loose-leaf calendar, the kind where the man behind the desk could tear off a day endured and throw those twenty-four hours away. He blew again, and the dust impaled itself on the uncapped pen that lay amongst the faceless heads doodled all over May 13.

Constance batted organically long lashes. Raising the loaded feather duster to her mouth, she took a deep breath. Her turn to blow. The mass of gray fluff separated into at least a dozen independent parts.

"Stuff it yourself, darling," she said with sugar, then stood and glided out of the room. The door was left ajar.

Dr. Kellerman spent the next minute observing the dust flurry descend over stacks of papers and periodicals on his desk, the stacks of books, digests and glossy magazines on the floor, and other assorted contents of the office. When all was settled, he introduced a new stimulus — fanned the air with a psychiatric journal — and observed again. He tilted his head back and watched a large flake drift towards his face, until a stream of smoke from flared nostrils sent it spiraling upward. The doctor held his breath and tracked the dust as it floated down. He felt the tickle as it grazed his chest above the scooped collar of his undershirt, then drew in his stubbled chin and watched the dust move over his sagging belly into a crease of his khaki shorts.

Joseph stared at his crotch. "Useless," he sighed, shaking his head. "What a waste."

Cigarette number five was used up, snuffed out, and laid to rest with the remains of the other four. Two more numbers came and went on the alarm clock as Joseph sat there, watching time pass away. Waiting.

He heard a door open and close, another door open and clunk

I. Joseph Kellerman

moments later, then Constance's distant "Hi, Delilah!" Muffled voices.

What is she doing out there?

He looked at the vase of fresh flowers Constance had set on the end table next to the yellow chair yesterday morning.

Ah yes, it's springtime again.

Suddenly very unsettled, Dr. Kellerman scanned the riffraff amongst the stacks on his desk, picked up a silver letter opener given to him many years ago by a client he wasn't trying to remember, and examined its tapered edges. He touched the sharp tip to his index finger, pressed and twirled until it hurt, then continued to twirl and press harder. He heard a door open and clunk and louder murmuring. He pressed and twirled. Another door opened and closed, and Joseph examined the indent in his skin. Then he glared at his skewed reflection in the dagger-like implement that had never been used for its intended purpose, only to clean the dirt from his fingernails and carve divots in the desktop.

"You don't even bleed, you inhuman schmuck," scoffed the warped man in the silver. "You're useless, too."

The much bigger warped man expelled some frustration with a grunt and, as he did, jabbed the letter opener between his legs, just missing himself. Had he meant to miss? Joseph wasn't sure. The letter opener stuck upright in the worn and very mistreated beige corduroy cushion.

There was a soft knock, and the right half of Constance's face appeared between door and jamb. Joseph looked up at her, and she looked at him, and then she put her whole head in the room. She couldn't see below his chest, on account of that big desk and its considerable load he hid behind.

"George is here, Dr. Kellerman. Should I send him in?"

"No. Give me a couple minutes."

Constance withdrew and began to close the door, then stopped as her boss looked down at his lap. In came the head again. "Do you need anything, Joseph? Something to eat? A drink?"

"Uh, no. No thank you, Miss Fairhart, just two minutes." He forced a quick smile and accidentally winked in the process.

Constance smiled and winked back as she turned the knob and closed the door without so much as a click.

Once more alone with himself, Joseph looked towards the yellow chair.

"Well, what do you want to do?" he asked without saying a word.

The one seated in the armchair stared at the upholstery, tracing the woven design with his finger. "I don't know," he mumbled.

"You don't know," said Dr. Kellerman.

And Joseph shot back, "Don't patronize me!"

"I don't understand."

"I hate when you do that, just repeat things all the time. Don't you have anything useful to say anymore?" The client was scolding the doctor.

Both Joseph Kellermans were speechless as both lit cigarettes. Neither could think of anything.

After a few mirror image puffs, the doctor shrugged. "I used to, I suppose. They got something out of coming here."

"Yeah, right," said Joseph. Inhale and puff. "You were pretty good with other people once in a while, you big fake. But somewhere along the line, you started to screw *them* up, too."

"What did *I* ever do?" the doctor protested, then surrendered to his alter ego with a wave of his hand. After a brief bout of coughing followed by a heavy sigh, he said, "I don't know how things got so bad."

The one in the yellow chair frowned at him like he'd said something absurd. "Oh, come on! Those women, Doctor Kellerman, what you did to them was horribly wrong. But one doesn't need a degree to figure *that* out. They were vulnerable. Transference, remember? But all you cared about was what *you* wanted."

"I've never given a shit about myself," the man behind the desk objected, staring at the cigarette he was rolling back and forth between his thumb and index finger.

"Not the way you should have. But at the same time, you've been so self-absorbed. I mean, what were you thinking? That you were helping them?"

The doctor shrugged again, then shook his head. "But it's not like I ... well, I mean, *they* wanted it, too."

"Oh, please."

"I know, I know," the doctor admitted. "It was wrong. I know what I am."

But Joseph wasn't satisfied with that. "You're a joke, is what you are," he told Dr. Kellerman. "You were a screw-up way before those women."

"I care about people," said the target of the ridicule, holding the glowing end of the cigarette a fraction of an inch from his palm. He could feel the heat. He said, "I just can't seem to —," then stopped because he didn't know how to finish the sentence.

And the other one shouted, "Shut up, you sniveling fool! Look at most of these people who still sit in this chair, and *you've* only made things worse. M.D., Ph.D. What a crock. You aren't worthy of the title."

The ashamed man behind the desk didn't want to hear any more, but the angry man in the yellow chair wouldn't stop. "Constance deserves it so much more than you ever have. You didn't merit anyone's gratitude. In fact, you don't deserve anything. So why don't you do everyone a favor and ... oh, never mind."

Another wave of the hand, this time by the imagined one.

"And?" the doctor prompted. He did want to hear this. He wanted the one in the yellow chair to be strong.

"You know what I'm talking about," said the client. "But forget it, you're too much of a coward to do that either."

"No, I'm not."

"Bull. You've been thinking about it for how long? You come close, but you don't *do* it."

"I should," said the doctor. "I'm useless."

Joseph crossed his legs and sucked on his cigarette. He raised his chin and blew a succession of smoky rings. "You don't have the guts, Kellerman," he said, squinting down his nose. "Besides, you suffer more being alive, and that's what you deserve. So, now then, what do you want to do?"

"I asked *you* first," the man behind the desk mutely asserted, then slapped his forehead with both hands. Ashes fell onto his leg. "You idiot," he said aloud.

"Huh?"

The voice of the next client, standing in the doorway, startled Joseph so much that he sat straight up and clamped his knees together. As he did, the letter opener still embedded in the seat cushion wedged into his crotch. "Nthng," he groaned through his teeth, trying to turn a wince into a smile. He grabbed his thigh and, with a twitch of the wrist, motioned the man into the armchair. As the man sat down, Joseph once again became Dr. Kellerman and the other Joseph disappeared.

The letter opener remained where it stuck for another forty-five minutes until the alarm went off.

Chapter 9

A peek through the mail slot of 4991 Hopewell Street as Orla Heffel made her way to the front office would have revealed little more than an expansive rump. Empty, that dim, dark-paneled hall with one frosted sconce was not quite three feet across. That itself would have been a bit tight for Orla. With the addition of fifteen stacks of newspapers from floor to her hip, along the entire length of that corridor, the squeeze was more than a bit. Orla moved another foot closer to the light and the next door with each labored step, disrupting a number of those *Boston Globes* in the process. By the time she made it the eighty-two feet from her gas guzzling sedan to the waiting room where she faced the kind of woman she'd always wanted to be, Orla was spent. She plopped onto the bench, halfway lying down, and fanned her decorated face with a parking ticket.

"Hello, dear. Would you like some iced tea?" Constance had gone from the front office into the kitchen to fetch the pitcher at the sound of the first footstep, the muffled slap of a flip-flop against Orla Heffel's heel. Her question received the usual one-shoulder shrug. "How are you today?" she now asked, pouring.

So far, the dialogue had been the same as on the preceding two Mondays not long before eleven. The week before that, Constance had offered bottled water, but Orla had complained for at least the third time that it tasted like sewage.

"Yeah, it's wicked hot," Orla wheezed, sounding as though a large cuff were taking her blood pressure right around her bulging middle. "It's all that global warmin' stuff."

"You think?" said Constance.

At the same time, Orla said, "Yeah, an I heard it's gonna be like, a hundred-thirty in July if people don't quit makin' pollution. Which is why *I* walk all the time, even if it's wicked fah."

"You walked all the way from — "

"I mean, cuz I like tuh do what I can, you know. Even if it *is* wicked hot."

Orla took the glass, without looking at the woman who finally handed it over. While she drank, Constance asked, "So how was your weekend with your sister?"

Orla swallowed. "Yeah, hey, I see you got them cookies again."

"Oh, I tried a new recipe. These are better."

Constance retrieved the plate from the corner of her desk.

Little did Orla know that the cookies she'd been given every third or fourth Monday for the past couple of years were sometimes sugar free, usually fat free, and always full of things nothing called a cookie should have been. But neither that nor the taste would have mattered. As always, Orla took the plate instead of a cookie.

Poor Orla, Constance thought, as she had nearly every Monday over the last ten years and two months. The problem wasn't the food or cigarettes, the booze or television, or the mood enhancers and other benign-sounding prescription drugs Orla had been taking for a decade. It was all of that and more. Addicted to addictions, she was a snowball of vices growing in size at increasing speed, as if rolling down a very steep hill. Constance had long been wondering where the bottom was and what would happen when Orla Heffel hit it.

Constance didn't intend to feed any of this client's compulsive habits. She brought the cookies for Joseph, but he never ate more than a few. Might as well share the rest. Besides, they were better for Orla than the candy she'd otherwise pacify herself with while she waited. She rarely arrived more than ten minutes early, but that was more than enough time for a Mars bar.

"Not *too* bad," said the woman now slouched upright on the bench, still chewing. "They ain't as good as Ma's, but, I mean—" Another bite, then, "She went tuh cookin' school. Graduated top of her class, Summa cum somethin'. Worked at this real fancy restaurant where all kindsa movie stahs go. Yeah, Ma was like—" Orla plucked a crumb off her considerable bosom and popped it in her mouth. "She was a real successful gourmet chef till she decided tuh quit an only take care uh me while I was growin' up. We did all kindsa stuff togethuh. *And still do.* Matter of fact, the othuh day...."

Orla continued babbling, as Constance stood there nodding and watching, not listening to the words as much as trying to figure out how to respond to them. She was still baffled about how to help this person, even after all these years. Orla never answered a direct question if it were about anything that mattered, and seemed impervious to indirect approaches as well.

"Pop's takin' Ma dancin' fuh their anniversary. Fawty-two yeis, ain't that cool?"

"Very," said Constance.

"Yeah, an he's gettin' her this real pretty bracelet. It's got like, diamonds and rubies and them blue things."

Constance smiled at a very serious woman. She'd never once seen Orla smile. At least Joseph did *that much,* now and then.

"Would you excuse me for a moment, hon?" She put her hand on Orla's shoulder, but Orla scrunched it and looked at the cuckoo clock.

Constance opened the waiting room door, stepped into the hall, then opened the door to her right and fumbled for the string. She clicked on the overhead light and went downstairs. In the basement, she clicked on another light and rolled up the sleeves of her blouse before plunging into the next drawer in line.

All those file cabinets full of manila folders stuffed with notes. An overabundance of details about thousands of people, as though Dr. Kellerman used to transcribe every word spoken from the yellow chair and every professional opinion thought from his. And Constance had read them all.

There wasn't much new material to read anymore.

"Hey, Con!"

"Coming, Orla!" Constance yelled back. She fingered through several more tabs, then closed the drawer, pulled the string, climbed the stairs, clicked off another light and emerged empty-handed, returning to the front office as Orla yelled, "Hey Con!" for the third time.

"Yes, Orla."

"Hey, member I toldja my cousin in Jersey asked me fuh that loan?"

"You might have mentioned it."

Constance didn't recall hearing that. Not even through the hole in the wall.

"Well, yeah, I wennuhead and sent him a couple grand. It's no big deal, though, he's good for it, and it ain't no skin off my nose. I mean, he's family, right? And I like tuh help people out when theyuh down an stuff. Like you an the good doctuh, devotin' yourselfs to people the way you do. It's pretty cool. People like us are kinda rayuh nowadays, uh?"

Constance stood with her arms crossed, looking as though she were contemplating Orla's comments. And she was. Like many other Mondays minutes before eleven, she replied, "That's awfully generous of you, you're a good person."

Constance never quite knew *what* to say to Orla Heffel. Not that she had to know, because, aside from pausing for a little praise from time to time, Orla seldom let her get a word in edgewise.

"Yeah," said Orla. Then she stopped talking long enough that Constance began searching for more meaningful words. But six seconds wasn't long enough to find them.

"So anyways, I got this cool present from Ma. It's this big-screen TV with a VC-Ah built in. An it's cool cuz you can like, be watchin' somethin', tapin' somethin' else, an like, have this box up in the cawnuh on anuthuh channel. It's cool."

Constance tried to jump in, as another cookie went from plate to mouth. "So you —"

"That's Ma faw yuh, though," said Orla. "She's always doin' nice stuff fuh me. I bet yaw ma's like that."

Constance forgot what she had begun to say. She hadn't thought about her mother in several hours. Not since she'd kissed her own palm, then touched it to Mom's photo before leaving the house, as she had done so many other mornings and evenings when she returned. One of her own personal rituals.

Sometimes it seemed only weeks had passed since she and Mom had sung *You Are My Sunshine,* like they'd always done before lights-out. And Constance felt as though it had been yesterday that her mother had braided her hair for her, as always, then let her use some makeup for the very first time. Constance had smiled at the pink lip prints on her mother's cheek, then left the apartment for just another day at school. As usual, she had kissed Mom on the other cheek when she returned. That time, though, Mom didn't wake up.

Constance had long since forgiven her mother for what she'd done, but how difficult the rest of those teenage years had been without her. Bob Fairhart was a caring and high-spirited man, but living with him and his partner had not been the same. Dad and Frank were always bickering. That hadn't changed a bit, not even after all these years.

Anger. The emotion, the look, the sound Constance couldn't bear. And she avoided it as much as possible. Just like Mom.

Constance had eventually come to understand her mother's depression, but she'd never accepted her solution. "If only you hadn't given up," a much younger Constance had often said to that photograph. "I could have helped. I know I could have, if you'd given me a chance."

Her only comfort had been her firm belief that Mom was now a happy a woman in a peaceful place.

But next to Bernie Babbish, Orla Heffel was the last person Constance wanted to discuss her mother with. And she knew she didn't have to. Orla wasn't really asking and didn't often wait to receive answers to her questions, anyway. Unless, perhaps, she was drinking or chewing or taking a drag, none of which guaranteed that she'd stop talking.

Still, Constance often used those opportunities to try to say something Orla might benefit from hearing, and Orla always acted like she hadn't heard a thing. So why did Constance bother any more? Because it was her natural inclination. At least, it had been since she was a fourteen year-old girl suddenly without a mother. Try to help even those who most people would deem un-helpable, beyond help, lost causes. People like Mom. Constance Fairhart would *not* give up!

But "Mmmm" was her response to Orla's comment. Constance was also preoccupied with that file she had been looking for since she'd hung up the phone at ten past eight, even when she had a client on the waiting room bench. She'd never misplaced a file.

Orla began another story, and the alarm clock sounded on the other side of the wall. The time was 12:58.

Constance's head and attention turned towards the closed door of the back office, as the muffled buzzing continued. "Excuse me another second," she said without looking back at the woman now talking about her parents' summer home on Martha's Vineyard. Constance tapped on the door as she turned the knob, but that was more out of habit than to announce her entry. She knew what she'd find in the next room.

Sure enough, the buzzing and snoring were competing to be heard. Constance walked over to the desk and pressed the snooze button. She'd stopped hating that annoying gadget Joseph had been using for half a decade. Wasted energy, since she had failed to convince him to stop setting the alarm the one time she'd tried. She had also attempted to talk him into radio mode. No luck.

I. Joseph Kellerman

Joseph was a very stubborn man.

The clock silenced, the only sound in the room was a nasal reverberation.

***

The hour between noon and one had become Dr. Kellerman's break, as he called it. Until one particular Tuesday in 1989, he'd seen a client in that timeslot each and every weekday, unless there was no client to be seen. And it hadn't been all that uncommon for someone to occupy the yellow chair between noon and one on a Saturday or Sunday, either.

Not anymore. Constance remembered the exact date Joseph had informed her that he would no longer see anyone during that hour on any day. February twenty-first, his fifty-fifth birthday.

That was also the last day he'd been outside of 4991 Hopewell Street.

The midday hour was supposed to have been the doctor's chance to "grab something to eat and read the paper for a change," but he never did either. As Constance had observed through the little hole, he had, for hundreds of those supposed lunch breaks, remained behind the desk and out of her line of sight, continuing to smoke when the eleven o'clock session ended. The newspaper also sat unmoved and untouched where Constance had left it first thing in the morning, on the front-left corner of his desk. She knew because she could see it from her side of the wall.

One day, maybe two years later, Constance had pulled her head back and spun around when Joseph had passed in front of her portal. For a moment, she'd thought he was coming into the front office. But the door had remained closed. When Constance had again turned, nudged, leaned forward and looked, she saw a profile she'd never seen through the hole in the wall.

Joseph didn't do anything or say anything. He just sat there in the yellow chair and smoked until the hour was up. He'd moved the clock to the front of the desk and set that dreadful alarm.

Constance had stopped checking on Joseph between noon and one. Nothing else appeared to be happening. Then, one afternoon, Constance heard the alarm go off as always, but the buzzing continued. She'd soon become more than a little concerned about the man on the other side of the wall when he failed to shut off that racket. Joseph did not like loud noise. He usually hit the button as fast as he could, then reset the alarm.

Unless he were asleep?

He *was* a deep sleeper, Constance had considered, having found him facedown on his desk a number of times when he happened to have a few uninterrupted minutes, if a client was late or lingered in the front office. Or cancelled perhaps. She'd begun poking her head in before sending the next client back, because, for weeks, Joseph had been dozing off several times a day.

Still, with that noise. Constance had started to spin around to take a look but remembered his one o'clock had entered the waiting room three minutes earlier. So she'd excused herself and knocked on Dr. Kellerman's door.

There was no response.

***

And sleeping was what he'd been doing when Constance rushed in eight months ago, before the last digit had changed from 0 to 1. She'd stopped to look at him then, the way she did now and smiled. The kind of smile one might make at a child if that child were to say, "Look, Mommy, the doggy's taking a nap," when, in truth, the old beloved pet has died. There was compassion in Constance's eyes while she watched the snoring man in the yellow chair. The floor lamp shined on his heavily whiskered face and uncombed hair. A cigarette was suspended between his index and middle fingers, mid-flick over the ashtray.

Amazing, thought Constance, shaking her head as she looked at the pile of gray matter. He'd smoked so much in the last decade, he could knock off ashes in his sleep and still hit the mark. Poor, dear Joseph.

Constance turned the knob on the lamp two clicks, dimming it to its lowest setting. She deftly removed the cigarette from his fingers, pressed it out, and set the ashtray away from the edge of the table. She watched the rise and fall of his chest for another long moment, before placing her hand on his shoulder.

"Joseph," she said.

The alarm hadn't woken the sound asleep man in the short-sleeved undershirt and khaki shorts, but Constance's soft voice and gentle touch did. His eyes opened and looked into hers for no more than a second. But no more than a second was always enough. She detected the familiar sorrowful smile in those murky windows to Joseph Kellerman's soul.

Before leaving the room and a groggy doctor to compose himself, Constance slipped the newspaper from the corner of his desk. He didn't even bring it out to the corner of hers anymore. Not that she gave him the chance. On her way out the door, she heard the usual click-click of the floor lamp, as Joseph returned it to its brightest.

En route to the next door, Constance passed Orla, who was slap-slap-slapping her way to the door from which she had just emerged. Constance entered the hallway and placed the newspaper on the pile closest to the front office. She relocated the paper on the bottom of that pile to the top of the next, and so on and so forth, down the line. From the bottom of the pile immediately inside the front door she withdrew the oldest *Boston Globe*. She opened that final door and dropped the paper into the steel trash can several feet below. If not for Constance's routine each day after one o'clock, the hallway, the front office, the back office and possibly the rest of 4991 Hopewell Street would have been, by now, filled floor to ceiling with Joseph Kellerman's newspapers, not to mention the rest of the stuff he couldn't bear to lose.

If only she could have lost that awful painting behind her desk *for* him. But she would never try that again. Maybe someday, Constance had often hoped, he would be ready to part with it on his own. She'd never expected that "not just yet" would mean this long.

In an odd way, though, that awful painting had become another normal part of the scene inside that building, and Constance hadn't given much thought to it in years. Now it was one dismal expression amidst eight cheerful pictures that covered the walls of the front office, along with three grinning masks, a file cabinet, two tall bookcases and several stacks of books, a console, a corner hutch, a "Have A Happy Day!" plaque above the bench, two hanging philodendrons, three thriving ferns, and a ticking clock that now refused to cuckoo.

As Constance sat back down behind her desk, Orla Heffel was maneuvering into the chair on the other side of the wall. Dr. Kellerman's assistant rarely bothered with the hole hidden by the corner of that poor excuse for art during this hour on Mondays, either.

Three minutes later, a muffled buzzing was heard by the devoted woman behind the front desk. He'd forgotten to reset the alarm for two o'clock. But that wasn't unusual at all.

Chapter 10

4991 Hopewell looked like a typical row house from the street, identical to those on either side. Brick walls, Rinceau ironwork, uniform windows and doors. Aside from some begonias on one stoop and a plastic dump truck left on another, a powder blue "It's a boy!" balloon tied to a handrail, and a name and an occupation on a brass shingle, there was nothing to distinguish one house on that street from another. On the other side of I. Joseph Kellerman's front door, however, things were much less usual.

If the sight of all those newspapers lining a murky hall wasn't enough to cause one to think that something wasn't quite right here, then several more steps and another door should have done the trick. Most of those who had gone that far either hadn't cared enough to turn around or they had not been paying attention.

The front office, which was also the waiting room, had become as crammed as the hallway, the back office, the downstairs kitchen, closets and bathroom, and the upstairs living area. Name it, and it was likely somewhere in that building. Countless clients had given countless gifts, most now many years old and covered with dust. Everything from a piranha petrified in a paperweight to a purple lava lamp and that silver letter opener with "I. J. K." engraved on the handle. There were enough books to fill a modest-sized professional library, over a thousand of which were amassed in dozens of piles precariously close to toppling point, and nested egg cartons that, all told, had accommodated round about six thousand eggs. Shoe boxes were filled with coupons, some for brands long out of existence. And there were all sorts of other items that had neither purpose nor value of any sort. The place looked like a bizarre bazaar.

Nevertheless, there was a bit of neatness and even some order to the disorder. The newspapers in the hall were folded as if they hadn't been opened, which all remaining had never been, and, due to the continuing efforts of Constance Fairhart, still in chronological sequence. The shelves and stacks of books were alphabetized by title and separated by subject or author, depending on which category the owner felt the more significant. All of the pens, money clips, cuff links and key chains that had been chosen especially for the doctor, so said the man who had given them — one a month for fifty-eight months — were stored in labeled containers, while a large supply of golf balls, given by clients who assumed Dr. Kellerman played golf, remained sealed in original packaging. An extensive assortment of neckties were arranged by dominant color on more than a dozen racks in Joseph's bedroom closet. The vast majority had never been around his neck.

But neatness plus order do not by themselves equal cleanliness, and Constance alone could do only so much with *so much*. So the dust collected and things sometimes molded within those brick and dark-paneled walls. Even a stuffed-up nose could detect the combination of furniture polish, moth balls and a hint of ammonia, the latter thanks to three felines that shared Joseph Kellerman's home and office and two litter boxes under that same roof. Those olfactory stimulants, along with years of cigarette smoke, could penetrate the most clogged of sinuses.

Constance was forever trying to keep up with the upkeep, but as soon as she'd wipe the last shelf or peel the cat hair off the final pillow or cushion with masking tape, several of each were again in dire need of same. Today, at half past two, she was in the process of seeking out regurgitated fur balls when the phone rang.

"Dr. Kellerman's office."

"Miss Fairhart, please."

"This is she."

"Miss Fairhart, this is attorney Mark Dunst. We spoke two weeks ago."

Constance tensed and put down the wad of paper towel and coagulated cat hair. "Yes, of course." She pinned the receiver between her ear and shoulder, then began unfolding a paper clip.

"Ma'am, this is a follow-up call to see if you've located the file on a Miss Linda Payne."

"Linda Payne," Constance repeated, giving no indication of the feelings that name brought to heart. She folded the former clip at the middle and began bending the ends of the wire back and forth.

"Yes. Linda Payne. You were going to search your archives and get back to me." The attorney sounded impatient.

Constance knew he had reason to be. "Yes sir, I've just finished looking," she told him. "But it seems we don't have that file here in the office."

Constance knew it had to be somewhere in that building.

"Why don't you let me take your number again," she said to the attorney. "I'll check our storage facility."

There was no such place. Constance snapped the wire in half.

"Please do. We'd like to get this matter resolved as painlessly as possible." Mark Dunst snickered at his pun, unaware of the concern written all over Miss Fairhart's face.

***

As Constance sat at her desk, still fretting about that call at half past five, she considered potential distractions. The best choice wasn't necessarily the one made, but it was the usual with many motivations. Spinning around, Constance nudged the painting to the left.

"I can — can't do — do it anym — more," cried the woman in the yellow chair, between chokes and sobs and scrubs of her running nose. She ripped a handful of tissue from the box, sending the box flying off the end table, up over the seatback, onto the floor. That made her bawl even harder as she rushed to grab the Kleenex, then back to the security of that chair.

"Mmmm" was what Constance heard from outside the scope of her view.

For ten minutes more, not a discernible word was heard between nose blows, and those staggered breaths and reflex snorts of one who has worked herself into hysterics, then tries to calm down before she's truly calm. The attempt was unsuccessful, the sobbing intense as ever. Constance spent most of that time facing the wall, staring at that little hole, not through it. Then she detected movement on the other side.

When she leaned forward to see what she'd heard, the yellow armchair and the weeping woman in it were blocked from sight, as Dr. Kellerman slipped between his desk and the book-lined wall, then passed in front of the hole. This was not usual.

Constance shoved the painting back into place with too much force, slanting it the other way. Had she not been so distraught, she would have worried that the two people on the other side of the hole might have heard the picture frame scrape the paneling. Had that crying not been so loud, they would have.

"Oh, please, no," Constance whispered.

The rest of the thought process was silent, but the voice in her head was not. It had been six years or so, she loosely calculated, since Joseph had ... engaged in an indiscretion with a client. And he would never do anything like *that* with Lucille McBride.

Would he?

Those others. Constance recalled three women, on five separate occasions between six and ten years ago — *they* had instigated it.

Hadn't they?

Or, at the very least, they'd wanted it, too.

The name of one of those women Constance was unable to forget. There was no excuse for what Joseph had done with Linda

I. Joseph Kellerman

Payne and two others. He was their doctor.

And *they* weren't in love with him.

Constance was saddened by the memory of what she'd never expected to see through the hole in the wall. But each time she had realized what was about to happen, she'd made things right — covered the hole and faced front — immediately working and concentrating as hard as she could on something else, while singing a snappy tune.

Dr. Kellerman had done the very thing Marta Von Schlossberg had so often accused him of, although it first occurred many years after her longest red nail had been pointed for the last time.

While a sighting twenty-two years ago had informed Constance that M was, in fact, alive and well soured, she didn't know the details about that earlier chapter of Joseph's story, or those that had come before. But that didn't matter. What she knew had happened at least five times on the other side of the wall had made her sick. And broken her heart. Constance would never again see Joseph the way she had for more than thirteen years and lived with the remorse that should have been his.

The remorse *was* his also, but that was something else she didn't know.

What Constance felt sure of was that Dr. Kellerman would have to answer for his unethical behavior. After all, how much longer could she manage to protect him? She was surprised her attempts had succeeded thus far. Despite it all, however, Constance still had a great deal of sympathy for the man she had worked and cared for for so many years. She didn't need any more details to understand the basic plot. She'd seen those numbers tattooed on his left forearm.

A minute or so later, curiosity got the better of Constance's other motivations and she moved the painting, exposing half the hole. Half was more than enough.

Oh, but of course, thought Constance, for, when she once again peered through, Joseph was on the far side of the room, pouring himself some coffee. The waterworks in the yellow chair continued, and Constance nudged the painting a little further left.

On his way back to his sanctuary on the other side of that oversized desk, Dr. Kellerman, who wasn't feeling quite himself today, stopped to scoop Bonsai off the back of the armchair. The black feline runt had been bumping heads with blubbering Lucille McBride for the past ten minutes. Watching the cat had been the saving grace of Joseph's mind for that short amount of time.

Bonsai, Rifka and Wadofur, once stray kittens Joseph had found on Hopewell Street and taken in on three separate occasions, nine, ten and twelve years ago, were the only creatures to which he'd been able to show the full depth of his affection for a very long time. Since he was a child.

To the onlooker's surprise, Joseph now transferred Bonsai to the same arm as the hand holding the coffee mug and, for a brief moment, placed his free hand on Lucille's shoulder. Years ago, that would have been out of character, but not quite so astonishing to Constance's eye as it now was.

The man who did it startled himself as well.

Joseph returned to his corner. He spent the rest of the hour behind the desk and out of Constance's sight, blowing streams of smoke across the chasm between doctor and client, cuddling his cat, and thinking far away, long ago thoughts.

Chapter II

"And he's so easy going?" Maggie continued. Many of her statements sounded more like questions than most of her questions. "He never rushes people? Or gets mad when things like, don't go exactly how he wants? He's not pushy at *all*."

Dr. Kellerman stole a peek at locks of silky, straight hair on a sheer white blouse over a clearly lacy bra over round breasts, as the client stared at her own happy vision. Maggie was seeing the man who'd captured her heart. Joseph was seeing a beautiful body and a sweet-tempered young woman unlike anyone who had sat in the yellow chair. That is, since Constance used to sit there years ago, though he hadn't looked at her quite the way he now did at Maggie.

She put her hands to her chin as if in prayer. "I don't know how it happened, but I think I've found the perfect guy."

Joseph wondered what a perfect guy was like. Nothing like him, of that much he was sure.

With a more solemn expression, Maggie crossed her hands over her chest. "If I could just leave the past in the past and like, be with him completely? *You* know what I mean."

Joseph nodded. Yes, I do, he thought, but didn't say. He hadn't said much of anything during this hour either.

This was Maggie Carlisle's third session with Dr. Kellerman. This was also the third time she had been to a professional confidante. Until her first hour in the dingy yellow chair, she hadn't really spoken to anyone about what had happened to her. She did tell her best friend not long after "the incident," as Maggie referred to the rape, but couldn't discuss it further than the fact it had occurred. She'd been angered by Jeanette's horrified look and slew of questions and made her promise never to tell a soul. It wasn't a big deal. She just needed to say it. Once. That's what she told Jeanette and herself, concluding with "And *that* is the end of it," without even a trace of a question mark. A few months before her first appointment with Dr. Kellerman, however, Maggie had found herself falling in love. And that's when she'd begun questioning everything.

***

Maggie scheduled the initial session in person. That was the only way she'd keep the appointment, if she looked someone in the eyes, having canceled three others over the phone, with three other secretaries. But she watched the woman she did not then know was Constance Fairhart neatly print "Maggie Carlisle" in the bottom margin of a page full of neatly printed names. In pen nonetheless. Friday at six p.m. This secretary was eager to accommodate Maggie's very busy schedule, what with a summer course, rehearsals and performances, her part-time job at the juice bar and, as of the last month and a half, volunteer work giving free cello lessons to underprivileged children. She'd even been considering another job, something to fill the gap between six and eleven p.m. or so when she didn't have a concert.

Over the past couple of months, evenings had become wonderful yet confusing and anxious times for Maggie. What if he invited her over or asked to come to her place? What if he wanted to do something more than play music or talk? She wanted him to want to, but ... still. It was easier to be busy.

Maggie had realized she did need to deal with what she'd so desperately wanted to forget, but it was on a whim that she first entered Dr. Kellerman's office. Hopewell Street was on her way home from just about everywhere she went. The other

I. Joseph Kellerman

professionals Maggie had almost seen had been recommended by fellow female members of the orchestra, who knew nothing of the reason she'd inquired about any good "counselors" they might know. She had been referred to two analysts, a psychologist, a crisis hotline she didn't call, and a psychic she hung up on when the woman said, "Madame LaRhonda speaking."

I. Joseph Kellerman, however, was a name Maggie knew only from a shiny brass shingle next to a gray, windowless door she'd passed at least twice a day, almost every day for years. And almost daily for a few weeks, she'd seen a young woman with spiky auburn hair cuddling with a black man on the steps next door to 4991. Maggie once even saw them seated *in front* of 4991, and that's when she stopped.

As she stood on the stoop above the hugging, kissing and whispering couple, frowning at the intimidating word engraved below that engaging name, the lady sweeping the steps next door told her not to bother knocking. "It's unlocked," she said and told Maggie to just go on in.

So she did, and another appointment was made.

Maggie felt better about the decision not long after opening that same gray door a few days later. She'd laid awake the night before, contemplating canceling yet again, but the image of that affectionate couple wouldn't let her do it. And the secretary had been so ... *nice*.

That same woman again smiled warmly when Maggie poked her head in the front office. "Come in, dear," she said, coming around the desk with her hands extended to the first-time client who hadn't yet committed the rest of her body to the room.

The secretary stopped a stride shy of the door and stood there with arms outstretched, as if waiting for a hug, and Maggie sidestepped in. One hand remained on the knob.

"Why don't you make yourself comfortable, and I'll get you some water," the woman suggested, taking Maggie's free arm and turning as if to lead her further inside.

Maggie didn't budge.

"Or would you prefer herbal tea?" the secretary asked.

"Oh, n — no thanks," said Maggie. "Just water would be okay?"

Comfortable, she was thinking. In a psychiatrist's office. I don't *think* so?

The doorknob was released and then Maggie's arm.

"Of course it's okay," said the woman who, at further close-range scrutiny, appeared to be around forty. "I'm Constance, by the way. Dr. Kellerman's still occupied, but I'm glad you're a little early. It's always good to have someone to talk to."

In a psychiatrist's office, thought Maggie. I shouldn't *be* here?

The unspoken words were clear in her blue eyes, which she averted from those that were prying into them.

Maggie began to wander about the room, touching knick-knacks, furniture, and plant leaves. Constance watched for several seconds, then closed the door and went to the corner hutch for a glass. With one arm behind her back, the younger blonde woman bent to examine a row of texts between marble feline bookends. "Oh ... he's a Freudian," she said to herself.

But Constance asked, "Who? Dr. Kellerman?" She looked over her shoulder, as Maggie did the same, frowning. "Oh, no he just reads a lot," Constance explained. "Wait till you see his office, he's got books by every psychiatrist who's ever *been* under the sun."

Maggie was relieved. "Bettelheim," she now observed, running her finger down the dusty spines of several more books stacked on the same table. She slid one out of the pile, flipped it open, and fanned a section of pages with her thumb. "I read some of this for a psych class?"

Constance wasn't sure how she was supposed to answer that. "Which one?" she asked instead. She had turned to the water cooler.

"Just an intro course?"

"What? Oh, no, I mean which book."

Maggie said, "Duh-uh," and knocked her forehead with the heel of her hand. "Um, *The Uses of Enchantment?*"

"Ah, yes," said Constance, watching the glass fill. "About the meaning of fairy tales." She turned and saw Maggie slide one of the marble cats over a little and add the Bettelheim book to the row of Freud texts.

Then Maggie turned her back to Constance and inspected the nearest bookcase. "Oh," she said again, concerned that she'd come to the wrong place after all. The top two shelves were filled with old picture books and children's stories. At eye level was Dr. Seuss, and Mother Goose was down below. Maggie stared at *Grimm's Fairy Tales* on the bottom shelf and said, "He treats kids. Dr. Kellerman, I mean?" She looked back at Constance, who shook her head.

For most of a minute there was no conversation between the two women on either end of the waiting room. One stood there holding a glass of water, watching the other, who continued perusing shelves, stacks and walls.

Why is she here, Constance wondered as the ticking of the cuckoo clock amplified. How can I help?

A vehicle with a holey muffler grumbled past the open window, followed by two chattering girls who thought someone named Vince was a geek. Then crying seeped through the wall, and Maggie said, "So you know he killed himself. Bettelheim, I mean?"

Constance tried to think of something suitable, some meaningful words. Nothing came to her soon enough, so a sober "Yes" was all she said.

"Some people say he was a total fraud?" Maggie remarked. "That he wasn't even a real doctor."

Christ, she thought, can't I shut up already. She wanted to go outside and come back in, to start over and do this right. Or maybe just go.

"Yes, some do," said Constance. And then she had one of her most habitual thoughts. She said to Maggie, "But there are more than two sides to most everything, don't you think? Especially people."

As with any author or topic Joseph seemed to have a keen interest in, Constance had read a number of books and articles by and about Bruno Bettelheim, the well-known child psychiatrist and survivor of Buchenwald and Dachau. Anything that might help her better understand the man sitting in the other room. When Constance had mentioned the revealing and often scathing information, falsified credentials and abusive treatment of patients, that had surfaced about Bettelheim following his death, Joseph's expression had gone from an open mouth and widened eyes to a knit brow and compressed lips in an instant. Then his face had returned to its most usual state: almost blank. With a quivering head, the doctor's only comment had been a monotone "I'm not surprised," before he'd returned to his office and closed the door. When Constance had previously mentioned Bettelheim's suicide, Joseph's reaction had been the same. She still wasn't sure what to think about any of it.

Maggie cocked her head and raised her brows at Constance's point. Yes, she agreed without saying so, there certainly *are* more than two sides to people. That Maggie knew all too well.

She continued looking around, rubbing one arm and then the other as if it were cold. "Hey, this sort of looks like my dad," she said and picked up the wooden bust, unaware that it very much resembled the man behind the desk on the other side of the wall. (Many years ago, a decent carver had spent some rather quality time in the yellow chair.) As she turned to show Constance what she was referring to, Maggie bumped a stack of files off the corner of the console. She dropped to her knees and the bust to the floor, and started scooping together papers and manila folders, like treading water. "I'm such a clutz," she groaned.

"Oh, not at all," said Constance, reaching to bridge the gap as she crossed the room. "Leave them. It's my fault, I shouldn't have left them there."

Maggie made one last scoop, shoved the mixed-up pile back on the table, and sprang to the bench. The drink was offered and accepted in silence, then swiftly gulped. Constance sat down and took the empty glass from Maggie, who would have shattered it in her hands at any moment.

Just then, the door of the back office opened and a red- and puffy-eyed Lucille McBride emerged. She eased that door back into place, then hastened to the next, clutching her black, patent leather handbag to her concave middle as she flitted across the room. As usual, her post-session smile was so exaggerated, her face would ache for several minutes after she allowed her lips to close, halfway down Hopewell Street. Lucille had gotten her Friday fix and was now ready to return to her duties. "Time to get home and get dinner going," she warbled.

Maggie scratched the inside of her wrist as she watched the woman zip through the front office, then turned to Constance, who rubbed her back side to side like an inverted pendulum, the way Grandma Hildy used to do when Maggie was a child.

"Take good care of yourself," Constance replied with a serious yet tender expression, as Lucille opened the door to the hall as though it were made of rice paper. Constance said, "We'll see you next Friday," then to Maggie, "You'll be fine, dear. Dr. Kellerman is a good man."

And the door clicked shut.

Maggie knew she could trust this demonstrative woman and, therefore, the still unseen man with the mysterious first name.

Dr. Kellerman's new client rose and approached the next door, as Constance went to the console. The door was opened then pushed an inch short of closed, as Lucille flew past the front window, and the bust and the Bettelheim book were put back where they belonged.

***

Two weeks following that initial session, Maggie Carlisle sat in the yellow armchair for the third time and continued her story, while Dr. Kellerman watched and listened from behind his desk and Constance did the same through the hole in the wall.

"It's weird, though. He's never even tried to kiss me, or touch me in any like, familiar way?" Maggie was uncomfortable with the topic of this very unbalanced conversation. Her hands gestured nonstop as she said, "I feel like he wants to, but it's like he's waiting until *I'm* ready? And even though I've never said a word about what happened, it's like he senses it? Like there's this connection between us that has nothing to do with words."

Dr. Kellerman was nodding, now gazing past Maggie's head towards the window. The mahogany-brown blinds that matched the wall were down and closed. No longer was it enough that there was paneling, plaster and brick between Joseph and whatever was out there. He didn't want to see it, nor it to see him. People could come in one at a time, if they still wanted to, but that was all he could manage. That was part of his penance.

Maggie slipped her hands under her thighs. She said, "I'm sure I give off vibes, though, like I don't want to be touched that way? But at the same time, I really do, and that makes me feel ... I don't know, weak, I guess? And it's frustrating, because, I mean, I want to get married and have a family someday." She looked up and squinted through illuminated smoke. "Okay if I move this a little?"

Dr. Kellerman nodded.

So Maggie slid the floor lamp back a foot and tilted the shade away from her. Now she could see him better.

"If I could just ... I mean it was *eight years* ago, and that's a long time to dwell on something? And even though I'm sure Mr.

Saunders —" Maggie smiled. "I mean Danny," she said, and her smile vanished. "I mean, I'm sure he's as great as he seems? But I have these awful visions. *You* know what I mean."

More nods from the doctor.

"Sometimes when I'm with him, I start to think about ... well, about being closer? And then all of a sudden I'll see what happened. I mean, I don't *try* to think about it? But it like, rushes into my head, and then it turns into Danny I see doing it? And it's not like I remotely think he would do something like that, so it makes no sense at all, and I keep saying the same damn things!" Maggie sat back with a sigh. Therapy was even tougher than she had expected. And she'd always thought people were supposed to *lie down* in a psychiatrist's office. "Sorry," she said, "but after a whole week, I can hardly remember what I told you the last time. Guess that must happen a lot, though? I mean, with other patients of yours?"

And Dr. Kellerman nodded.

Had Maggie been watching him continuously, not to mention had there not been that bright light in her eyes until less than a minute ago, she might have noticed that the doctor's slow, rhythmic head-bobbing had seldom paused since the beginning of the hour. Then again, she might not have. There were much more important issues on Maggie Carlisle's mind.

"But, anyway, Danny is nothing at all like that asshole. And Brian didn't love me. I was like, his conquest or his trophy or something? But I'm so much more than that? Than a body? And that's *all* he got. So why the hell should I let that poor excuse for a human being affect me so much? I mean, I deserve to be happy."

In the front office, Constance was now nodding too.

You don't need me, thought Joseph as he once again looked at the young woman on the other side of his desk. Don't waste your time with me, I'm no good for you.

But he was glad she was there. The timing *was* right. Something had been stirring within Joseph Kellerman for a long while, and, entirely unrealized by Maggie, her genuine spirit and enthusiasm for life and love despite what had been done to her were drawing that something closer to his surface.

After a couple of involuntary coughs, the lines on Maggie's forehead disappeared as her thoughts jumped to much more recent events. "I met Danny at The Java Joint last night. He showed me pictures of his family."

"Family," the doctor heard himself say as he pressed out his cigarette.

"Yeah, I haven't met them. They live in Vermont, so I'm sure I would. Or I will eventually if things, *you* know ... progress." Maggie peeked over the arm of the chair at the two cats curled like a black and gray yin-yang on a green velour pillow. She smiled at a thought and said, "So anyway, he showed me pictures? And told me stories about the people in them. It was really nice."

"Nice," said the doctor.

"Yeah, I got to know a lot more about him. I think that's so important, don't you? To know about someone's past? Where he comes from, about his family. I mean, isn't that a big part of who we are?"

No response.

"So anyway, it was a really nice evening. And romantic. *You* know, in that subtle kind of way?"

Constance heard an "Mmmm."

Then Maggie said, "It's like, they have these couches there? At the coffee shop? And he was sitting next to me, and just the sides of our arms were touching? And our legs a little? But even though that was all, it was so ... I don't know."

There was a blissful, faraway look in Maggie's eyes as she dragged her upper teeth over her lower lip. An expression she had made no less than once a day from the time she'd first realized what romance was until the moment, eight years ago, she'd stopped believing in it.

But then there was Danny Saunders.

"That's just it, though," said Maggie. "*Those* kinds of touches?

I. Joseph Kellerman

I can't get enough of them. Like when he touches my arm when he talks to me, or puts his hand on my back? And sometimes when we aren't even touching at all, there's this energy."

The doctor said, "Energy?"

And Constance nodded again, this time with a dreamy expression of her own.

"Yeah, it makes me feel calm and safe," said Maggie, "like I really matter to him? I mean, I know that must sound corny? But it's the most sensual thing I've ever felt." Maggie was still glancing over the arm of the chair at a pleasing scene only she could see.

Joseph was seeing things, too. Not corny at all, he thought. This is ... nice.

Maggie giggled, self-conscious, but looked at the doctor as he put his hand back down on the arm of his chair. What she hadn't seen was that he had moved a switch on the clock only he could see, because it was blocked from her view by the stack of files Constance had placed on the desk first thing that morning. That stack was blocked from Maggie's view by a stack of psychiatric journals behind a cardboard box full of golf balls. The previous two times the alarm had gone off while Maggie was in the yellow chair, she'd nearly jolted out of it, which in turn had made Dr. Kellerman's chair screech and the man in it smack the clock.

As the last two numbers now did a synchronized, silent flip to 00, he nodded and looked at her. Doctor and client both looked away at the same time but for different reasons.

Eye contact. Not something Joseph was comfortable with, especially with someone who wasn't Constance. Although he'd thought a number of times since he had first seen his new client, Maggie did look a little like her. Most of all, the hair.

"He asked me to go to the mountains with him. Him and some of his friends," said the taller and less familiar of the two women in the building. "Three married couples are going, Danny and I, and one other guy. Another music teacher? But he's from Berklee. Oh, I told you, right? That Danny ... or, well, that Mr.

Saunders was one of my professors?"

Constance nodded yet again, but Dr. Kellerman's head-bobbing had stopped. Now he just sat there, doing nothing.

"Yeah like, ten times probably," Maggie replied to her own question. "Well, anyway, they reserved these bunks at this cabin for the weekend? It's like five miles from the road, above the tree line, so we have to walk and like, carry everything?"

Yeah, yeah, Joseph was now thinking. Whatever. You're sweet, though, so go on.

Maggie said, "To be honest, though? I don't know what I would do. I mean, if just the two of us were going? But with all those people, it's not like...." She sighed again and, after another peek at the cats, told the doctor, "Part of me wishes it *were* just the two of us? But I still need more time. I mean, just a little." She showed him exactly how much, as if holding a marble.

Maggie looked from Dr. Kellerman, who'd resumed nodding but now with a bit of vigor, to the clock on the wall behind her. "Oh, it's after seven," she said.

Surprised, Constance checked with the cuckoo clock that hadn't made a peep in a decade. Sure enough, it was five past. Strange. There was a distinct moment of silent tension going on in the back office as Constance moved the painting to the right.

Maggie slid forward to the edge of the yellow chair. She crimped her lips and raised her shoulders and eyebrows, as though they were all connected by a single muscle. "Well, thanks for letting me ramble. You know, I'm glad I decided to do this. I think this is exactly what I needed."

As she stood to leave, the doctor lifted his chin from his hand, his elbow propped on the knee of his loosely crossed leg.

I'm glad you came, too, he thought but didn't say. He just smiled a little. And nodded, of course.

Maggie looked at the expressionless eyes staring back at her neck. Then, for the first time in twenty minutes, Dr. Kellerman moved a body part other than his head. He picked up a small pad and scribbled something Maggie couldn't decipher, not even when she accepted the paper from him and held it six inches from her face.

"Well, see you next week!" she said with gusto, overcompensating for another awkward silence and her own discomfort, then left the room.

Dr. Kellerman saw her crumple the paper and stuff it in her canvas bag on the way out the door.

"You're such an ass," Joseph chastised the doctor. "What did you do that for? *Lazy jerk.* Is that all you know how to do? Write prescriptions?"

"She said she's been experiencing some anxiety. Didn't she?"

"She said she's a little stressed out. You know, why don't you try talking to her for a change. Or is that too much to ask?"

The doctor sat and stared.

So Joseph said, "She came here to see you. She's paying to see you, for you to listen and, hey, maybe even help her out. And you give her drugs she doesn't need."

"She didn't come to see me," Dr. Kellerman replied in a repentant whisper.

"Oh, no? But aren't you the guy who's supposed to save everybody? It's your name out there!" Joseph tittered. "Now I know where the expression 'shit on a shingle' came from."

"Okay, so I screwed up," said the doctor. "I just ... I don't know, I just did it. I got stuck."

"You got stuck."

"It's been happening lately."

"Lately? Oh come on, Joe, really."

"Don't call me that."

"Okay, *Isaac.*"

***

While a silent battle ensued in the back office, Maggie spent another few minutes out front.

"How'd it go?" Constance asked.

"Good, I guess? I don't know, I'm still trying to get the hang of this talking-about-it thing. *You* know what I mean."

Constance rubbed Maggie's forearm. "I do. But the hardest part is over. And you should be very proud of yourself. You did this all on your own, coming here."

Maggie gave Constance a light hug, which was reciprocated and then some.

"Okay, well I'll talk to you next week," Maggie said once she'd been released. "Oh, and I'll try to remember that tape this time?"

"I can't wait to hear you play." Constance meant what she said, which was most often the case.

Relief from another session's passing caused Maggie to laugh a bit harder than was warranted. "I doubt you'll be able to hear me screw up," she told Constance. "There are more than like, fifty of us in the string section alone."

"Well, then you'll have to treat us to a solo performance one of these days, won't you?"

Through the open door to the front room, a defeated man in an old oak chair heard Maggie's good-natured response and parting words. He knew so well the look on Constance's face as she said, "See you next week." And Joseph smiled, too.

Chapter 12

On a Tuesday eight months ago, Bernie rammed his back against the seat, grabbed a leg, and propped one black sneaker on the edge of the yellow chair. "That bigheaded *prick*. Thinks he can get any piece of ass he wants just cuz he's freakin assistant manager. Yeah, well, he don' know jack." Bernie snapped his gum four times, a sound that always made Dr. Kellerman jump, then chewed with his mouth open. He rotated his eyes with over-the-top disdain before shooting that hostile glare of his across the desk. "*I* can get it, though," he bragged. "Any time, if I wanted." Bernie wished he could. He was sure *that* would make him feel like a man.

Dr. Kellerman did stare back, but not at Bernie.

The guard shoves her through the door, then follows, undoing his belt.

Joseph shook his head. Don't think about that, he told himself. This isn't the right time.

He'd happened to hear his client's most recent few sentences, while searching his mind and, with his eyes, the room for the next diversion. Dr. Kellerman had been listening to Bernie Babbish for so long, it was anything but interesting anymore.

But he did feel for the guy. It wasn't like it was Bernie's fault he was so disturbed.

"See, I work a lot," Bernie explained. "And them girls at the market ain't my type. I gotta have somebody who can handle me, cuz I don't do none o' that mushy crap. My mother didn't raise no *priss*."

Here we go again, thought Dr. Kellerman. Not that he'd had the least bit of hope for anything different.

***

The alarm was about to go off. Bernie waited, arched forward in his seat, looking bored to death and picking his teeth with a thumbnail, as Dr. Kellerman scribbled.

Bernie could always count on Doc. All those years he'd been there, in his office Tuesday after Tuesday without fail, when Bernie made it to the yellow chair. The place to get some *stuff* out of his system until the next time. Bernie was quite sure that was the only reason he hadn't done to Mother any of the marvelously evil deeds he imagined doing.

And the doctor knew this was a precarious situation, one that warranted a more proactive approach, as opposed to the current no-approach-at-all, to prevent with any certainty Bernie's violent fantasies from coming true.

Bernie *had* made some decent progress in earlier years, most notably during a hiatus of several months spent at a clinic Dr. Kellerman had referred him to. But after his release and return to the yellow chair, Bernie had deteriorated to a worse state than he'd been in when he'd made his first appointment.

Dr. Kellerman had continued to sit there and listen, or at least appear to be listening, to Bernie's tirades, write prescriptions, and feel guilty about it all. Despite the guilt, nothing much had changed.

Mother had given Bernie life, but she'd taken it from him, too. Bernie knew Doc understood. *He* never ridiculed or laughed at him. And, thought Bernie, Doc always gave him just what he needed. Today he'd informed the man with the prescription pad that he needed a good lay.

I. Joseph Kellerman

Bernie practically belly flopped onto the desk and ripped the paper from Dr. Kellerman's hand as the clock buzzed, then kicked himself upright when the noise ceased. This Tuesday, however, the befuddled client sank back to the yellow chair. He stared at the strange words. Looked like "Oslo Heffer" maybe. But the phone number was legible.

***

At two o'clock the day before, Orla Heffel also had been given a page from Dr. Kellerman's prescription pad, as she had been every few months for most of a decade. If it hadn't been for those pills, she knew things would be much worse. Thanks to the good doctuh, Orla always got just what she thought she needed, not to mention an hour a week to talk to someone who didn't ridicule or laugh at her. And *he* didn't interrupt. She hated when people did that. Dr. Kellerman was a great listener — much better than Constance, thought Orla — and his rates were the lowest around.

They hadn't changed in well over a decade.

One thing that had changed was the instant each minute fifty-nine became minute zero-zero. That used to be an awkward reoccurrence for the doctor and sometimes took him a number of additional minutes to muster the nerve to say, "Well," and lean forward, his hands on the arms of his chair and elbows raised as though he were about to get up. Sometimes he did have to get up, but even that didn't always work. In particular Mondays at two o'clock and Tuesdays at noon. Hence the alarm clock's move from Joseph's apartment to Dr. Kellerman's desk. He didn't need it upstairs, because he didn't sleep much at night. Too many disturbing dreams far too often. The clock was useful downstairs though, to signal the end of each long hour, especially those hours with Orla and Bernie, in case the doctor's mind wandered or the person in the yellow chair wasn't ready to leave.

Dr. Kellerman often stared at that old clock radio, the kind with white digits on flipping black flaps, and watched the numbers change. His favorite flip was from :59 to :00, though he hated the nerve-wracking noise that accompanied it.

Like everyone else who visited the yellow chair, Orla had learned to stop talking when the buzzing began, even if the sound lasted for only a split second.

"Yeah, so if I decided tuh do it, I'd give the money tuh charity," Orla had continued between puffs on her third cigarette of the hour. The room was filled with a haze of smoke. "A thousand bucks tuh lose weight. Geez. But I don't know." Inhale and puff. "It ain't like I need it or nothin'. I make real good money at the bank. Toldja I got promoted again, uh?" Inhale and puff. "Yeah, they wannuh make me manajuh."

Orla had been collecting unemployment for almost three months, ever since she'd been fired from the tobacco shop for sampling too much of the inventory.

"But I don't need money tuh lose a few," she now told Dr. Kellerman. "Not that I wannuh, really. But if I did, I could. I could do *anything* if I wahnned. Yup, I could quit smokin' *right this second.*" Long inhale and puff.

Orla knew those last few statements were false. If only she could find something better. Something good to take her mind off other things.

Oy, thought the doctor, who'd been screwing and unscrewing the knob on his center desk drawer for the preceding four minutes. Give me a break already.

Then he felt guilty for thinking such a thing and changed his tune. So out of control and alone she is, so unfulfilled. He snapped, twisted and pulled an unused cigarette in half, then felt guilty about that too.

"I could get a guy if I wahnned," Orla had informed the one with the prescription pad. She wished she could. She was sure that would take her mind off things. "But I gotta find somebody who ain't into all that winin' and dinin' and gooey stuff," she specified. "I don't got time fuh games."

I. Joseph Kellerman

Once again the numbers flipped, and that last statement became true.

When her hour in the yellow armchair was callously up, Orla began her usual extraction. Her dress, which matched the cleaner areas of the upholstery, had been bunched at her thighs when she'd wedged herself between those inflexible arms an hour earlier.

If only he'd get a bigguh chayuh, fuh chrissake, thought Orla, as she had on many a Monday over the past nine years and eight months. Paid him enough money, you'd think he could affawd a freakin sofa.

Orla's heavy breathing and all thinking stopped when she looked at the piece of paper handed across the big desk. Something like "Bornio Balls" and a phone number.

And that had been the start of a very unhealthy relationship.

***

The elderly man who lived in room twenty-four on the second floor of the boarding house thought the ceiling might cave in. It had all started sometime back in late 1992 for reasons unbeknownst to him. But every Wednesday at one a.m., from that week on for many weeks to follow, he'd vacuumed chips of plaster and white dust off his carpet when all the commotion and banging upstairs stopped at that wee hour of the morning, just in time for the movie on Channel Four.

Beginning at thirty-five minutes past midnight on Wednesdays like clockwork, the bed in room thirty-four on the third floor of Bobbie Dee's bounced in time with the flashing sign outside the window. After the usual second round, Orla was past due for a smoke, so the box spring heaved another submissive groan as she dismounted, grabbed her pack of unfiltered Marlboros and the remote off the crate-turned-nightstand, and raised the volume. Just in time, every time, for the one a.m. movie.

On the other side of the lumpy mattress lay Bernie Babbish's limp frame, his catatonic expression unchanged since thirty-five minutes past midnight, with one brief exception; the second round never worked for him.

Orla took another slug of beer to wash down a couple of pills, one more than prescribed by her allergist, and chased the drink with a mini chocolate donut. Late night black-and-white movies were her favorite.

I was right, Orla thought, as she watched the pretty pictures and even prettier people on the black-and-white television. Sex *was* helping get her mind off her imperfections. At least, it did every Wednesday for twenty minutes or so. Dr. Kellerman had fulfilled yet another of Orla's needs by producing this Bornio guy. She lit another cigarette and, for a fleeting moment, considered the possibility of switching to Lites.

I was right, thought Bernie, his head spinning. Sex *did* make him feel like a man. Or while it lasted, anyway. But Bernie still hated Mother as much as ever. And he hated that he loved her. Most of all, he hated himself.

Maybe he needed a stronger pill. Maybe what this Oslo broad had in that little orange bottle over there would work for him also. Finding out what that something was, however, and asking to try a few would involve conversation, which had no place in their relationship.

Bernie Babbish was the only person Orla Heffel *wouldn't* talk to.

They were two lost souls seeking what they truly needed in all the wrong places. Especially 4991 Hopewell Street.

Chapter 13

"I just stopped fighting," said Maggie to her fidgeting hands. "I mean, I thought he might kill me if I didn't? So I lay there and tried not to think. It seemed like it went on forever." She glanced up in the doctor's general direction, as she'd been doing every minute or so since 6:01, then back to her lap, a dirty yellow armrest, the floor. "All I wanted was for him to finish and get the hell out. Of me, my apartment. My life. But I guess in a way he's still in it, isn't he? Since I can't stop replaying it in my head."

Dr. Kellerman was staring towards Maggie's down-turned face, but he wasn't looking at her either. He was hearing the words but thinking of things long past. Thinking of them in a way he could live with.

"Go!" the guard growls, shoving her back inside.

The ten and a half year-old boy, who now thinks of himself as just Josef, doesn't know the girl's name and can't see her face. Only the back of her nearly bald head. She isn't as frail as the others.

He's sure it's a girl.

The guard peers outside, as she sits, shivering, on a lower bunk, her arms around her sunken middle. He approaches her while undoing his belt, walking past the petrified boy who's watching.

Without a word between them she turns and kneels, as if she knows the routine.

The bugs are making Josef's ulcerated skin crawl. He wants to run away, but he can't.

The girl leans across the wood, as the guard stands over her and unzips his trousers. Such a tiny sound is earsplitting.

The boy doesn't understand what's happening. He chants a Hebrew prayer, though he no longer believes anyone is listening. Still, he tries anyway. There's nothing else he can do. The Kiddish is the only one he knows by heart, and his own words have never worked at all.

"Baruch ata Adonai —"

The guard crouches and yanks the girl's baggy pants down so hard he nearly pulls her off the bunk.

"Eloheinu melech ha-olam —"

He's on top of her unpadded spine, ramming her forward.

Josef feels the pain, too. It runs up his back and down his legs.

"Asher ki-d'shanu b'mitz-votav v'ratza vanu —"

The boy is struggling for air.

But the girl doesn't make a sound as the bunk squeaks, squeaks, squeaks, and the guard grunts.

"V'shabbat kodsho b'ahava," Josef continues in desperation, as the girl grips the far side of the bed. He can see her white knuckles and feels the cold wood on his own hands. He hears himself chant, "u-v'ra-tzon hin-chilanu," and the guard lets out a hard groan. The room is quiet, and the boy stops praying. Once and for all.

The guard stands, arches his back, zips his pants, buckles his belt and smoothes his uniform. He reaches into his coat pocket, then tosses a chunk of molded bread onto the floor and walks with a stiff, official stride out the door, leaving the bare-bottomed child stretched across the bunk.

So it had been that young Josef Kellermann learned what sex was.

"And when he slammed the door and left," Maggie continued, her eyes filled with tears, "I just lay there and didn't move for like, I don't know how long. My whole body hurt, but I tried not to feel anything. And in a way it worked? I became numb inside? And I sort of stayed that way for a long time."

The doctor said, "Yes."

And Maggie told him, "I tried to pretend it hadn't happened. To block it out and act like nothing had changed? That didn't work."

"No."

"So then I told Jeanette, I said I just needed to get it out. To say it and forget about it? Which obviously didn't work either. But then...." Maggie was thoughtful, as the tears receded.

"But then?" said the doctor.

"But then it was strange. I mean, for a long time, it felt like it had happened to somebody else? Like if I remembered it, I was *watching* the whole thing? Like it was a movie? Isn't that weird?"

Dr. Kellerman nodded, staring at the image of a man who looked very much like himself. The action remained the same with the rapid flashes of memory, but the face of the woman changed with each forward motion of the man's hips. Meaningless sex. That's all it had been. Fulfilling a basic need, like breathing or eating. A fact of life, of staying alive. There was nothing spiritual or emotional about it.

Like that guard and young prisoner.

As the scene repeated, Maggie's voice now a murmur in the background, the woman beneath the man changed once more. Joseph now saw Marta's accusing eyes, over and over again. Eyes he'd never wanted to look at.

Her nails are digging into his scalp.

That part had been real, numerous times. But in Joseph Kellerman's imagination, the blood began to trickle from beneath the man's hair, down his neck, his back and sides, onto the bed. The bed Joseph hadn't slept in for almost twenty-four years. He blinked several times, erasing the disturbing images that loomed between him and sweet, sincere Maggie.

"But that's not how it was supposed to *be*," she said, her gaze now focused through the center canyon of the desk. As far as she could tell, the doctor was listening intently.

In a way, he was hearing her again.

"Not supposed to be," he mumbled.

"Not at all. I mean, I'd imagined it a lot. And I thought I wanted it to be with Brian? But obviously it was just physical to him. He wanted it and was going to have it with *me*, whether *I* was ready or not. So he did. And it meant nothing to him? And I guess *I* didn't mean anything to him, either." After a moment of contemplation, she added with a pointed finger, "You know, Dr. Kellerman, as far as I'm concerned, I'm still a virgin. Because what he did to me? That was *not* making love."

What had been plaguing Joseph's mind for the past fifteen minutes at last faded away to reveal the sanguinity that washed over Maggie's face as she lowered her hand. "Someday I'll be ready," she said. "And it'll be as special as I always imagined. I mean, I know it will, because it'll be based on love, trust and friendship. Everything that's good and beautiful. And *real*."

A faint smile appeared and remained on the doctor's bearded face, as Maggie Carlisle described her most precious fantasies for the rest of the hour. The scenes in Joseph Kellerman's mind that followed along with the young woman's words were nothing like those which had come before. Ever. They were wonderful things Joseph had never experienced outside of his own imagination and then only when a client described them. No one had ever done so quite like Maggie.

To have so much time, he pondered with a touch of envy as he watched her leave the room. If only I had that. The time to make it right. You don't know how lucky you are, my dear girl.

Chapter 14

"Hello, Mr. Babbish."

"Miss Fairhart, ma'am. Wow, you — you're looking lovely."

"Oh, why, thank you."

Bernie was looking apologetic, his head bowed and shoulders pulled in as if to make himself even smaller. "Is that a new dress?" he asked, sitting. "It's awful pretty."

"Well, thank you again. But no, I've had this for years, actually." Bernie looked disappointed, so Constance added, "Although, I don't think I've worn it on a Tuesday in a very long time."

"Oh, yeah, okay, I remember now. Yeah, but I was just sayin', you know, that it's *nice*, that's all."

"That's sweet of you, Bernie, you're such a gentleman."

To most men, Constance's tone would likely have sounded condescending, as if she were speaking to a child. To Bernie, however, it was a wonderful compliment she had paid him. He was a gentleman, and that's exactly what he wanted to be.

Now he looked pleased. And, for the moment, he was. Bernie smoothed the gelled hair above his ears, then folded his hands in the crook of his lap.

***

When Bernie Babbish arrived each Tuesday, he acted much like the daughter Mother had always wanted. "Bernie" was short for Bernice, but he was and always had been a male. And he'd never desired an additional X chromosome. His mother, on the other hand, had had other ideas from the start. Her son's given name was the absolute least of it.

Mother Babbish hadn't wanted a child at all in the first place, but accidents happen, as they say. And she said she'd accidentally had sex with the garbage man. Or had it been the meter-reader man? She couldn't remember.

It had been both and the little maintenance man in 4B, but that made no difference. For her own very disturbing reasons, Bernie's mother didn't want *any* man in her life. So she was determined not to have one, regardless of what some doctor had announced around the middle of 1951, give or take a year or so. Bernie never had bothered to find out when he'd been born, nor did he really care.

Neither did Mother. She'd sat up in the hospital bed, written "Bernice Babbish" with no middle and no father's name, and signed the bottom line of that long since misplaced birth certificate, then swallowed another pain killer like she often did and went back to sleep.

So it had come to be that Bernice Babbish entered the world. No less than six years after that incident, "she" started to realize a strange feeling inside, a feeling that something wasn't right. The pigtails and dresses and nail polish were the same, but none of the other girls Bernice played Doctor with in the stairwell had one of *those*.

Mother didn't care. He was a she, and that was that, no matter what the rest of the world said. Bernice was a little young lady with a tiny penis, she'd told him, and young ladies do *not* stand up when they use the facilities.

Bernice had continued to do and behave as he was ordered, because the punishment was too much to handle and the threats of cutting the abnormality off far too terrifying. He'd tried very hard to be Mother's little girl.

As Bernice had grown older, the resentment and self-loathing had grown stronger and he'd started to fight back. Not against Mother or the kids who taunted, but the feminine habits and confusion he couldn't seem to shake. The fact that Bernice was of small stature with somewhat unfortunate looks didn't help matters at all.

***

Bernie, as he'd insisted everyone but Mother call him since around the time of puberty, now poised with legs tightly crossed, posture perfect on the waiting room bench, tending to his cuticles as the cuckooless clock approached his very own hour.

There was muffled buzzing.

"Excuse me for a moment, Mr. Babbish." Leaving the cover letter from attorney Dunst and the first page of the enclosed document upside down on her desk, Constance picked up the second page, passed the exiting client with yet another "See you next week" and stepped through the open door.

"Dr. Kellerman?"

"Yes, Miss Fairhart." He was lighting the cigarette pinched between his lips, so the words sounded more like, "Yz, Mz. Frhrt." He tossed the lighter onto a stack of journals, slid a sandaled foot off the corner of the desk, then turned his chair and, from his collar bone down, his body in her direction. Besides the Birkenstocks, he was wearing those fifteen year-old khaki shorts and a white undershirt of similar age. July or January, it made no difference; the temperature inside that building never fluctuated more than five degrees.

Dr. Kellerman gave his assistant a glance, along with a puff of smoke.

Constance cupped a hand over her mouth and nose. "This place smells like an ashtray." She had been saying that for years.

"Srry," he said, as he had so many times for nearly as many reasons. The cigarette was still hanging from his mouth, bouncing as he spoke. "Wnt one?" He held the pack out to her.

Constance pursed, puckered and twisted her lips as she shook her head, but tender amusement showed through nonetheless.

Joseph shrugged and tossed the pack onto the desk calendar. He propped his elbow on the arm of his chair and smoked, his head tipped to the cigarette as he examined Constance through squinted eyes. She still looked twenty-seven when he did that. Younger even.

What if he *could* turn back the clock, twenty-three years back, and start over? Perhaps fifty years back. Or more. Could he change other things too? He made himself stop thinking about it.

"Hello!"

"Huh?"

"I *said,* Dr. Kellerman, sign this."

The first time, it had been a polite request. Constance stretched across the desk, placed the partial document in front of her boss, and slapped a pen down on the paper. "Are you sure that's a regular cigarette you've got there?"

She received another mischievous glance. That was one of the few emotions that ever showed through on *his* face anymore.

Joseph grabbed the pen with a dramatic swipe of the hand, but looked down only long enough to position the point on the proper line.

Constance knew he wouldn't care what he was authorizing this time either. His signature resembled "I. LpXrllw" much more than "I. Joseph Kellerman."

Joseph was forever signing "I. LpXrllw" on things Constance placed, slipped or slapped on the desk in front of him. If this were something she thought the least bit interesting or worthy of comment, she'd already have been summarizing the data. He knew that; that's how it always was. If this were something important, she would have left it for him to read. Otherwise, the assistant instructed and the doctor did as he was told. That's how it had been for a very long time, which was better than fine with him.

Joseph liked when Constance told him what to do. He preferred it that way. Don't ask, he'd often thought when she gave him the option of yes, no or otherwise. Just make me.

But Constance never went quite that far.

"Thr" was the next sound that emanated from behind the smoke, as the paper covered with all those little words, some of them being "Linda" and "Payne," flew back across the desk. As Constance stooped to pick it up, she grabbed a crumpled calendar page out of the wastebasket and scored a bull's-eye on Joseph's forehead. She stood, turned on her heels, and walked with exaggerated purpose towards the door.

"I'll send in your next client, *Doctor*."

When Constance reentered the front office, Bernie Babbish was standing, staring fiercely at the cuckoo clock. She'd wasted two of his minutes!

***

By half past eleven, Bernie was midway through his usual transformation. He'd gone from chitchatting about the gossip of the week he'd read in the tabloids when not bagging groceries to bitching about what this stuck-up checkout girl or that nitpicky customer had done to piss him off during the last seven days. He had begun the hour with a mellifluous tone and dainty gestures. Once again, he'd become absurdly masculine, his legs spread and the arms of the yellow chair jammed into the pits of his, as he forced bodily noises and cursed.

At ten minutes before the end of his hour, Bernie was launching into high gear. This time, his big complaint was a coworker's habit of snapping her gum. That was the past week's very displaced issue.

"That *cow*," he snarled, "poppin' that grape shit she's always gnawin' on."

As if you don't, thought Dr. Kellerman.

Bernie dislodged some phlegm, swallowed, and said, "Chews her cud all freakin day, blowin' an suckin' like there's no tomorruh. I'm tellin ya, if Mother hadduh been there, she'duh grabbed that ass-lickin' bitch's tongue and yanked it clear outa her pukin' ugly head!"

Delightful was the next unspoken response. I don't want to hear this.

Dr. Kellerman ignored his conscience when it asked, "What happened to your compassion, Joseph?" He began mouthing the names of the fifty states. In alphabetical order. Backwards.

But it didn't really matter to the one still raving in the yellow chair. Bernie had years ago stopped pausing throughout his customary diatribe to see if Doc had anything to say. And Dr. Kellerman had ceased having any comments for Bernie Babbish years before Bernie had stopped waiting for them. The little man who sat and slumped in the yellow chair, Tuesday after Tuesday from eleven to noon, continued spewing all the anger he didn't know what else to do with, while the doctor tuned out.

And that's just it.

Like Bernie Babbish, a rather large percentage of the clients Dr. I. Joseph Kellerman still spent an hour with each week had been coming to sit in that yellow chair for many, many consecutive weeks. Also like Bernie, most of those people rarely missed an appointment. They were the ones who didn't want to stop coming. And they were the ones who didn't come early. If they did arrive several minutes before their scheduled sessions, they didn't have all that much to say to the woman who'd occupied that front office on the vast majority of days for more than twenty-three years. Or they didn't care to listen.

The many clients that *had* come, gone and eventually not come back during the past decade-plus had done so for either of two reasons. The first being the feeling that they and the doctor just weren't right for each other. Or perhaps all that time over all those days they had arrived a little early had done them a lot of good. Not that most of them seemed to realize that the accumulated pre-appointment time spent in the presence of Constance Fairhart had been the most therapeutic hours they had spent in that building.

Following their unofficial sessions in the waiting room each week, numerous clients then spent a rather productive, emotive hour in the yellow chair, working through their innermost thoughts and feelings by speaking, for all intents and purposes, to themselves. Especially over the last four years or so. The breathing, smoking and sometimes nodding doctor sat in the corner on the other side of his desk, so the clients didn't *feel* like they were talking to themselves. For many, that process had paid off, whether they recognized how it was happening or not. The majority of those people had no conscious idea, some didn't care, and a handful of others said they couldn't afford the fees. Constance knew better than they, of course, how out-of-date Dr. Kellerman's rates were, but she didn't press the point. Not even for Joseph's sake. Constance also realized people had good reason for not wanting to return to that dulled yellow chair.

So did Joseph. He knew he wasn't much more than an old body in another worn-out chair in a row house with a name and occupation apparently still out there on that embarrassing brass shingle. He was able to recognize through the haze in his mind what kind of man he'd become. And he knew that all that remained of his dignity, not to mention his livelihood, was owed to the benevolent woman who acted as liaison between himself and the worlds on either side of that distant, heavy door. Through her eyes and her window dressing people saw Dr. I. Joseph Kellerman.

The rest of the professional psychiatric community no longer called upon the man who continued to age inside 4991 Hopewell Street. He wasn't one of them anymore. And that's how they thought of him, too. When they happened to think of him. It was a near miracle no one had made an official issue of his unprofessional conduct. Up to this point, Dr. Kellerman had slipped through the cracks, thanks in large part to the well-intentioned efforts of Constance Fairhart.

With one significant exception, humanity had forgotten, or at least disregarded, Joseph Kellerman. And that was how he wanted it. Or so he had thought for a very long time. He was now, he felt, less than nothing. He felt guilt. And he felt ashamed. Despite all his schooling, reading and studying, however, and all the good he had done for many, Joseph understood himself the very least.

***

"Mother sure wouldn'a put up with that bullcrap," continued the fully metamorphosed Babbish, who grabbed what little of himself he had. "You don't get no second chances with *her*."

Mother Babbish always became the central topic of Bernie's fits. She figured into everything he knew was wrong with the world. And she had everything to do with all the things Bernie knew were wrong with *him*. His face began to flush as he snorted and grabbed himself harder.

"'Pull down your dress, Bernice! Pull your shirt up, Bernice!' Always flappin' her freakin fat gums. 'Little girls don't chew with their mouths open, Bernice!' Yeah, well, I'll show that dickmuncher how fat old hags chew. I'll rip out her freakin yellow, rotten teeth!"

Just as Mother had threatened to do to him with pliers when he was eight. To Bernice's relief, she had only extracted two molars.

A throaty laugh came from the client now slumped so low in the yellow chair that he could barely be seen through the hole in the wall, as another puff of smoke streamed across the desk and Constance's view. A few seconds later, at the blunt end of Bernie Babbish's latest hour, nothing had changed from the week before. Or the thousand or so weeks before that.

Chapter 15

"See you next week, Dr. Kellerham."

"Kellerman."

"What's that?"

"No, nothing. Take care, Mr. London."

"I'm Linden."

"Right. Sorry."

Well, that was only his fourth visit. Dr. Kellerman passed the rest of the minute recalling the number of hours he'd listened to the guy blather about his other nine personalities, who refused to see a psychiatrist.

Kellerham, Kellman, Kelly. Whatever. Joseph didn't really care what anybody called *him*, as long as it wasn't by his given first name. Once in a while someone would ask what the I stood for, but Joseph never did repeat the same answer. He'd made up first names such as Ichabad, Igmont and Irkle, ignoring one argumentative client who said she'd always thought Irkle started with an E. How names were spelled didn't matter to him at all. An f or a ph, one n or two. Whatever. Dr. Kellerman told one guy that the I stood for nothing, but that Miss Fairhart would say it was i for ignominious, insufferable, impious and impalpable invertebrate, or some such string of impressive and self-deprecating adjectives attached to a vague but meaningful label that would render the recipient of the rhetoric speechless. Sometimes Dr. Kellerman didn't answer the question at all.

So why, then, was I-period etched on that nameplate next

to the front door for all the world to see? No one but Constance had ever asked.

***

"Come *on*, Joseph," she pleaded, kneeling before the desk with hands clasped and a beseeching look in her always expressive eyes. "I've known you for five years, and you *still* won't tell me your first name?"

With lids at half-mast, he shook his head.

Constance rose and performed her most authoritative guise, standing as tall as she could at five-foot-two and affixing her hands to her hips for added effect. Something she did often when dealing with the immature imp she worked for. "I mean it," she said, fighting that persistent smile with everything she had. "I'm going to hand in my resignation, effective immediately, if you don't give it up."

But the harder she tried and more frustrated she got, the more impish he became. Again he shook his head, this time with eyes wide.

Constance grabbed a pen and prescription pad off the desk, positioned as if to write, and gave her best impression of a serious threat. "This is your last chance, Kellerman."

"Well, maybe the Blue Moon will take you back now that you're all grown up," he replied, then shielded his face as though she were going to strike.

"Look," Constance growled, "if you don't like your name, if it's something embarrassing or ... whatever, then why the *heck* is it on that shingle of yours?"

"Why don't you just say fuck and get it over with." Joseph made himself chuckle with that one.

Constance continued as if he hadn't spoken. "Not to mention your business card and your monogrammed handkerchiefs."

"Someone gave those to me," he said.

I. Joseph Kellerman

He had no idea who that had been.

"Well, whatever! If you hate the name, then drop the fucking I!"

Constance was taken aback by Joseph's next response. She'd expected the usual. Some kind of exasperating, childish remark or an immediate change of subject. Or, if nothing else, at least a vague grin for the uncharacteristic expletive she'd thrown in at his suggestion.

Instead, his mischievous expression gave way to one of serious reflection with a definite touch of melancholy.

"My father gave me that name," he said. "And he was an extraordinary man."

Constance sat down on the very edge of the yellow chair and waited with breathless anticipation for him to elaborate. The result was unsatisfying, but that certainly didn't surprise her anymore.

"He should never be forgotten, Constance," Joseph said with glazed eyes.

Constance couldn't help but fixate on the sound of his voice speaking her first name. He'd never called her anything but Miss Fairhart. Question after question began surfacing in her mind, but she didn't dare let them pass her lips for fear of interrupting his train of thought and this rare and precious insight into Joseph Kellerman's past. Not to mention his heart.

"I'm nothing at all of the man he was, but, at the very least, I honor him by using the initial. It's insignificant, I know, but it's something. And I must never forget."

As if he'd caught himself in an unintentional confession of a crime, Joseph abruptly closed his mouth and stood. Before disappearing into the front office and then upstairs, leaving a puzzled young woman behind, he said, "Never mind. Just call me Joseph."

And that had been that. When it came to I. Joseph Kellerman, Constance didn't push too hard, though perhaps

she should have.
   She knew she should have.
   But she never had.

* * *

By 12:08, Dr. Kellerman could no longer distract himself by doodling noses on his desk calendar. So he picked up the clock and moved to the other side of his desk. He set the alarm for 12:58, then placed the clock on top of the box full of golf balls. Taking his other seat, Joseph tried to let his troubled mind go. Today it took another two minutes to begin.

"It's all right, Josef."
The boy hears the voice but doesn't see her.
"Mama?"
"Over here," she says.
Josef crouches and peers around the corner of the barrack. "Be careful, Mama, they mustn't see you."
"Sweetheart, your legs!"
Josef's frostbite has become open, infected wounds.
"Yes, but I did it," he says. "I kept my arms up the whole time. We were punished for something, I don't know what. We had to kneel with our arms in the air, but I made up lots more of the story and watched it in my head. And I didn't get hit once. I didn't even feel the cold after a while. I know how to do it. And I work hard, but only hard enough, so I can keep going. Like Papa taught me before, in the other place. When they aren't looking, I rest, even if it's just for a few seconds. I know how to do it!"
"You're a strong young man, Josef. Very brave."
"I'm doing it for you," he tells his mother. "I'm going find us a way out and take care of you, I promise."
Josef reaches to touch her hair, but she ducks out of sight as a guard passes. Josef waits until he no longer hears the crunching footsteps.

"Mama?"

"Yes, sweetheart."

"Will we ever dance again?"

"Of course," she whispers. "Soon. God will see to it."

"Do you really believe that?" Josef asks, looking into his mother's eyes. That's where he finds his answers.

But she disappears as someone shouts at the back of his head. "You!"

Josef turns to a gun.

"What are you doing?" the guard at the other end of that gun asks.

Josef says nothing. He raises his chin and stares straight ahead, just like Papa did.

Something diverts the guard's attention. He walks away, leaving the boy with a churning gut. A shot is fired nearby, and Josef runs for the latrine.

The groans, the vomiting, the putrid air. Those fetid pits and gaunt, ailing bodies of the men and women who use them are separated by transparent cloth. There's no privacy and very little time. Finishing up as quickly as his intestines and sore backside can, Josef determines to get as far from this wretched place as possible. But before he's able to escape, sudden commotion and the wails of several women on the other side of the cloth make him turn.

"No, Rachel, no!" one of them urges, looking down into the pit.

What Josef sees when he leans a bit further makes him heave, though there's nothing left in his stomach. A young woman he saw carrying her bread ration has dropped it into the latrine. And she's gone down into the excrement to retrieve it!

Gagging, Josef escapes as fast as his weak legs can carry him. Wherever he looks there's something just as dreadful. And more so. Death, disease, starvation, torture—everywhere, always. He frantically searches for a place to hide, but the only safe haven he can find is inside his head. So the boy closes his eyes.

"*Dies ist alles nicht echt,*" said a nauseated Joseph Kellerman, as the child had repeated over forty-nine years earlier. And a new scene began.

"Josef," she says softly, waking her son. "Come, we'll dance."
How wonderful it was to rest for a while with Mama. Her touch is medicine.
She helps Josef to his feet. The pain in his back and legs diminishes as the music plays.

You Are My Sunshine faded into Joseph Kellerman's ears.

Mama's hair shimmers. There are no walls or barbed wire fences now, only cobalt-blue sky. Around and around they glide, big circles across a field of wildflowers. He feels so alive, so completely happy, as they float together on the music. How he loves to dance with—
What was that?

In the front room, Constance had dropped a twenty-pound bag of cat litter, and Joseph looked over the side of the yellow chair.

Josef looks over the side of the bunk.
The one who was on the edge of the bed below has died, and someone pushed him off. They lie five and six on a bed for one.
The thin layer of straw on Isaac's bunk is foul. He feels the wet on his legs. The one overlapping him is very ill and can't climb down to relieve himself. Josef thinks maybe it would be better to sleep on the concrete.
No, it's much too cold. Better to share some body heat and human filth than freeze to death on the floor.
Isn't it?
Josef raises his head back onto the bunk, and it spins.

I. Joseph Kellerman

Joseph grabbed the arms of the chair and closed his eyes. With a few deep breaths, the wooziness subsided. He lit another cigarette and continued watching the oddly edited film.

Another transport. Swoosh-bang! Bang!
And another. Bang! Bang! Bang! The bolt being shoved into place, he hears it over and over again.
This time, there's no room to crouch. He has to tilt his head back to breathe.
Bang!
"It's all right, Josef," she says. "I'm here."
"I know, Mama."
They lean on each other, for how many days he doesn't know. Maybe the next place will be better.
Bang! Swoosh-bang! And lifeless bodies fall out, to the ground.
Josef staggers from the train, gulping air. He walks, runs ahead, rests while the others catch up. Run ahead, rest. Must keep up, the ones who fall behind are shot. Must keep going for Mama. He doesn't know how long they walk. Maybe a week or more.
Yes, more.
Josef sees his swollen, bleeding feet, but he doesn't feel them. They look so bad, he knows he should feel them. But now Josef feels nothing at all, not even the boils that cover his arms and buttocks. He sees the hills of rotting bodies and feels nothing. He sees the near-skeleton of a man cutting and eating the raw flesh of another, who died hours ago. Still, Josef feels nothing. A man comes to yet another squalid barrack full of emaciated, lifeless souls —some dead, the rest almost —and cries, "We're free! We're free!"
And Josef feels nothing.
Free? But the dying is far from over. Typhoid fever is rampant. Starvation, misery and desperation are everywhere. And in its midst there is still a little boy.
Why?

A numb, helpless Josef Kellermann sits and waits. Does he want to die

The man in the yellow chair nodded, then shook his head.

Is it three years later now? The boy is still alive.
Why?
Josef is on a ship bound for the States. That's all he knows. But he doesn't care. He does as he's told or does nothing if nothing is instructed. Sits and waits, sits and waits. Working was better. He wants to be busy.
Josef doesn't know the fat man with the gold tooth who introduces himself as Mister Smith and takes him to a house like none he's ever seen. The only thing that brings a detectable response from the boy is the sound of his first name coming from those stranger's lips.
"Mein name ist Josef!" he shouts, clenching his fists and eyes. "Mein. Name. Ist. Josef!"
The only part of Mister Smith's reply that he understands is "Speak English."

Dr. Kellerman's mind went dark and silent right on time.

***

"Joseph," Constance said softly, a long moment after she extinguished his cigarette and moved the ashtray away from the edge of the table. When she placed her hand on his shoulder, it was time to stop pretending and open his eyes.

Chapter 16

A slight change in Dr. Kellerman didn't go unnoticed, but it wasn't anyone seated in the yellow armchair who saw it. Constance was the one who detected the difference, as her boss plodded down the stairs from his apartment. At first she wasn't sure what that difference was. But when Joseph lifted his head, nodded and said his usual "Morning," his longtime assistant realized. He was not only freshly shaven, something he usually was only once a month at the beginning of the month, but there was not a single shred of blood-stained tissue on Joseph's smooth face.

"Good morning, Joseph." Constance watched him pass her desk. "I picked up some groceries on my way in. Thought maybe you could use a few things."

She knew he was well aware that she'd done his shopping.

A few steps from his office, Joseph stopped. "Oh, thank you," he replied with a rueful smile and downcast eyes. He buried his hands in the pockets of his khaki shorts and nodded, but didn't know what else to say.

Neither did Constance.

Joseph had never asked her to bring him food or anything else to speak of, but he hadn't needed to. Constance had figured it out for herself. All those deliveries all those weeks. And the *Boston Globe* was still on the stoop when she'd arrived, morning after morning. Sometimes, there were two or three newspapers waiting by the door if she had taken a day or two off for a holiday or weekend. And Delilah said she never saw the doctor pass by anymore.

But he *is* still a rather busy man, Constance had reassured herself when the truth of the matter had begun to sink in and make her very uneasy. Seemed reasonable enough that he order meals and groceries. But why pay extra for deliveries when *she* could pick up a few things on her way in, or when she went shopping *anyway*? And what difference did it make if he brought in the paper or she did? And Delilah wasn't *always* around. Maybe she and Joseph had been missing each other for a while. Maybe he went out at night?

Or maybe not.

So Constance delivered the papers from the stoop to Dr. Kellerman's desk and stocked the downstairs kitchen. Gradually the food disappeared, and immediately she replaced the missing items. Weeks had turned into months and months into years, and the routines had continued. Now they seemed normal.

"Thank you," Dr. Kellerman repeated before moving on to his office.

***

Today, Constance spent a bit more time than usual facing the wall behind her desk. Although she couldn't see him, she always knew what Joseph was doing. Or not doing.

Regular puffs of smoke wafted into her view, with only a short respite during the two to three o'clock session. The doctor had probably nodded off, but Constance knew very well the client now seated in the yellow chair wouldn't notice. He was the one who kept his eyes closed the entire hour until the clock buzzed. Said he had to pretend he was hypnotized in order to "release" like that.

Another hour and session later at the sound of the four o'clock buzz, Constance pushed the painting to the right and spun in her chair to face her desk. Seconds later, the client reentered the front office, and, this time, Dr. Kellerman followed.

"Goodbye, Cheryl," said Constance, looking up from the

ledger. "See you next week."

"Yep, thanks, Constance. Bye, Dr. K."

Dr. Kellerman raised his hand as he walked to the front of the desk, then both hands went to his pockets. He leaned in to check the appointment book.

"Something I can do for you, Joseph?"

"No, thank you," he said, but he continued to lean and look. "We still have that six o'clock, then." It was more a statement than a question.

Constance tried not to sound curious. "Yes," she replied, studying the ledger to enhance her performance. "But if that's too late, we could probably arrange something different for next week. I'll talk to Maggie about it, if you'd like."

"No, no, I was just checking."

Joseph waited and so did Constance, keeping her eyes on her work. "Something else, Dr. Kellerman?"

"Hmm? Oh, no, mm-mm."

He headed towards his office, as the next client rushed in and apologized for cutting it so close. What the man meant was that he was sorry he hadn't left time to chat with Constance before his appointment.

Joseph stopped short in front of the door, and the client nearly ran into his back. "But thank you, Miss Fairhart," the doctor said. "I appreciate your help."

Constance nodded. Something certainly was a bit off today, but aside from his nickless, mid-month shave, she couldn't quite put her finger on it.

***

The waiting room door opened on schedule.

"Hi, Lucille, good to see you."

Lucille McBride looked forward to her time in the front office, because Constance seemed to want her company. She was the only one Lucille knew who ever treated her like that.

"Good to see *you*," she replied.

Lucille closed the door, then sat down on the bench as though afraid to dent the cushion. She clutched her handbag to her stomach and looked at the braided rug, as Constance got up and went to sit beside her.

"How are you today?"

"Oh, fine, fine," Lucille replied and began fiddling with the silver cross that rested on her chest. She was a bit nervous, despite the fact that she'd been showing up twenty minutes early each Friday for most of the past four years. Lucille felt so flawed next to such a confident woman. How she admired her!

Constance put her hand on Lucille's shoulder and felt sharp bone beneath a thick rayon-acetate blend. The black dress was much too heavy for such a humid day. "Can I get you anything?" she asked, knowing full well what the answer would be. "How about iced tea and a cookie."

"Oh, no, I couldn't, I'm watching my weight."

Lucille was almost dangerously thin.

"Foo on that," said Constance. "You're beautiful just the way you are."

Unlike the more subtle change in Dr. Kellerman, there was a drastic difference in Lucille's appearance. Constance still wasn't sure what to say about it, but there was no avoiding the subject a moment longer. Lucille was eyeing her for a more specific comment, visibly concerned.

"And your hair is lovely," Constance added. "The color really brightens your face."

Well, that last part was true.

Lucille let go of her pendant, relieved. "I didn't think you'd noticed," she said.

There was no way anyone could *not* have noticed, even if they had never before seen Lucille McBride. She'd gone from a medium-brown flap that hung, straight and limp, across her forehead and down to her shoulders, to beyond bold and uplifted.

"It's called Scarlet O'Hara," she told Constance. "Richard pointed it out in church. He said he loved that young woman's hair. The pretty girl I told you about? The one with the pierced nose?"

Constance glanced from Lucille's eyes to her slightly upturned nose, but saw nothing unnatural. I'd rather see a nose ring than you lose any more weight, she thought.

"So I asked her at the picnic that afternoon," Lucille continued. "I asked what shade it was. It was her God-given color, she said, but her boyfriend calls it Ripe Cherry. So I told Belinda. That's the young lady at the beauty parlor. I told her I wanted to be a Ripe Cherry, too. Belinda said she didn't have anything by that name, but that Scarlet O'Hara would be the closest shade. So here it is!" She touched the sides of her heavily sprayed semi-beehive.

Constance noticed the line of dye along Lucille's temple, the edge of her conspicuous cheek, and around her ear. She said, "I'm sure Richard loves the new look."

Constance knew what Lucille's husband was like. Not that she had met him.

"Oh, but he works very hard," Richard McBride's wife explained, her expression dampening. "And he's so tired when he comes home."

Constance watched the woman whose cold left hand she covered with her warm right one, as Lucille's angular face began to struggle with emotion. Lips twitching. Erratic blinks.

Lucille produced a tentative smile as her eyes went back to the floor. "And he'd had such a difficult day at work," she said. "You see, there's this new man that just ... well, Richard has been twenty-two years with this company, and he's the best they've ever had. But now this younger man comes along from some expensive school. And Richard, he's from modest means. He's worked so hard to make a good life for his family. I'm grateful to him, of course." Her voice now strained, as though her throat were closing, Lucille covered Constance's warm hand with her other cold one and said, "But this new employee, he's had the formal education, and these days that means they can slide right in over the heads of those with the experience. Richard has good reason to be upset. He's been in the warehouse for twenty-two *years*. He knows where everything is! And then to appoint this new man from Cleveland, of all places, Director of Marketing ... well, Richard has every right to be upset. *Every right.* So he's had a lot on his mind." Lucille looked up to meet a skeptical yet benevolent gaze. "So why should he notice something as silly as this awful hair color?"

Lucky for the woman who didn't know how to respond, the door of the back office opened and Dr. Kellerman's four o'clock emerged at 4:50.

"Gotta run," said the man in the spandex tights and tank top. "I'm filling in for the five-fifteen. She pulled a quad."

"Take care, Jasper," Constance said, as the departing client opened the next door. "See you next Friday! And don't forget to stretch!" That's what she usually said to him. Except today she'd said it ten minutes early and most of it after he'd left the room.

As the man's bald head bounced past the window, Lucille looked from the cuckoo clock to the woman whose hand she was still holding, then back to the clock. Her time was not up yet!

"I'll be back in a minute, dear," said Constance, standing as much as possible. She sandwiched Lucille's upper hand between her captured hand and free one, and said with conviction, "I like the new color. It makes a statement. It says, '*I'm Lucille Scarlet McBride,* darn it, *and I'm alive.*'"

The woman blinking back a raging flood and fighting the undertow at the corners of her mouth loosened her grip. She could not have smiled if she had tried.

***

When Constance entered the back office, Dr. Kellerman was fumbling through the shallow and overflowing center drawer of his desk. "Thought I had another pack in here," he said, bending for a better look. The doctor's rear end and the chair it was in

I. Joseph Kellerman 141

were pushed into the corner.

Constance picked up the wastebasket. She had emptied it the evening before, so the only things in there were an empty pack of cigarettes and yesterday's crumpled calendar page Joseph had torn off last night. Another day down, that one covered with lips. Thin lips, fat lips, smiles, frowns, puckers and twists. Just like today, she noticed.

Constance watched her boss search the same four corners of that drawer a few times over. "Well, I wouldn't be sorry if you didn't," she said, whapping him on the head with the Brookstone catalog he'd apparently been reading. "Watch, I'll be the one who ends up with lung cancer."

"Hmf!" was the response she got.

That's me, Joseph was thinking, always hurting the ones I get close to.

Why do I keep bringing him those awful cigarettes? The thought perplexed Constance, until she put it out of her head the moment it concluded. There were chores to do.

She set the wastebasket next to the yellow chair, then retrieved a box of Kleenex from the closet. A quick survey of the inventory before closing the door indicated that it was time to buy another case of tissue. Plenty of light bulbs, though.

On her way out of the room, she placed the box on the end table next to the yellow chair and injected her final comment of this routine visit. "If the cigarettes don't kill me, that cologne certainly will." Constance crinkled her nose and waved her hand in front of her face.

A louder "Hmf!" followed her out the door.

He hadn't been wearing it earlier. As a matter of fact, she didn't remember ever having smelled cologne on Joseph Kellerman before. Except, perhaps, many years ago following a lecture when she'd been able to get close enough to smell it. Constance's sensitive nose knew the toilet water she now couldn't help but inhale from across the room must be at least as many years old as she had been sitting at that desk out front. Yuck was the comment the voice in her head added.

When Lucille entered the back office, her lips trembling in anticipation for her cleansing cry, which would be a whole eight minutes longer today, she found her psychiatrist sniffing his left armpit.

Chapter 17

Constance had had a number of close calls over the years. Keeping one ear tuned to the front door wasn't easy while there was so much to watch and listen to through that little hole. And all those newspapers had a way of softening people's footsteps as they moved towards the waiting room. On numerous occasions, Constance had barely had time to push the painting back to the right before the next client entered. Many more than a few times, she hadn't had a chance to do even that and had twirled around the instant the door had opened. She'd invested in an adjustable, swiveling chair about fourteen years back, which made it much easier to turn quickly, not to mention quietly, and she'd once reinvested since. But it was a marvel no one had ever noticed that hole in the wall behind her head all those times she had failed to conceal it. The most anyone had ever said was "I think your painting's a little crooked."

Maggie didn't notice that either when she walked in on a peeping secretary.

"Oh, hi!" Constance exclaimed, spinning. She exhaled when she realized Maggie had been rifling through her canvas bag as she'd come through the door.

"Hey," Maggie replied. "Sh-h-h-oot."

"Something wrong, dear?"

Constance heard how phony her concern sounded.

But Maggie was oblivious. "I think I lost my keys," she said, still busy in her bag. "I got to the door and like, forgot where I was sort of and went to grab them?" She paused and looked up.

"You know like, when you go to a friend's house and feel like you're at home, so you go to get a glass from the cabinet next to the sink, where they're supposed to be? And then you open it and see like, wheat germ and granola instead, and you go, 'Oh, right, this isn't *my* kitchen?'"

"I'm so glad you feel comfortable here," said Constance, but Maggie didn't appear to see the connection.

She cocked her head, blinked a couple of times, then resumed her search. "There's no way I'll get into my apartment without my keys. My landlord's hardly ever there, and he's always three sheets to the wind when he is." Maggie set her tote on the desk and continued to root around, with plenty of rustling and jangling in the process.

"Where do you remember seeing them last?"

In the bag up to her elbows, Maggie paused to think. "Well. I took them out to unlock the storage closet this morning? To get strings? And then I set them down ... on the shelf, I think? Shit, I hope I didn't leave them in the closet."

And on to unpacking Maggie went. A hairbrush, a jumbo-sized bottle of hand lotion and a paperback with a long-maned, bare-chested man on the cover were removed from the bag and placed on the desk. More manipulation of unseen items, then a balled pair of white socks, a tube of baking soda toothpaste and pepper spray joined the extracted pile.

Maggie sighed. "I'll have to go all the way back after my appointment. Hey, um, you don't happen to have your car?"

"I'm sorry, no."

Constance had never learned how to drive.

"Or I don't know," said Maggie. "Maybe I should go now."

"Here," said Constance, turning the phone. "Perhaps someone can check for you. Might as well try to track them down, before running all over creation." She opened a drawer and brought out the phone book, but Maggie was already dialing.

"Hey, who's this?"

Constance thought she asked as though calling home to a house full of siblings.

"Oh, hey, Hal, it's Mag ... I'm good, but, hey, do me a huge favor. I think I left my keys in the storage closet? Would you be a sweetheart?"

She waited, inspecting something on the rug it seemed. Constance heard Maggie's foot rubbing at whatever that something was. Then some side to side, ho-hum what's-taking-so-long head bobbles.

Maggie drummed her fingernails on the desk. "Probably forgot what he was looking for," she told Constance. "He can't even remember the notes if he's not reading. Hey, did you find them? ... You checked all over, the shelves, the floor? ... Damn. Well, thanks anyway ... Yeah? ... Uh-huh." Eye roll. "Hey, that's great, Hal. Well, I have to run, okay? Somebody's waiting to use the phone ... Okay, you too! Man, Dr. Kellerman's lucky *he's* not a patient," said Maggie, finishing the sentence as she hung up. "Hal's the nicest guy? But he can like, talk the ears off corn. I think he's around seventy or something, but he can still play really well."

"No luck, then?" Constance asked for no other reason than to change the subject back to keys, before Maggie took this one and ran with it.

"Oh, wait! Duh-uh." Heel of Maggie's hand to forehead. "You had a lesson after rehearsal, dipwah."

Then she told Constance, "Little Kimmy Warner, she's so cute. The cello's bigger than she is."

"So you took your keys out at the school," said Constance, moving things along.

"To get into the practice room, yeah." Gasp! "Can I use the phone again?"

Constance sat and stared, her mind wandering off to fantasy land while Maggie dialed, waited, talked, waited, rubbed the rug with her foot, drummed her nails. Just as the dashing man in a black tuxedo knelt and took Constance's hand, the marriage proposal was interrupted by, "Shit. Well, thanks anyway."

And Maggie hung up.

"Did you lock the room when you left?" Constance suggested, though she had no idea how she managed such logical thought so soon after an irrational one had been cut short. "If so, maybe you used the key."

"No."

"Well, let's see then. Where did you go from there?"

"Joy's."

Constance picked up the receiver and held it out. "Perhaps you left them at *her* house."

"Joy's Juice Bar."

"Oh, well — "

"Closed," said Maggie.

This was getting tired, as was Constance's arm. "Well," she said, pressing on, "could you phone her at home? Maybe she could open the bar for you to look. Or maybe — "

"Hey, hang on a sec," said Maggie. She went back to the hall.

Constance put down the phone and stared at the array of abandoned items and lumpy bag in front of her. What else could be left in there, she wondered, then realized she was hitting her own bag with the side of her jiggling foot.

That same tan vinyl pocketbook Constance had owned since its predecessor had begun to show signs of aging after more than a decade of daily use and frequent cleaning. She'd been so happy to find a perfect clone, with the same half-circle wedge of a clasp and snap pockets. Constance had been delighted to discover, when she'd turned that half-circle in line with the rectangular slot, raised the flap, and removed the wads of white newsprint, the same tan vinyl cosmetics purse. She loved the little "pop" it made when she closed it. And Constance had purchased a new wallet too. Same color, same configuration, although she'd had to settle for a zippered change compartment instead of another pleasing "pop."

Most of an evening had been spent transferring the familiar contents of the old pocketbook, cosmetics case and wallet into the new. Constance had laid the items out on the dining table like some homespun game of solitaire. The first row consisted of a hairbrush, two keys on a heart-shaped key chain, and an old compact, its cake of powder and unblemished pad still separated by a plastic disc. Row number two was a bottle of vanilla-scented cologne, nail clippers and half a roll of peppermints. A pen and small spiral notebook, its pages filled with neatly printed notable quotes and random things to remember, had a row to themselves.

Each of these items had been tidied up as necessary. Every last bristle, both keys and key chain, the compact and other containers wiped. The outermost, lint-covered peppermint discarded. Entrails of torn-off notebook pages removed from the spiral. And the pen fitted with a new tube of ink.

Then came a short row of cards. A library card, a Visa without a balance, an ID displaying a smiling cardholder, the buy-nine-pair-of-pantyhose-get-the-tenth-one-free punch card. Below the cards, Constance had set out fourteen wallet-sized or clipped-to-wallet-size photos in chronological order. First was herself at age eight, posed with sixteen year-old brother, Charles, not two weeks before he'd gone to live with his girlfriend's family on the night of Dad's big revelation that Frank had been more than just a business partner for years. Next was Charles at twenty-three, with Beth on their wedding day, he in tails and she and baby-to-be in her voluminous white gown. Baby then became Ethan Patrick at age two hours. He had those big, blue Fairhart eyes and ephemeral cap of dark hair. After that was a Christmas family portrait of Charles, Beth and four year-old, by then very ash-blonde Ethan, who'd inherited his mother's curls and round face. The pictorial time line jumped to Lori Mae at her christening, a bald-headed baby in what looked like a miniature version of her mother's wedding dress. That baby turned into a five and a half year-old, ash-blonde, curly-haired and round-faced little girl.

And more pictures of the kids as they'd aged, lost and regained teeth, and graduated from elementary school and middle school. As they, by then, lived their lives through the mail into Constance's wallet. She had purchased an extra set of clear vinyl sleeves the second time around, so fewer photos would have to be slipped between the backs of two others. So she could look through them more easily, on the bus or while standing in line in the checkout aisle, and watch the kids graduate from high school and college. And get married. And so on.

What would *my* children look like? Constance had pondered the thought as she'd transferred those pictures of Charles and Beth and young Ethan and Lori, one by closely studied one, into the new wallet. By the time Ethan's first child entered that same wallet, Constance had long since stopped wondering about that altogether.

***

Some clunking and then "Yea!" came from between the front office and front door. A happy Maggie reappeared, holding up a large ring with a plethora of dangling keys.

Constance was reminded of a baby toy. A red plastic key, a yellow plastic key, a blue plastic key.

"They were in my cello case," Maggie announced.

"Good," said Constance, then she smiled too. "Oh, you have your cello!"

"Yeah, I got a ride from a friend of mine? I have another one at home, but I wanted to practice with Hildegard."

"With your friend?"

"No, with Hildegard."

"Oh." Constance was confused.

"Actually, it's my grandmother's name," said Maggie. She shoved her bag and loose items over, gathered her crimped, muslin skirt, and sat sidesaddle on the edge of the desk. "She was a violinist."

"How lovely," said Constance. "You practice with your grandmother."

"No, Grandma Hildy passed over."

"Oh."

"Yeah, I got carried away when I signed up for music lessons. I was like, wow, a monster violin? My parents weren't thrilled, though, they had a Volkswagen Bug at the time."

"Ah," said Constance, for lack of anything more meaningful to say.

"But, anyway, Grandma Hildy was an incredible musician. And my other one's Arthur? After my grandfather?"

Constance finally got it. "Oh, Hildegard is your *cello*."

"Yep, Arthur and Hildegard Carlisle. Grandpy couldn't play a note, but he loved to listen to Grandma."

"How nice," said Constance, standing. "Well, everyone should have some music in their lives. Music, art, anything creative, it's good for the soul." She walked around to the door Maggie had left open as usual and peered into the hall. A large black case was propped against the third oldest stack of newspapers. "What's Hildegard doing out there alone?"

Maggie joined her in the doorway and leaned farther, her hands on Constance's shoulders. "Well, it's kind of a tight squeeze? What is it with all these newspapers, anyway?"

Constance stepped back inside the waiting room. "I think we can get Hildegard in here for a little soul food, don't you? That is, if you wouldn't mind playing something."

"I'd be happy to. But if I don't make it through in the next five minutes, come extract me and Hildy from the hall."

***

By the time Lucille McBride reentered the front office at six, her eyes bloodshot and nostrils raw, Maggie was seated in the middle of the room in what used to be Constance's desk chair, immersed in the first bar of Beethoven's *Sonata No. 5*. Lucille couldn't help herself and stayed until almost five past before realizing the time and rushing out the door. She feared dinner would be much too late tonight. Richard would be starving!

Maggie played the final notes, drawing the bow slowly across her instrument. As she did, something made Constance, who was leaning against the front of her desk, staring at the far wall, turn her head to her left. Perhaps it had been that smell.

He was standing inches inside the open door of his office, just out of Constance's sight. She'd been so captivated by the music and the daydream it had inspired, she hadn't noticed Joseph's presence for the preceding five minutes. Neither had Maggie.

He was mesmerized. Her chest pressed against the neck of the cello. Legs spread to envelop the belly. The way her golden hair swished in front of her face. Maggie's eyes were closed, long lashes against soft cheeks, as she bowed. Back and forth, back and forth. Joseph ached from pounding heart to throbbing loins. How he longed to change places with that instrument, to be in tune with that beguiling young woman.

Had Constance been able to see Joseph's uncharacteristically expressive eyes, she might have detected at least some of what he was feeling during *Sonata No. 5*. Somehow, though, she had a gut instinct that something wasn't as usual. The meaning of it all, however, had not yet begun to sink in.

Chapter 18

"So you want wunnuh these?" Orla held the plate of two remaining cookies out to Dr. Kellerman. There was no way she was going to remove herself from that chair twice in one hour, so if he wanted one, he was gonna haftuh get his freakin ass outa that chayuh ovuh theyuh and come get it.

Joseph had been wandering around his mind, trying desperately to find something to keep it off of certain things, but, during the past fifteen minutes, all he'd come up with was empty space and dark shadows. He had just happened upon a lighted, open window and, through it, the mesmerizing sound of *Sonata No. 5* when Orla's unusual gesture slammed the window shut.

"Oh!" he said with a start, "No, thank you."

"Con gave 'em to me, but I'll split 'em with ya."

"Thank you, Miss Heffel, but no. I, uh, I had a big lunch." The doctor patted his growling stomach.

Joseph had been the beneficiary of Constance's alternative cookies, as he called them, for over two years now. Tasted a bit like sawdust and borscht, he thought, but he didn't care and would never say. He liked that Constance made them for him and thought it was nice she brought extra for the clients. Although, watching Orla Heffel eat disgusted him. Orla disgusted him, and he felt guilty about that too.

Long ago, Dr. Kellerman had tried to see the beauty in her. He'd tried in his mind and sometimes with words to peel away the layers of this woman still sitting in the yellow chair on Mondays between one and two o'clock after all these years. But he'd never been very successful, and Orla had only become more grotesque. In his eyes and hers.

Is it all due to circumstance? Joseph had contemplated the question on a number of occasions, when bits and pieces of Orla's stories rang so untrue he knew reality must be somewhere in the vicinity of the exact opposite. What's her *real* story? Orla never answered when he used to ask in one way or another. Would she be someone entirely different had other things been different? Who had been the little girl Orla? That innocent child with tender, clean skin, pure body, and future of hope and possibilities. What had happened to her? How did she become ... *this*? Will the real Orla stay trapped in there forever? The doctor still wondered these things when he couldn't help but think about the woman sitting in front of him, way on the other side of the desk.

Orla Heffel wondered much the same when she thought about herself, so she tried not to. So she smoked and ate, drank and watched television. She took pills. She picked at her face, then tried to hide the scabs and scars with multiple coats of concealer. She worked and shopped when she could hang onto a job, and talked and talked to nearly anyone who would listen. In Orla's opinion, Dr. Kellerman was now an even better listener than he used to be during her earlier years in the yellow chair.

"Suitcher self," she said and took another bite.

Dr. Kellerman had long ago stopped trying to fill the semi-silences while Orla Heffel masticated, and Orla didn't care that he didn't seem to care. She wasn't interested in anything the doctor might have said anyway. He knew it, she'd convinced herself that she knew it, and so had the person on the other side of the hole in the wall.

Maybe I should try again, Dr. Kellerman thought as he listened to Orla chew. Yes, I should try. He began mulling over a potential question or comment, as Orla continued with today's story. When she had to talk about herself, and she knew that's what she was supposed to do in therapy, she pretended to be someone else and made things up.

"So anyways, me and Ma hang out all the time, like real good friends. We go tuh the movie-e-e-s, muse-e-e-ums, spa-a-a-s. We're even thinkin' of goin' tuh Europe, just us girls."

Orla had been telling certain lies for so long, she almost believed what she was saying was true. If someone had told her her mother — whoever she had been — had left her in a dumpster when she was hours old, that Orla had spent the next six years in an orphanage and another twelve bouncing from foster home to the street to foster home, Orla would have called the informant crazy and almost believed that too.

"Ma's always checkin' up on me," she told the doctor. "An I gotta admit, that does kinda bug me sometimes, her buttin' intuh my business. But, I mean, she worries about me an everything. I'm her only kid, so you know how it is. An she's always spoilt me. That I also gotta admit. I'm always tellin' her she don't hafta keep bringin' me stuff all the time, but she don't listen. Yeah, that's anothuh thing that does kinda bug me about her. She just don't listen."

Dr. Kellerman was listening, and he shook his head.

"But she's real cool, though," Orla quickly added. "Don't get me wrong. I mean, all my friends say they wish they had moth-uhs like mine, an I sure don't take it fuh granted. Yeah, I'm real lucky. I appreciate how she's always doin' stuff fuh me an makin' me stuff. These are okay, but I gotta say, they're nowheres near as good as Ma's." Orla broke the last cookie and held the smaller section out to Dr. Kellerman.

He put up his hand and shook his head again.

Orla didn't want to share what had been made just for her, but she wasn't thinking straight today. How could she?

As she would tell Constance over the phone the very next week, "The doctuh was actin' kinda wee-id, like somethin' was eatin' at him or somethin'." That's what Orla's take on it was. He'd acted so phony, so interested in what she was saying. She even thought she heard him "mm-hmm" a couple of times. Orla was sorry to have to cancel her appointment on such short notice, she told Constance, then hacked into the receiver. But maybe the following week the ductuh might be feelin' bettuh, too.

***

A Monday without Orla Heffel was a day Constance didn't straighten the newspapers in the hall, as she had once a week almost every week since the squeeze had gotten to be more than a bit. When Orla did come, and she usually did, Constance would wait until Orla had made her way back to and through the heavy gray door when her hour in the yellow chair was up. Constance would then proceed to the hall.

Joseph did have a need for a certain order to his life and the many contents of his building. Without being asked, Constance had long helped fulfill that need as best she could. But she had no idea why she continued to straighten those papers Joseph didn't read anymore. He hadn't been in the hall in two years. Constance had come to that conclusion herself, when *Boston Globes* had begun piling up in the front office. On the corner of her desk. Up to that point, Joseph himself had always brought the day's paper out to the hall and placed it on the pile closest to the waiting room door. For the past two years, Constance had taken care of that part of the routine as well.

When she'd first come to work for Dr. Kellerman, there'd been only one thigh-high pile of newspapers inside the front door. Two weeks' worth. When that pile had grown to Constance's waist height and then multiplied all the way to the next door, she'd initiated the first of her secret routines. Each day, after Joseph had placed the newspaper on that nearest pile with only a quick open and close of the waiting room door, she'd waited until the departing client was out of the building and Joseph was back in the back office with the next. Then Constance had moved those newspapers until the oldest *Boston Globe* was outside in the trash. She'd been relieved Joseph never seemed to notice that the pile nearest the front office did not get taller.

He had noticed and wanted her to stop. It would have been far less embarrassing if she'd gotten rid of them all. If only she'd *made* him get rid of them. Just do it, Constance, he'd often thought and still did after all these years. Distracted? Yes. Completely oblivious? Not to everything. Joseph didn't have to go into the hall to know what Constance was still doing with those newspapers. Even if a client were seated in the yellow chair, talking away, Dr. Kellerman could hear the door open and close, then the next door open and the paper hit the trash can. His ears were well-tuned to certain sounds.

Please, get rid of it all, he now thought each day when Constance slipped the paper off his desk. Do it, no matter what I said or did before. Make it all go away, and don't bring more. *Don't let me stay in here!*

But Joseph never said a word about any of it. Not about the newspapers, the groceries, the junk mail she didn't throw away before he saw it. The damn painting. He had a hard time asking for anything, even for Constance not to do something. She was trying to help, and he didn't want to hurt her feelings. Joseph would never forget what *that* was like.

Constance remembered, too. After that deeply disturbing incident on her second full day as Dr. Kellerman's assistant, she had tried to do and keep things just as she felt he wanted. Or at least make them seem that way. She'd been very careful not to push too hard.

***

Orla's over-permed head passed outside the window, and Constance proceeded to the hall. As she once again straightened newspapers, she considered the routines. The one she now did after waking Joseph each day at one, and the one she'd been doing on the vast majority of Mondays, minutes after two for the past ten years and six months. Since he no longer entered the hall, Joseph wouldn't notice if the papers had been disrupted by Orla's hips. He wouldn't notice if they weren't in chronological order. He wouldn't notice if they were gone. Lately, Constance had been considering getting rid of the whole lot. It was a thought process she'd never had before, but something had changed. What that something was, she couldn't quite put her finger on.

But what if he did go into the hall, she now considered as she reached the pile closest to the front door. Then he would notice if the papers had been disrupted. If they were out of order. If they were gone. What would happen if there were a change in his routine, a change in what was familiar? Joseph was fragile, of that much she was sure. What if he got upset? A lot of what-ifs streamed through Constance's mind.

What did not come to mind was the fact that many of the routines, as peculiar as some of them were, had become no less than almost normal to her. They were now as much a part of Constance's life inside 4991 Hopewell Street as they were his, and, in a way, she was the one who couldn't let go.

She opened the front door, waved to a man whose dog was urinating on the lamppost, filled her lungs with fresh, late summer air, then went back to the waiting room to do the best she could with a rag and a can of Old English.

***

Though Constance maintained a certain modicum of order on the first floor, she left the upstairs to Joseph. In fact, she'd climbed those steps to the second floor only once in twenty-three years and four months. She remembered the date, because it was a February twenty-first. Joseph's forty-eighth birthday.

Years earlier, Constance had done some sleuthing, searching through the wallet Joseph had left unattended on his desk, to find out when he'd been born. He was as stubborn about withholding that information as he was about the meaning of the I, which was another thing she'd hoped to discover inside that wallet. Like everything else with the doctor's name on it, though, the ID card divulged only that frustrating initial. At least it revealed the other bit of information: 02/21/34. Soon afterwards, Constance's attempt to make Joseph happy with a cake ablaze with forty lighted candles had informed her that he did not want to acknowledge, let alone celebrate, his birthdays. But she remembered them nonetheless. Especially February 21, 1982.

On that day more than eleven years ago, Dr. Kellerman's first client had been sitting in the waiting room since eight minutes before the hour. At eight past, he'd still been sitting there, and Constance had had enough of the waiting and worrying. But she'd been apprehensive about knocking on that door. So she had continued glancing at the clock that still cuckooed each time the minute hand hit twelve and six, and chatting with the client, whose headphones were on his ears. At 9:10, Constance had made the decision she'd best go up and check, praying it wasn't too late.

***

"Dr. Kellerman?"

The soft knock and then a somewhat more solid one produced no response.

"Joseph?"

Neither did the hesitant inquiry through the cat hatch at the bottom of the door, so Constance tried the doorknob and found it to be unlocked. In she went, tiptoeing. She felt like an intruder. With caution and a pounding heart, she made her way through the clutter.

As she passed the couch, one third of which was covered with books, Constance noticed a scrap of cardboard push-pinned to the wall where a painting would have made much more sense. It was the piece of cardboard she'd torn from the back of her notebook a dozen years earlier! But she didn't even *have* that phone number anymore. (Not that Joseph had called a second time.) She didn't hesitate despite the surprise, but continued through the living room, past the kitchen to the slightly open door of Joseph's bedroom.

Constance would be forever grateful for her luck when she managed to get out of that apartment without being detected. She would have been so embarrassed!

And that's exactly why *he* never mentioned it to *her*.

There he sat, on the edge of the bare mattress, when Constance peeked in. She didn't understand what he was doing. But the more she watched, and she watched for most of a minute, the more it looked as though Joseph were pretending. He was smiling. He was sitting sideways with one leg off the bed and his arms up, as if his right hand were behind an invisible neck. And his left? Toying with an imaginary ... something. He looked as though he were supposed to be sitting on a very tall person's lap.

Constance made good use of the opportunity to exit swiftly, as her boss of almost a dozen years threw his head back and began to laugh like she'd never seen or heard him laugh before. Constance had no idea what may have been so funny, but she was not at all amused.

When her hand reached the knob and as she proceeded to turn it, Joseph's laughter became a wail that sounded like agony. Constance wanted to cry. She didn't know whether to rush back to the bedroom or out of the apartment, but there was no time to consider and reconsider.

Constance yanked a bit too hard. The door flew back, toppling a freestanding pile of books. The intruder held her breath and listened.

Nothing.

So she tiptoed out. By the time Constance reached the bottom of the stairs, she'd managed to compose her exterior self.

I. Joseph Kellerman

"The doctor will be right with you," she announced, trying to sound at ease and hoping her statement was correct. Had the client heard that heartbreaking cry? Apparently not. Constance could hear the lyrics through those headphones on his ears.

Four minutes later, a rather disheveled man emerged from the second floor, just after a tri-colored kitten burst through the hatch.

***

February 21, 1982, was the first and last day Dr. Kellerman had ever been late for his duties. His cheeks and chin dotted with blood-stained bits of tissue, he couldn't look at Constance that morning as he'd rushed past her desk, motioning for the client to follow. "Morning" was barely mumbled. He was mortified.

How long had she been up there?

The same February twenty-first had been the beginning of Joseph's more obvious and extreme deterioration. Until then, he'd managed quite well to keep up the professional front, to do his job passably. He was not the doctor he once had been, but he was still good enough. That had changed, right along with his shaving habits, his cigarette consumption, his note-taking and choice of clothing.

With the exception of three women, on five occasions, and then in just a physical sense, Joseph had not only withdrawn from clients more and more as days passed, but from Constance as well. He'd long been trying to hide from his own mind and, in time, kept himself hidden from the rest of the world. A row house on Hopewell Street had become much more than I. Joseph Kellerman's office and residence. That building had become his self-made prison.

Chapter 19

"How could I have been so stupid," said Maggie. Today, even her rhetorical questions sounded like statements; she was in a very bad mood. She'd skipped Tai-chi class, called in sick to the juice bar, and completely spaced it and missed a lesson with a first-time student whose single mother had to work three jobs to just squeak by. Maggie felt horrible. She had dressed for the doldrums, too, in a plain gray t-shirt, a gray, hooded sweatshirt, and jeans that were faded almost to gray themselves. Her usually loose and well-groomed hair had been twisted into a sloppy coil and run through with a chopstick. She looked from her untied sneakers to her infallible friend sitting beside her on the waiting room bench and said, "Such a stupid mistake it was to trust that guy."

"You're not stupid," Constance replied, absentmindedly patting the hand of the innocent young woman, who she hadn't been watching much today. Constance was drained, but still she tried. She focused her weary eyes on Maggie's and said, "You're an honest, loving person. What happened wasn't your mistake *or* your fault."

"I know, but ... I don't know."

"But nothing," said Constance. "You aren't to blame for *his* violence." She'd thought of that comment two Fridays ago but hadn't found the ideal opportunity to use it until now.

Maggie looked up at the "Have a Happy Day!" plaque and shook her head. "I feel like I must have provoked him somehow. I mean, maybe Brian was right. What he said that night when he

... you know, when he did what he did to me. Maybe it *had* been too long. We'd been seeing each other for like, six months. Most couples sleep together way before that."

She checked with her friend again but found her staring into space. So Maggie gave her a poke in the arm and said, "Don't they?"

Constance smiled a little. "Sometimes it's much longer," she said. She spoke from experience and then said to Maggie, "But there isn't some kind of schedule we're supposed to follow, you know that. You weren't ready and didn't consent, and he had absolutely no right. There's *no* excuse."

Both women were silent as first Constance and then Maggie looked over to the far wall, behind the desk. They both winced.

"I thought I was in love with him." Maggie rested her elbow on the back of the bench, her head on her hand. "I told him the most personal things. He could be so sweet and like, really charming. And I was really attracted to him. So, I mean, I know I flirted a lot and everything."

Constance just listened.

"But I had told him more than once that I wanted to wait until I got married. Or engaged at least, and he said that was all right, was how he put it. He didn't tell me he wanted to marry me, but he said he was a patient guy. Yeah, well, what a load *that* was. But I believed him, and so I felt like it was okay to mess around a little. And it was fun. I mean, the anticipation. I thought about it all the time, like every time I looked at him and even when I wasn't with him. It was ... exciting."

There was a period of nothing but clock ticking and traffic passing and intermittent murmuring from the next room, as Maggie remembered.

Constance was remembering, too. She'd heard certain words more than others — love, attracted, anticipation — and her mind had wandered away from the context in which they were spoken.

Over the last few months, Constance had been missing certain feelings she hadn't had in a very long time. When Maggie talked about Danny, she missed those feelings even more. But this was about Maggie and Brian, and what he had done to her, Constance reminded herself. She turned her head and tried to pay attention.

"But, all of a sudden, he was totally a different person," said Maggie. "Or maybe he wasn't, but I'd never seen that in him. Maybe I didn't want to, I guess, but I sure didn't know the monster that came over that night. I mean, it was to supposed to be like any other Friday we didn't go out somewhere. He'd bring the lo mein and fried rice and some tapes, we'd have dinner, then watch a movie or listen to music, and cuddle. That's what we always did."

Constance acknowledged with a nod.

"But not that night," said Maggie. "I opened the door, and then it was just ... I mean, one second I was giving him a hug and, next thing I knew, he was on top of me. And he was a *big guy*. And he started tearing my clothes, and I tried to stop him, but he beat the crap out of me. I think the only part of me that wasn't black-and-blue or scratched up was my face."

Constance's attention shifted back to the far wall. Recently, M's painting had stopped seeming so normal. And now much less abstract.

Maggie lowered her head and volume, as if she didn't want to hear her own words, and recalled what else had happened on the floor of her apartment in all its painful detail. Constance, meanwhile, watched the scene play out in front of her eyes, but it wasn't Maggie and a faceless man called Brian who she saw.

There's a creak, and the yellow chair and the weeping woman in it are suddenly blocked from view. Then he stands in front of her. He offers a handkerchief, and she takes his wrist. Hand over hand, she pulls him towards her, but he doesn't resist. He kneels and there are two profiles. Hers moves towards his, and she kisses him. After a brief pause, he kisses her, and the painting is pushed back to the right.

There's a creak, and the yellow chair and a different weeping woman are suddenly blocked from view. Then he stands in front of her. He kneels and there are two profiles. His moves towards hers, and the painting is quickly pushed back to the right.

There's a creak, and the yellow chair and Linda Payne are suddenly blocked from view. Then he stands in front of her. He kneels and there are two profiles. His moves towards hers, and the painting is quickly pushed back to the right.

He kneels and there are two profiles. He pulls Linda towards him. They disappear from view, and the painting is very quickly pushed back to the right.

Linda leaves the yellow chair, and that chair is suddenly blocked from view. Then the yellow chair is empty. The other chair creaks, and the painting is much too quickly pushed back to the right. Seems neither of them hear it scrape the paneling, because the creaking continues.

And I sing an up-tempo rendition of Sunrise, Sunset *as I vacuum.*

M and I have something in common after all, thought Constance, as the bottom right-hand corner of the painting came back into view. This was a most unexpected thought she'd first had a decade ago, spoken by the voice inside when she saw what she'd never wanted to see through the hole in the wall. The thought had eventually become a subliminal state of mind that Maggie Carlisle's story, though itself a murmur for the last few minutes, once again translated into words inside Constance's head. M's heart had been broken also. And then, as the voice of the young woman sitting beside her faded back in, Constance had the most disturbing thought of all. Maggie and those three women on five occasions, they too have something in common.

"And he acted like he hadn't done anything wrong," said Maggie. "He walked up to me and said, 'What's up,' like nothing had happened! Can you believe that?"

Still staring across the room, Constance nodded, then shook her head.

Maggie said, "I didn't know what to say or do, or how to feel about anything. I just wanted to get the hell out of town. I guess I thought I could run away from the whole thing, somehow. But no matter where you go, your past sticks to you like a tattoo. It's like trying to run away from *yourself.*"

"Mm-hmm," said Constance.

"I do sometimes wonder about him, though. If he ever thinks about what he did, or if he's ever felt the least bit sorry. If he's ever felt guilty."

Constance continued to scrutinize the painting. *That's* why Joseph had kept it, she was sure.

And she was right about that much.

"I wonder if he's got a girlfriend," said Maggie, "or maybe married and seems like a regular guy, and nobody around him has a clue. It's like, I have this real cliché vision sometimes. I see him in this white, like, Cape Cod-ish sort of house with a picket fence and rose bushes and all that, and he's sitting in a Lay-Z-Boy, reading the paper. And then I see this pretty woman in a rocking chair, sewing or whatever. And they have their two-point-two kids and their nice life, and everything's all hunky-dory." Maggie sniffled and said, "It isn't fair."

Following a brief hiatus while she rummaged in her bag, then tended to her eyes and nose, Maggie's demeanor changed. She looked at her friend and said, "Hey, I just realized I have no idea?"

Constance heard the question mark and turned back.

"Are you married?" Maggie asked. "I mean, you don't wear a ring, but that doesn't necessarily *mean* anything."

It wasn't often that anyone in 4991 Hopewell Street asked Constance Fairhart personal questions, though many had wondered about her. She answered with a subdued smile and without hesitation. She said, "No, not exactly."

Now Maggie was the one who nodded.

For a moment, Constance thought that was the end of subject. She hoped it was. Not that there was anything in particular to hide. She just preferred to separate her life within this building from the rest of her world. Her other world. Discussing one while in the other didn't feel right. And, for so long, Constance had been *not* talking about that other life while immersed in this one, she almost didn't know how anymore. This was not the time, nor did she have enough time, to explain. And she was in no mood to try.

But Maggie persisted. "Well, you've been in love," she said.

A few mechanical ticks and a U-Haul went by before Constance realized that too had been a question. She looked from the window to Maggie and said, "Oh, sure I have. And I've been with him for more than twenty years."

To Constance's relief, the direction of the conversation changed.

"So, how do you know for sure?" Maggie asked, then rolled her eyes. "God, I sound like such a kid. But that's how I feel lately, sort of awkward and nervous, like a teenager. It's not just because of what happened."

"The rape," said Constance without thinking. That's often when she said the most meaningful things, when she didn't try too hard. And this was something Constance didn't need to think about anymore. She frowned and said, "He raped you."

There was a pause, then, "Yes," said Maggie.

"And you're angry."

"Yes, and hurt. He broke my heart."

Constance said, "Yes."

"And I made it worse," Maggie added, "because I didn't deal with it."

Yes, Constance thought but didn't say. She did say, "But you're dealing with it now, and you've got plenty of time."

Just then, the sound of claws in kitty litter came from the back of the house. Scratch, scratch, then a fuzzy gray form zoomed out of the kitchen into the waiting room, up the stairs and through the cat hatch, as two women watched and Maggie's thoughts shifted. "It's always been such a big thing to me," she said. "Finding someone to spend my life with."

"Of course it is," Constance replied, still looking up at that door.

Maggie looked from that same door to Constance. "But it's scary," she said, "trying to figure out who to trust with your heart, and then who's the one to give it to? Don't you think."

"Yes."

"I mean, most guys aren't anything *at all* like Brian. And Danny's like, the best person. It's just that I worry sometimes? I mean, there are so many men out there, and I think I could love a lot of people?"

Constance's gaze returned to her young acquaintance. She opened her mouth to say whatever would come out, but Maggie said, "I guess I'm afraid to commit myself one hundred percent, and then meet somebody else and find out I have feelings for him too. I see it happen to my friends all the time, and I don't want to go through all that? *You* know what I mean."

"There are different kinds of love" was the next spontaneous comment.

"True," said Maggie with a slow nod.

And Constance continued, searching for words as she spoke, letting her mouth roam with her mind for a change. "We shouldn't be afraid of or ... or not allow ourselves to love people just because ... well, just because we make a special commitment to one man."

Her thoughts bounced back to an earlier part of this conversation and subconsciously to an earlier Friday evening at six-something. Oftentimes, what someone in the yellow chair said touched the heart and stuck in the mind of the woman watching and listening through the hole in the wall. When Constance didn't try too hard, some of those words occasionally and unintentionally became hers. Sometimes, like this time, said to the person who'd uttered them in the first place.

"You know, Maggie. And I hope this doesn't sound ... something."

"Say anything? I promise I won't think it's motherly."

Constance laughed.

"Oh, I mean not in a bad way," said Maggie. She'd never had with her mother the kinds of conversations she had with Constance. And Grandma Hildy had died before Maggie was ready to have them. They'd only gotten as far as female physiology.

"Well, I was going to say, there's a difference between sex and making love. And just because intercourse ... happens, there isn't necessarily affection or intimacy."

Constance often paraphrased those parroted words.

Maggie concurred with more big, slow nods. She wished *she* could speak so openly like that.

Constance couldn't help but think of those three women yet again. Those three women who had transferred the intimacy of what they'd shared of themselves with Dr. Kellerman in words, onto the physical acts he performed with them. What had Joseph been thinking? What did he feel for those women? And how does he feel about what he did? That's when the no-nonsense voice in her head asked, was *that* rape, too?

Constance couldn't stop replaying and rehashing it all, over and over in her mind, no matter how hard she tried not to. Even after all these years and, due to present circumstances, especially not the three occasions that had involved Linda Payne. The other two women had soon afterwards taken their injured feelings elsewhere and must not have said a word about Dr. Kellerman's misconduct, because nothing had ever happened to him. Linda Payne, however, had continued to arrive a minute or two before four, each and every Thursday, then spend her usual hour in the yellow chair, acting as though she were unaffected by the doctor's sudden and continued disinterest.

But things had apparently not been as they'd seemed.

Will I be able to save Joseph this time? Constance wondered how much longer she could avoid telling him what she'd known for months had become of his long-time client, who had stopped showing up almost a year ago. She knew she couldn't — *should* not — continue to stall Attorney Dunst, who, at the request of the parents of Linda Payne, was investigating the circumstances of their daughter's suicide, found naked in an armchair, an empty, unmarked pill bottle in one hand and Dr. I. Joseph Kellerman's business card in the other. Linda's death had occurred seven months after her last hour in the yellow chair, but Constance knew that wouldn't matter.

Joseph would feel responsible. He'd lost patients to suicide before and both of those times had been consumed by guilt. Day after day, Constance had said, "See you in the morning," to the man bent over the deceased's file, only to find him bent over the same file and still dressed in the same clothes first thing in the morning, morning after morning, murmuring, "What have I done? What have I done?" But he hadn't had sex with *them*.

"Certainly not if someone forced themselves on you," Constance now added to her speech. She'd managed to get back on track after skipping only a couple of beats. "On the other hand, you can be very intimate with someone without there being *any* sex."

Again, it was from experience that Constance spoke. She was now thinking of the man in the other room, with whom she still felt a somewhat peculiar closeness despite everything and without physical contact or any meaningful words.

"But when there's both," Constance told the still-nodding young woman next to her, "it's the most wonderful feeling. I'd say that's how you know. It'll make you feel good on many levels." She thought she'd finished her stream of consciousness but tacked on an impulsive footnote. "I believe it's perfectly okay to have intimate relationships with more than one person, to love more than one man. I don't mean I think it's all right to *make* love with more than one at the same *time*, but — "

Constance realized what she'd just said and put her fingers to her sudden smile.

The two women on the bench laughed, as Lucille McBride emerged from the back office. Her eyes and nose were only moderately pink.

Chapter 20

The beige chinos she hadn't seen him wear in almost as many years as there were gray doors on Hopewell Street. The white, button-down shirt. The loafers instead of old Birkenstocks with broken buckles. And not near as many cigarette butts in the ashtrays. In addition to the clean-shaven, nick-free face, those were the more superficial changes Constance had observed in Joseph over the past few months. She'd even thought she felt the weak flutter of gastric wings.

Then there were the other differences. The lucid moments she'd heard, though couldn't see, through the hole in the wall, when he'd had a verifiable response that hadn't first gone from her lips to his ears in passing, and the fleeting sparks in those cavernous dark eyes. The lifelike expressions were obvious to Joseph's long-time devotee.

Every now and then in recent weeks, Constance had felt as though she were watching a man she'd known many years ago. Though there was now as much gray as gingerbread brown in his thinning head of hair and more lines on his face. Though his once stout shoulders bowed a little even when he attempted to sit up straight, and his nose had become somewhat bulbous with age. To Constance, Joseph was still very handsome. Despite everything, she'd never stopped seeing the beauty in him.

And there had been that brief exchange earlier in the day.

***

Dr. Kellerman followed his eleven o'clock client into the front office at the buzz of noon and waited as the third party left the building. From the middle of the room, he watched the man pass by that one unblinded window. For many years, it had not been usual for Joseph to look out to the street.

Constance was intrigued by his presence but not surprised he said nothing until she spoke first. "How are you?" she asked. Seemed as good a question as any.

"Maggie Carlisle," he said, turning to face Constance but not quite making eye contact. "You've gotten to know her?"

Joseph seemed to be in rather good spirits and smiled a little.

"Well, yes, I suppose. We chat some." Then, after a pause he didn't fill, she asked him, "Why?"

With an intense frown, the doctor began to pace in front of her desk, one hand behind his back, the other stroking his chin. "Well, Miss Fairhart, sometimes young ladies feel more comfortable talking to other *women* about ... things of a certain *nature*. So, if she should happen to tell you something, mention anything that might be at all helpful to me in handling her case, please do let me know." Dr. Kellerman stopped moving and stroking, and looked at her. "Would you?"

Constance could only nod. Where was *this* coming from?

Then Joseph nodded. "Good" and, after an awkward gap, "Thank you, Miss Fairhart" was all he said before returning to his office and closing the door.

***

When Constance first came to work at 4991 Hopewell Street, numerous and lengthy conversations regarding the clients had followed between her and the doctor. At first, he spoke and she listened, intently on both their parts. Constance always had an array of questions for the competent psychiatrist, who also held a Doctoral degree in psychology, and he gave captivating answers. As the assistant had felt more at ease in her role, the division of dialogue had trended ever closer to equal. Joseph had enjoyed those private conversations as much as she did, and much more so than any he had with other doctors. Time went on, and Dr. Kellerman and Constance Fairhart had become more like partners than employer and employee.

As more years went by, however, the unscheduled hours and evenings they spent sitting in the back office, he in his chair, catty-corner to the yellow armchair she was in, had dwindled, as had the intensity and quality of the conversations that took place therein. Not long before those talks ceased altogether, Dr. Kellerman had taken up permanent residence on the other side of that oversized desk. He seemed miles away by that time.

Since then, the conversations about anything much that mattered had been quite one-sided — Constance to Kellerman — and carried out in a casual manner that afforded no clue to the preoccupied doctor about his assistant's knowledge of things she wouldn't otherwise have known had it not been for one little, well-placed hole in the wall. His note-taking had declined to dribs and drabs of repeated textbook quotes, his responses to clients to essentially the same, an occasional "Mmmm," "Mm-hmm," or parroted words. A substantial amount of what Constance had said in passing over the years did manage to seep through to Joseph's mind and heart, and her comments often became his to whoever was sitting in the yellow chair. Once in a while to the person who'd said them *to him* in the first place.

* * *

"I was disappointed he couldn't ride up with us," Maggie continued. She was recounting her weekend in the mountains with Danny and the others, while fiddling with the cuffs of her sweater. "But I had a great day with his friends, though. Well, our friends. I mean, the weather was perfect when we hiked in? And he and Bill were supposed to be at the hut by like, five or six. That's what they call those cabins, by the way."

I. Joseph Kellerman

There was a subtle smile from the doctor.

You have nice hands, he was thinking. Delicate. He tried to imagine their touch and ran a few of his own fingers down his smooth cheek.

"So anyway, Danny had told me they'd be done by noon and then they'd jump in Bill's truck and head up. He was really apologetic, but I'd never get mad about a thing like that? I mean, it like, came up last minute, so ... And I would have waited and gone up with him after the meeting, but Bill was with him, and I figured I shouldn't be too clingy? I'm a lot younger, and that might have seemed a little childish maybe."

"Childish" was the word Joseph heard come out of his mouth. Oh beautiful, what an intelligent thing to say, Kellerman.

Joseph was having trouble concentrating on the peripheral details Maggie was giving. He watched her lips, those hands, the rest of her wholesome, effervescent self, occupying his mind as he waited for Maggie to take it away with her. He stroked Wadofur as he watched the vision in the yellow armchair.

I bet your hair is just as soft, he thought.

"So anyway," said Maggie, "Bill and Danny get to the trailhead around four, which we know because Tammy has her cell phone and Bill has his. And we talked to them right before they started hiking. And so, later on? When the weather does a one-eighty? I mean, *you* know how the Whites are. They say if you don't like the weather, wait a minute?"

Now Joseph's smile was forced. And? And? Where are we going here?

He was nodding and Maggie talking, as the painting on the other side of the wall was straightened. Constance had heard this whole story already.

Maggie was saying, "So when it gets real nasty in a matter of like, an hour? And then gets dark eventually? Well, I get really uptight. Tammy couldn't get a signal to call them again, so at nine? We're still waiting. I was worried sick when it got to be like, ten o'clock, and no Danny. Or Bill. I mean, people have *died* up there?"

Joseph's knee had begun to react to his impatience. Within seconds, Wadofur jumped across the desk to curl in Maggie's stable, skirted lap instead. The sight of a cat in that cradle held the waiting man's attention. His eyes were riveted to the spot. That is, until his mind became otherwise occupied.

Maggie's words weaved in and out of his fantasy.

"Thank God," she says, rushing into his arms as he walks through the door, out of the raging wind and driving sleet. She snuggles under his jacket. "I was so worried."
"It's okay, baby, I'm fine," he reassures her.

Maggie told the doctor, "And then he said, 'We could have holed up and waited it out, but I wanted to be with you?'"

She holds on tight.
"Somebody was about to lead her own one-woman search party," *Tammy tells Joseph as she walks up beside him.*
"She's a sweetheart," he replies, nuzzling his face against the golden hair of the beautiful young woman he's holding.

"And he didn't let go," said Maggie.

He feels her warm body against his and tries not to let it affect him. He's unsuccessful, but she doesn't seem to notice.
She has noticed, but it's comforting and thoroughly exciting. For the first time, she's not at all uneasy with their closeness.

"If he'll wait just a little longer for ... *you* know, the rest," said Maggie.

Of course he will. Joseph would wait forever. And even if forever never comes, he'll still be right here, loving her.

    And such is how the remainder of the hour was passed. Maggie continued to describe the sensual, yet unconsummated, romance of the weekend she'd spent with Danny that had made her pulse race and imagination run wild. The experience had the much the same effect on the half listening and wholly fantasizing doctor. Though they hadn't spoken to each other about what they were feeling, Maggie and Danny knew what was happening. It had been happening for a long time, and the time was almost right to take their relationship to a new, wonderful level. They had been intimate in many ways, but now she was almost ready to give her trust and herself to him completely.

    And that's what Maggie Carlisle shared with Dr. Kellerman in all its heartfelt detail for the rest of the hour and a bit into the next. Joseph enjoyed every moment of their intimate time together.

Chapter 21

"So, tell me about your sister," said Dr. Kellerman to the man in the yellow chair.

Joseph smoked until another digit flipped. Then he told his image, "She was four years older than I."

"And?" said the doctor. He knew the client was still getting used to this talking-about-it thing.

"And she was my friend. My best friend."

"What did you do together?"

"Well," said Joseph, then he paused to think again. "We invented games. Card games sometimes. We'd use the tops of cigarette boxes for cards and pretend while we played. We were always pretending."

"What did you pretend?" Dr. Kellerman asked.

"Oh, all sorts of things. One of us would start off and the other would join in. Rosa would usually go first, though. And she was much better at it. She'd say something like, uh … Well, let's see now."

Joseph stared at the clock, but after two more flips nothing had come to him.

"Pretending helped," the doctor suggested.

"It did," the client agreed. "It made us less afraid. Or a little, anyway."

"Afraid of what?"

"Of everything. Of the unknown. Of being caught."

"Caught?" asked the doctor.

"When we'd sneak out," said Joseph.

I. Joseph Kellerman

"Of where?"

"The secret hole in the wall."

"What wall?"

"The *ghetto* wall!" Joseph snapped. He was aggravated with himself. "I'm sorry," he said and told Dr. Kellerman, "Once they sealed the ghetto, my sister and I would crawl through to try to get extra food. We'd take off the, uh, the arm bands, the Stars of David, so maybe no one on the outside would know. And we had these pockets hidden in the linings of our coats, and we'd take things to sell or trade."

The client knew the doctor's next question, so he said, "Whatever people would give us or whatever we could find. Like pieces of material, silverware. Jewelry sometimes. Or sometimes we had nothing, so we would, you know, *ask* for food. A carrot, a slice of bread, an egg. Anything."

"And what did your parents think of this?" Dr. Kellerman wanted to know.

"They didn't like it. No, Mama especially. She was afraid that the next time we'd go, something would happen. She'd always make us promise we wouldn't do it anymore. But I disobeyed."

"What about Rosa?" the doctor asked. "She went back out, too. Didn't she."

"But it was *my* idea," said Joseph.

"Are you sure?"

"Yes. Well, that time it was. Mama wasn't feeling well, so I wanted to get something more for her to eat. They made her shovel snow all day."

Joseph frowned and looked at the clock again. The time was 12:13. At 12:14, the numbers faded with the cigarette smoke.

"Let's look for a pumpkin," Rosa says while brushing the dirt off her knees. "A big one, so my fairy godmother can turn it into a carriage for us, and we'll all ride away."

"To where?" her brother asks.

"Far away, to the countryside. We'll find my prince, and when I put my foot in the glass slipper, it'll fit perfectly, and then he'll invite us to come live in his palace." Rosa looks around and takes Isaac's hand. "Come on," she says, leading him quickly towards the main street.

"If we find a pumpkin," Isaac tells his sister, "I'd rather have it turned into wiener schnitzel."

"But if we have the carriage," Rosa explains, "we can go to my prince, and he'll give us a mountain of wiener schnitzel and anything else we want. New clothes, new shoes, bicycles like we used to have."

"And coats," Isaac chimes in, holding the collar of his closed where the top two buttons used to be. "And Mama needs mittens."

The children pass more quiet buildings and parked cars, and turn the corner. As they near the shops, they slow their pace and try to act like this is where they're supposed to be.

Rosa lets go of her brother's hand. "There's a pretty maiden," she says, giving Isaac a nudge. "Go on, talk to her."

He takes a step backwards. "You go."

"I went first last time," Rosa reminds him.

So Isaac stuffs his hands in his pockets and approaches the woman with the fur-lined boots. They look warm. He wishes he could bring them back for Mama.

"Excuse me ... miss?"

The fur-lined boots stop.

"I was wondering if, um, if you might have anything you could spare? Something to eat maybe? It's for my mother."

The fur-lined boots disappear.

Moments later, Isaac feels an arm embrace his hanging shoulders.

"Come on," Rosa says. "She was just in a bad mood. She kissed her prince this morning, and he turned into a frog."

Brother and sister move along in the safety of the crowd, as the sister talks of her prince's kingdom, its green hills dotted with wildflowers, and sparkling lakes teeming with big orange fish, and tree branches bent to the ground with giant apples and peaches and pears.

In the midst of painting a delightful picture in Isaac's hungry mind, of a grand celebration with song and dance, meats and cheeses and a towering cake, Rosa stops in front of a white-haired woman with a covered basket. Two pale gray eyes glare out of a mass of wrinkles, and Rosa says, "Pardon me, ma'am, but my name's Cinderella, and this is my brother, Prince Ishak."

"Cinderella doesn't have a brother," the old woman says.

Isaac moves behind his feisty sister and tries to shrink.

"Says who?" Rosa challenges, hands to the hips she doesn't have.

The old woman replies, "I have never in all my life heard any mention of Cinderella having a brother."

"Just because you haven't heard of Prince Ishak doesn't mean he isn't real."

"I'm not," he mumbles, and his sister's heel strikes his shin.

With a smirk, the old woman looks Rosa over. "Well, even so, if you're Cinderella, then your brother wouldn't be a prince, now would he? You certainly don't come from royalty."

"Oh, yes we do! Our papa's a mighty king, and he's off at battle right this minute, fighting for your freedom."

"I see," the old woman says. She shifts her basket to her other arm as if it's heavy. "How terrible for you, then, living with your wicked stepmother."

"She's our real mother, and she's not wicked," Isaac protests over his sister's shoulder. "She's beautiful!" He turns and stomps away, putting meters between himself and that nasty witch. He stops and leans against a building, his eyes on passing feet. Minutes later, he sees the pair he's been waiting for. "Cinderella!"

"There you are," she says. Rosa drops something in one of her brother's outer pockets. "One for you, one for me."

Isaac knows a potato when he feels one. "One for you, one for Rapunzel," he corrects her, and brother and sister head back towards where they came from.

"She said she'd try to find us a pumpkin," says Rosa with a skip and a hop, "big enough to make a carriage for the four of us, and Ellie

and her mama too. She goes to market every week at the same time."

"But how will we hide a pumpkin?" Isaac asks. "It won't fit in our coats."

Rosa tousles his hair. "You silly little prince."

Isaac doesn't understand what's silly, but he smiles anyway. Rosa always makes him smile.

Away from the safety of the crowd, brother and sister quicken their steps and lower their voices.

"I wish we could get more," Isaac says. He stops and transfers the potato to one of his hidden pockets.

"Next time," Rosa tells her brother, tugging him along. "Our fairy godmother said she'd take care of us."

Isaac curls his upper lip. "She's not anybody's fairy godmother."

They turn onto the side street, Isaac trailing his sister. The wall is straight ahead. The street looks deserted. Just a few empty vehicles along the curb.

"Someday," Rosa says, "you and your princess, and Mama and Papa can have your own palaces next to mine. And Grandpa and Grandma will come, and Uncle Benjamin."

"And Auntie Evy?" Isaac asks.

"Yes, of course. They'll find us, and we can all live in the valley together, by the river. And you'll all come to my palace for supper, every night. Mine will have lots of windows, and huge pillows to sit on, and unicorns and rainbows painted on the walls. And there'll be a stage where we can have plays, and we'll invite people from all around. Now tell me what your palace will be like, Prince Ishak ... Isaac?" Rosa turns around. "Isaac, what are you doing?"

"The potato," he says, peering under a car. "It fell out. The stitches came apart, I think."

"Well, hurry up."

Isaac runs around to the other side of the vehicle and drops to the sidewalk.

"Hey," says Rosa, "it's her."

"Who?" Isaac asks, now on his stomach, reaching.

I. Joseph Kellerman

"The lady who gave us the potatoes."

Isaac's fingertips barely touch the one he'll give to Mama. "Where?" he asks, stretching farther.

"Back there."

Isaac sees his sister's feet on the other side of the car. She's facing the main street. With his fingertips, Isaac rolls the potato towards him and gets his hand on it.

Rosa says, "What is she...?" then draws a panicked breath. "A big, bad wolf!"

Isaac knows what that means. As Rosa dashes behind the car, he jumps to a crouch and looks back up the street. A uniform is standing next to the witch, who's pointing directly at them. Then the uniform starts moving.

Rosa grabs the back of Isaac's coat, as another uniform rounds the corner. "Run, Isaac! Run!"

"And then what happened?" the doctor asked.

The client shook his head. "I don't remember."

"Are you sure?"

"I'm sure."

"Joseph."

"I'm sure!" he yelled silently.

Joseph looked at the clock. His knee started bouncing. 12: 44. Damn, he thought. He glared at the numbers, concentrating hard. He just wanted to watch the minutes go by. Don't think, he told himself. Don't think, don't think, don't think!

And such is how the man in the yellow chair spent the next fourteen minutes, until the alarm finally went off.

Chapter 22

Constance browsed through the glossy brochure, studying pictures of carefree people drinking colorful concoctions with miniature umbrellas and tropical fruits sticking out of them. Some of the travelers reclined in beach chairs. Others played shuffleboard or lounged by the side of a kidney-shaped swimming pool, which didn't look much larger than the organ itself. Next came the itineraries and dates, the special offers, the number to call. Constance fingered the corner of the last page, contemplating. This was much more difficult than choosing art.

She'd been rejecting or ignoring the enticements a former client, a travel agent, had been dropping off on her desk and mailing to the office from time to time for almost three years. Hawaii, Tahiti, Paris. Lately there had been cruises to all sorts of exotic locales. Constance hadn't taken a vacation in almost half a decade, and she had not even considered doing so since returning from the last one.

That is, until yesterday, her fifty-first birthday.

As though suddenly possessed by a will that was not her own, Constance pushed her chair and self away from the desk, shoving it forward in the process.

At that same instant, the man watching digits flip heard a muffled scrape.

Constance stood with conviction and marched herself over to the door, giving it a knock that meant serious business was at hand. Dr. Kellerman barely got "Yes?" out of his mouth before she had walked in and thrown something over the desk. The brochure fell into his lap.

"What's this?" he asked, staring down at a buxom woman in an orange bikini, who was smiling at a smiling man with hulking pectorals. Teeth and breasts were all that Joseph saw.

"A *va*-cation," said Constance as if he had never heard the word.

His "Oh" was followed by silence. He'd thought she was coming in to say, "See you in the morning." She always did that.

Joseph felt a chill. He said, "But I don't really need one."

"*Me*, Dr. Kellerman. Although, you could certainly use one, yourself. But that's a lost cause, now isn't it?"

He didn't try to respond to that. He just sat there, his eyes locked to hers, which were full of what looked a lot like anger. Her pink lips were not even slightly smiling when she said, "Tell you what, though, I'll bring you a souvenir. How about one of those paperweights with sand and little starfish? And, ooh, maybe a mini shark in it, too. If it's under glass, it can't hurt you."

Constance didn't know why she was feeling annoyed with Joseph today, but she wanted to shake him.

He wanted her to shake him. He wanted her to yell at him for real, to force him to talk about something that mattered.

Joseph still said nothing. He hadn't felt this type of uneasiness in years. Constance had taken maybe a dozen vacations since becoming his assistant and never for more than a week at a time, although there'd been no specified guidelines. She and the doctor had never discussed vacation or sick time or, for that matter, any other terms of her employment and few job requirements to speak of. She'd left the office following her first time in the yellow chair without even asking how much she would be paid. After three weeks of waiting for him to bring it up, she had finally broached the subject.

***

"Excuse me, Dr. Kellerman?"

A twenty-seven year-old woman with a very low checking account balance stood several feet away from his desk, hugging her waist. He'd been reading a client's file and hadn't heard her enter the room through the door that his last client had left open as the doctor had requested. He looked up and smiled a little.

After a few motionless seconds of staring, Constance said, "Um," took another step on the balls of her feet, and lowered her heels. When the doctor leaned forward, hands folded on his desk, she added, "Well, I was wondering. When would payday be?"

Joseph's arms flopped on his legs as he sat back. He was stumped. Marta had been in control of the accounts ever since she had appointed herself guardian of all that was his.

"Uh ... oh" was Dr. Kellerman's response to his new employee's more than reasonable inquiry. Then they stared at one another again, until they both heard a mid-hour cuckoo in the front room.

"I'm sorry," the doctor said. "I should have paid you already, shouldn't I?" He started shoving papers, books and magazines around on his desk. "It's supposed to be every week, isn't it? Oh, my. Let's see now, where'd that checkbook go?" Drawers were opened two at a time and the contents stirred, some of which ended up on the floor.

"Oh, it's on my desk," Constance at last remembered and pointed to her left to show him where that was. "I paid a few bills that came in. I just figured, you know, you're busy with other things. But if you'd rather, I could just leave them for you."

"No, no, that's fine. Wonderful. Perfect, actually. I'm sure you're much better with finances than I am. Why don't you go ahead and write your paychecks too."

Constance was baffled. She'd never heard of such a thing. Then again, she'd never had a job anything like *this* before. "Well ... okay," she said and, raising her heels off the floor, turned in place. Constance had taken only one step towards the door before she realized something very important had been left out of the instructions. So heels up, spin, and "Dr.

Kellerman?"

"Mm?"

"Um. How much?"

Pause.

Then "How much what?"

"Money. How much do I write the check for?"

And another pause.

"Oh," said Joseph. He thought about this as he pinched and released his lower lip, ran an index finger across the underside of his nose, then reached around his neck to scratch a past or future itch. Nothing came to him except "Whatever you think is fair."

Joseph wasn't sure why Constance laughed, but he did smile again and this time wider, when she said, "You're funny, Dr. Kellerman. But really, though. How much?"

Really, he thought but didn't say, whatever you want. And then some. You're worth much more than money. Take everything.

***

The rest of that conversation had involved more staggered nonsense, as each party waited for the other to make a decision. In the end, a heavy door had been opened and closed, and Constance had glanced at her watch. The four o'clock client had cancelled, but the five o'clock always came early. Constance had stated the time as a closer door was opened and closed, to which the doctor replied, "That sounds great."

So it came to be that Constance was able to live much more comfortably than she ever had before. And it was not at all uncommon for the doctor to tell her, to insist, that she write herself an extra check for random amounts. If he saw something in a shop window, for instance, something he imagined his companion wearing to dinner or a show or dancing perhaps, the amount on the price tag would become the bonus he wanted her to have.

She'd often wondered about those strange numbers but never

inquired. Discussions about business issues other than those of the clients were so exhausting for both of them, both of them avoided those topics as much as possible.

As far as Joseph was concerned, everything was better left to Constance's discretion, like a mother making decisions for a child. In a way, that's how it became, and more so over time. Constance did what she thought was best, as he'd requested. And, to Joseph, what *she* thought was best was always perfect. With certain routine exceptions, Constance would tell him what she was doing or going to do or what she had already done, and Joseph would nod and say something like, "Okay, good. Yes, that's wonderful." Following the shameful incident regarding the switching of the paintings, Joseph had been very careful not to criticize. As long as she was happy, he could function.

As long as she was there and they were together, everything would be all right.

***

Other than those sporadic vacations, when she often traveled no farther than the suburbs, as well as a day or two spent at home now and then for major holidays, Constance had been to 4991 Hopewell Street all other weekdays and numerous weekends since April 13, 1970. She had taken no such thing as a sick day regardless of the state of her health, which was generally above average. On one rare occasion when Constance had the flu, Joseph had been so overcome with concern and anxiety at his inability to express it, he'd smoked two packs of cigarettes, unfolded three boxes of paperclips as well as the boxes, and jabbed his seat cushion five times in nine hours. He'd even eaten all twelve alternative cookies on the plate on the corner of Constance's desk, three each of the four times she'd rushed to the bathroom, when he had a few minutes between clients. And he'd heard that same door open and quickly close eight other times during the day, while he was trapped behind his desk. But Constance hadn't gone home until the last client had left the building at 8:02 p.m. Joseph had never asked her not to leave early or take time off, but he hadn't encouraged it either.

When Constance was gone, Joseph felt very uncomfortable. Without her, he had to deal with matters he'd grown all too accustomed to avoiding. Sitting behind that big desk or carrying out studies and acting the doctor was one thing, though it had become a very lackluster performance. Really *inter*acting with people was quite another. Talking with people on their side of the desk, let alone in the front room, was too personal. He felt exposed.

When he was to be alone for more than a couple of days, Joseph would turn off the answering machine and let the telephone ring until the caller gave up. But he did listen to the outgoing message once in the morning when he came downstairs and once in the evening before going back up for another sleep-deficient night.

"You've reached the office of Dr. I. Joseph Kellerman," said the pleasant voice on the machine. "We're so sorry no one can take your call at the moment, but if you'll leave us your name and phone number, someone will return your call no later than the next business day. If you do not wish to receive a return call, please try us again. We look forward to talking with you *very* soon. Thank you, and have a great day!"

Constance Fairhart was the one who returned any messages and answered all calls.

In her earlier days as Dr. Kellerman's assistant, Constance had once attempted to phone him while she was vacationing in Tampa. When she'd gotten neither answering machine nor answer for several days, she had begun to worry. Another day of the same results had passed, and she was quite beside herself, so much so that she'd called the police and asked them check on Joseph. He'd been embarrassed but not upset with her when she returned to the office shortly thereafter.

Since then, Constance had continued to ring him while she was away, but she would have been surprised if Joseph or the machine had picked up. Instead, she'd arranged for someone else to check in on him. Just to be sure. Now a twenty-eight year-old woman with spiky auburn hair, ears pierced from lobe to cartilage, and no apparent freckles, Delilah was the person Constance relied on for peace of mind when she couldn't get there soon enough to see for herself.

***

Doctor and assistant stared at the brochure on the desk between them.

"When?" he asked.

Constance hadn't yet considered that particular detail, but replied, "Oh, three, four months maybe. There's a two-week cruise in January that looks nice. Two-for-one deal."

Irritable though she still was, that last bit of information Constance instantly wished she hadn't mentioned. The comment was unnecessary, and somewhere in her intuitive heart and mind she knew what it did to him.

Joseph picked up the brochure and turned the pages with single-handed jerks. "I'm sure it'll be great," he said, obviously staring through what he was pretending to look at. Constance could see his jaw tighten, his ears lifted. "Take pictures," he told her, then rolled the brochure into a tube. The way his body began to shake, she knew his knee was bouncing.

Constance always regretted telling him she would be leaving. And she'd never stayed away for *two* weeks. Now with tenderness in her voice, she said, "You know, Joseph, I could arrange for a temp."

He held up his hand. "No, don't worry about that at all. Just make your plans. And write a bonus check while you're at it." He peered with one eye through the telescope he'd made. "These people look awfully fancy," he said. "Take five hundred. Or a thousand rather. I'm sure clothing must be expensive these days."

"Oh, no. No, that's far too much."

Again, Joseph put up his hand, this time accompanied by a deep frown. "Go on, young lady, write the check and make the call." He handed over the telescope and dismissed his assistant with a backhanded wave.

Constance left the room much more slowly than she had entered, blowing out a long-held breath between the door and her desk. On an envelope, she began making a list of things to buy and do just before she'd go on the cruise she now felt committed to: 2 gal. milk, 10 lbs. flour, 2 doz. eggs, 2 jars herring, ham, cheese, mustard, yeast, butter, 2 bags kitty litter, 2 cartons cigs. Ask Delilah to bring in mail & newspaper. Constance crossed out "& newspaper," but the list continued to grow.

Chapter 23

Constance's photos from vacations and other special occasions caused both pleasure and pain for Joseph, but he wanted to see them. He'd sit down in her raised chair behind that little desk and study each picture more than most people would. Even more than those who had taken or were in them.

"What's this?" he would frequently ask, pointing.

Leaning in, Constance would ask, "What's what?"

Joseph would turn his head to look at her, then, "Uh — the — uh," he'd often stutter as her braid fell past his face. She always smelled like vanilla. He'd look back at the photo, reposition his finger, and say, "That."

"Oh. I don't know. A bird, maybe?"

Whatever it was Joseph was pointing at was usually well in the background and too small to be identified. What, or, rather, who he was truly interested in was in the foreground and sometimes touching his shoulder. If there were someone else in the photo, Joseph tried to overlook that bothersome detail. He wanted to see only what she had seen, where she had been. Not with whom.

They were snapshots of Constance Fairhart's life. Her life outside 4991 Hopewell Street. Things Joseph had never been able to share with her. The pictures made him smile a little and, once in a while, a bit more than that. They made him melancholy, and they made him jealous. But most of all, they made him feel incredibly lonely. There was a whole world out there he didn't want to share her with. Still, he couldn't seem to help himself. Curiosity and longing often overwhelmed his resolve to ignore both.

I. Joseph Kellerman

But there hadn't been any pictures for almost five years.

Joseph seldom asked Constance anything of her life beyond that building, the rare exceptions being about those infrequent vacations and holidays. It was not at all that he didn't care or wasn't interested, but it *was* much easier to imagine Constance existed only within those walls. Within *his* life.

And she felt much the same. The time she spent at 4991 Hopewell Street was separate and unique.

There was nothing Constance wanted to hide from Joseph. She wanted him to know her as much as she yearned to know him. Back when they used to sit together and talk, sometimes late into the evening and ostensibly about the clients, Constance had injected much more about who she was — random details about growing up in Bridgeport, jobs she'd had, favorite pastimes. There had been numerous comments with reference to movies and books that affected her, galleries, shows and social gatherings she attended. There'd been some sporadic, more profound and emotional disclosures. Constance had told him about Mom and once even alluded to a certain man she had been admiring. A certain man she wanted to be closer to, but wasn't sure if he felt the same about her.

Joseph had been gripped by a strange fear he'd never experienced and couldn't name. If it were something he'd studied, he was unable to identify the specific feeling firsthand. Then Joseph had informed himself that she couldn't be talking about *him*. And as for the remote possibility that she was? Well, it was best she let it go. But he had said nothing more than a yawning "My, it's been a long day."

Though Constance's heart had dropped when Joseph had stood up and walked to the door, not much hope was lost. She wasn't about to give up *that* easily.

But unlike most people Constance had befriended over the years, Joseph Kellerman had never bared his soul to her. Not even a little and no matter how much more she'd craved that from him than any other person she'd ever met. At first, she'd subtly probed to learn what was hidden beneath the surface of the man she thought about day and night. Even when she was with someone else.

No results.

When from time to time she had been a bit more direct in her questioning, Joseph had closed up tighter. So she'd eased off and tried to accept the situation for what it was. What it was was not what Constance had dreamed about the night after the day she became Dr. I. Joseph Kellerman's assistant and numerous nights thereafter, until it was clear that it was not to be. She'd still had her daydreams, but Constance had needed more than Joseph Kellerman was capable of giving. Though part of her heart had moved on long ago, Constance had not given up, nor would she ever, on the man behind the enigmatic eyes.

Joseph was hard-pressed to comprehend how she had continued to put up with him and be so loyal for so long.

"You don't deserve her," the jerk in his upstairs bathroom mirror had chided many times. The conversation that followed was always, in essence, the same.

***

"No, I don't," the man leaning on the sink agreed, closing his eyes as he replied. He opened them, and the one glaring back at him spoke.

"She'd be much better off without you. You should do her a big favor and let her go. She's wasting her time here."

Eyes closed, and Joseph said, "Fire her? Oh, I could never do that. She's too ... perfect. And it's her decision. If she wants to leave, she will."

Eyes open.

"Well, she hasn't left yet," the man in the mirror pointed out. "No matter how much of an ass you are, she stays. So you'd better do something about it."

"I've tried," said Joseph, looking down the drain. "I mean, we don't really talk anymore. We used to talk for hours."

He massaged the bridge of his nose, then looked up again. These man to man-in-the-mirror to man conversations required some skill in order to work. The eye tricks made his head throb.

"So?" said the reflection. "What has that accomplished? Other than hurting her."

"You don't think she cares that much."

"You know she does. You could see it. How she would come sit, say something, then wait with those big eyes. And then what did *you* do? Nod like an idiot and 'mmmhmmm'. If that much. One day you couldn't shut up, the next you ... you shut down. But she kept trying, and you kept her locked out. You know she was upset that day you locked yourself in your office. Goodnight! That's all you said when she knocked and tried to turn the knob. And then you watched her through the window. You just watched her leave! Why?"

Joseph shrugged.

And the mirror image said, "Because you were scared, that's why. It was getting too comfortable, so you pushed her away."

"No, she was getting too attached," Joseph explained. "I didn't want anything bad to happen. I made sure it didn't."

"Still, she's been so good to you," the other one added. "That's how Constance is. She cares about people. Even lost causes like yourself. But she'd be much better off with someone else. She's wasting her life on you."

Joseph frowned into the sink. "She's just my secretary, you know. Not my wife."

"God forbid."

"God?" said Joseph, glancing at the toilet. "If there *were* one, maybe she would be."

"Impossible to say. If a lot of things had been different, maybe. If *you* were different."

Joseph pounded the porcelain.

"Calm down, Kellerman!" the man in the mirror ordered.

Joseph closed his eyes and took some deep breaths. He said, "She's a great help to the clients too. That's why she stays. Because of them."

"You're sure about that?"

Joseph tore off a square of toilet paper and wiped a smudge off the faucet. "I don't know," he said, still rubbing what was already polished. "But if I thought she were here just for me, I would tell her to leave. You bet I would."

Laughter came from the mirror, and the rubbing stopped for a moment. "Oh, right. You'd be lost without her."

The rubbing resumed. "But I wouldn't do that to her," said Joseph. "I wouldn't let her stay in here. Look what's happened to everyone else I've gotten close to." He ignored the warped little man in the shiny faucet and rolled the tattered toilet paper into a tiny ball.

"Yes," said the one in the mirror, "and those you used for ... whatever it was you thought you were getting. You can't win, Kellerman, and neither can anyone you get close to in *any* way. You'd better stay away from everybody."

"But I'm a doctor," Joseph mumbled.

"Doctor? Oh, right, I forgot. But, please, do them all a great service and just sit there. Look interested, but don't try to help. You'll only cause damage otherwise."

Joseph threw the tissue pellet away and looked sideways at the edge of the mirror. "Then I suppose I shouldn't be talking to *you* either." He stepped back in front of the sink.

And the other one said, "No, you shouldn't. Makes you look crazy."

"You're a loser," Joseph grumbled.

"Yes," the man in the mirror agreed, glaring back at the one in the bathroom. "And so are you."

Chapter 24

Dr. Kellerman was on hands and knees when Constance stuck her head into his office. She had been in the basement, once again searching for the Linda Payne file, when she'd heard him begin to call.

"Rifka!" he repeated for the fourth time, but no longer in the singsong style of his three prior appeals.

Constance couldn't see the man and had no idea where the cat might be, but she could hear things bumping and sliding beneath the desk. A thud was followed by a howl.

"Joseph, what *are* you doing under there? Besides knocking yourself silly." Grinning despite herself as usual, Constance walked into the room and set hands to hips. But her smile was overcome by concern in an instant, when Joseph's voice became more agitated.

"Come *on*, Rifka, *please!*"

Constance got down on her own hands and knees and looked under the desk, coming face-to-face with a very disconcerted, perspiring man.

"Can't find her," he said as he crawled through, pushing boxes and Constance out of the way. Joseph was on his feet and in the next room before she could turn to see the floor lamp fall on the yellow chair. She heard a door hit a wall and something crash, followed by another howl.

By the time Constance righted the lamp and entered the front office, there was a man burrowing into the coat closet under the stairs. All she saw were moving garments and a pair of stirring beige pant legs. Rustling, grunting, clunking and a muffled "Rifka!" was what she heard, as shoes and other items began catapulting into the room. A shoe box opened midair, spilling five years' worth of cancelled checks on its way to her feet, which hopped aside to avoid the next projectile. Joseph was last to shoot out of the closet, just after an empty briefcase caught Constance on the shin as she reached to part the thrashing coats. He almost knocked her over, but the now even more frantic man didn't seem to notice. He began whacking at ferns and philodendrons, breathing heavily.

"She was here before!"

"Before?" said Constance.

"Before that ... that guy left!" In his current state, Joseph could not recall the name of his client of twenty-four angry years. "She was on my lap," he panted. "With me the whole time ... and then he left ... and the door ... and now she's gone!" He leaned over, hands on his knees, stiff-armed, as he struggled for breath.

"Wait a minute, Joseph, calm down." Constance put her hand on his heaving back. "I'm sure she's napping in a nook or cranny, like she always does. Goodness knows there are enough of them in here." She reached out with her other hand to touch Joseph's arm, but he was already on the move again.

"She followed him!" he yelled from the hall. "He let her go!"

"Joseph."

"She's *out there!*" He pointed at the front door.

Constance couldn't believe what was happening. After all, under-reaction was Joseph's usual M.O. He was now turning circles — step, turn, step, turn — his fingers buried in his hair. Constance had no idea what to do, much less what to say.

Without warning, *Boston Globes* began coming to pieces. Joseph's windmilling arms whacked knuckles and newspapers against the wall behind him.

"It's o-kay," said Constance, trying to sound as serene and confident as possible. She kept reaching out to touch him, to rub

I. Joseph Kellerman

his back or take his arm, but he was moving too furiously. "I'm sure she's in the office, right under your nose," Constance reassured him. "A cat could disappear for days in there. Not to worry."

Joseph didn't hesitate in his paper-throwing, so she tried a stern approach.

"Listen to me, Joseph, we will find Rifka. Try to relax now, you're scaring her with all that yelling."

"*Rosa-a-a!*"

Constance was as startled by that shout as she was by the wild look in his dark brown eyes, when Joseph turned on her. He grabbed her arms, his grip tight.

"It was you," he charged in a rasping whisper, with what looked and sounded a lot like hatred. "You didn't protect her. You *ran away.*" Joseph was getting progressively louder again.

"I ... ran away?" said Constance, her voice quavering.

"And now she's out there alone," said Joseph. "And probably *dead!*"

Constance recoiled, nearly falling backwards as he let go along with that final word and bolted for the door. Joseph grabbed the knob he hadn't touched in four years, seven months and six days, then turned that knob and pulled.

And, for a moment, everything stopped.

***

Though the same and similar sounds and people had passed by Dr. I. Joseph Kellerman's row house for decades, they had done so mostly unheard and unseen by the man who had lived and worked and hidden inside its walls for thirty years and seven months. For three years or so before the last time Joseph had opened the front door, he'd left for little more than brief and sporadic trips up the block to the bakery or produce stand, to take out the trash or retrieve the paper from the stoop, or to fulfill an occasional professional requirement. For at least a decade before that, he'd come and gone much like anyone else would come and go, yet still he heard little and saw even less. Except when it came to Constance Fairhart. Otherwise, he'd become far too distant from the world around him to notice much at all.

But outside I. Joseph Kellerman's walls, life had gone on.

Next door, the woman in the turquoise apron had swept those steps most days since 1965, greeting her neighbors whenever she'd had a chance. For three of those years, she'd watched scowling Marta come and go from 4991, but quit saying hello, goodbye or anything else to her after the first few attempts at being sociable seemed to fall on deaf ears. That same woman had also witnessed Marta's final exit when she'd let out a loud "Rrraaah!" and slammed the door. As Marta had stormed up the street, with a large framed picture under her arm, the young woman had smiled with pleasure at the bitch's departure.

The sweeping woman had grown older as she'd then watched plain but pretty Constance come and go, day after nearly every day, year after year. She was a much nicer neighbor than Morticia, the woman had thought. Although, Constance didn't exactly live there either.

The children outside had grown older, too. For several years after meeting the silly lady with the white pumps, Delilah had continued to play with her rag doll on the steps and jacks on the sidewalk, while her elder brother passed many of his own childhood days playing hockey in the street with his friend. In time, the little girl had exchanged pigtails for a ponytail and her doll for little boys. They'd sat out front, giggling and nudging, pulling at Delilah's hair, tugging at her dress. Meanwhile, her brother and his friend had tired of hockey and eventually looked as though they were bored with life in general. They'd hung out on both sets of steps doing nothing much at all. Constance had often had to negotiate around four or more children to enter the building.

Many more days had moved on to the past, as the boys who'd teased Delilah matured into teenagers who French-kissed and felt up instead of poked, pulled and tickled. Delilah's brother and his pal had turned from boredom to deals and drugs on the nearby corner. And Constance Fairhart had continued to walk up the street and climb those same six steps from sidewalk to stoop nearly every day, always with a cheerful "Hello!" to Delilah's mother and the same to Delilah, who would take a breather from making out long enough to greet Constance in return. About the two boys who'd grown into young men in trouble, Constance had become more than a bit concerned. She'd gone on passing by, however. Too many other people needed help inside 4991 Hopewell Street.

Several months before Rifka disappeared or, as Joseph feared, possibly met her demise when she may have accompanied Bernie Babbish out the door, the young woman who'd played with a rag doll as a child gave up a sleazeball who'd groped and called her pussy as a joke, in exchange for a courteous man with a sincere smile. He gave Delilah a bouquet of tulips and baby's breath "just because." Then they'd sat, kissed and cuddled in front of 4991, without so much as a glance at the young blonde woman who stepped around them and, after weeks of agonizing, finally opened the door. Delilah's mother had put down her broom and sat on those clean steps of hers, her arm around her drugged-out son while he rocked.

The morning of the day of Rifka's disappearance, Constance had smiled happily at the bride-to-be she'd watched grow up on the sidewalk and both sets of steps, and sympathetically at Delilah's mother and brother. She'd turned the knob and pulled, but, as always, paused before stepping inside. Constance had kissed her pinkie, then touched it to the first initial on the shingle that hung next to I. Joseph Kellerman's gray door.

What Joseph saw when he opened that same door a few hours later hardly resembled what Constance or anyone else would have seen. He had trapped himself inside for years, where he could better handle and control the bits and pieces, the fragments of memory that could no longer be suppressed or avoided. But the walls Joseph had built had begun to crumble and the distant visions grown clearer and louder and more and more frequent, until the barriers collapsed under the weight of it all. Today, losing Rifka had sent him over the edge.

After a moment of stillness between the two worlds, Joseph's senses were bombarded. The midday sun was a blinding searchlight. A car horn honked a few blocks away, but it became instead a piercing siren. A single dog's bark transformed into a pack of snarling canines, bearing their sharp teeth just out of his fixed line of sight. Joseph couldn't move, not even turn his head or close his eyes, and make it all go away. All he could do was hold on tight as the scene before him began to sway and skew. That's how it was when he yanked open that last door, the one through which anyone *but* Joseph Kellerman had come and gone, from and to 4991 Hopewell Street, for almost half a decade.

People are gathering.

A woman came down the steps next door and stood on the sidewalk, watching. A younger woman and her fiancé stopped smiling at each other and turned to look up at the petrified man in the doorway.

That much was real. Only in Joseph's wide eyes did more and more people come to stare at him. They looked as though their images had been pressed in Silly Putty, then stretched every which way.

Cars are stopping. People are leaning out the windows, looking. They stand in the street and on the sidewalk. A little boy with a hockey stick steps forward and points.

The finger was pointed at Joseph. This time, he'd become part of the vision, no longer just an observer.

I. Joseph Kellerman   201

They begin to laugh.
The guards are laughing on the other side of the wall, taunting as Rosa cries. I hear thumping and slapping, and she cries louder.
If only she could have run faster. She was right there, behind me, but she didn't come through the hole! I waited, but she didn't come through! She's always gone through first, all those other times when we came back with food. I should have waited on the other side. I should have protected her.
She's screaming, "Isaac! Isaac!"
I hear another thump. And another.
"Please, Isaac!"
What are they doing to her?
"Isaac!"
Thump.
And now there's only laughter.
What have I done? I should have helped her. I should have fought them, so she could go through first. What am I going to tell Mama and Papa?
What have I done!
Wait.
Who's that? I know that voice. "Isaac!" it calls, "Isaac!"

The timeline had jumped ahead almost two years, but the memories were as accurate as could be.

Papa appears, crouched with his arms extended.

Reaching out to his son, who was standing in the doorway.

"Come, Isaac!" he calls. And there's a blast, and there's blood everywhere. It's on my hands and my face, I can feel it. It's in my mouth, I can taste it. And Papa is staring at me.
Papa?

Papa?

Joseph felt the scream deep in his gut before he or Constance heard it. When the sound burst from his lips, the intensity shocked him more than anyone else. He hadn't felt so much in such a long, long time.

Constance raised her hands to her open mouth. She didn't know why exactly that blaze of emotion had erupted from the core of Joseph Kellerman, but somehow she understood. After all, this was the man she had cared for and taken care of for over twenty-three years. The man she had admired and learned from and still to this day respected, no matter what anyone else may have thought of what he'd become. No matter what he had done.

Constance had no specific knowledge of what had happened to Joseph before she'd first seen the young, dignified man standing at a podium, and not much more between then and the time he'd called, apologetically offering her a job. But those numbers tattooed on his forearm had been enough of an explanation for Constance when she'd first noticed them on her fifth day as Dr. Kellerman's assistant.

Joseph had employed Constance Fairhart as his own caretaker and confidante. Although, that was something he'd known, at the time and for years to follow, only in his subconscious. And he certainly hadn't given her a chance to fulfill the more important of the two roles.

Constance had said she wanted to do the kind of great work he had done. Well, Dr. I. Joseph Kellerman had been, and continued to be, her single most challenging opportunity to do so. For a very long time, Constance had felt on the verge of complete failure. Over the last several months, she'd been perpetually confused.

And now this.

She had been watching in stunned immobility from the other end of the hall. The scene looked as though someone had pressed pause on a human remote control the instant Joseph had opened the door. For several seconds he'd stood motionless and silent, his one hand clutching the knob, the other the jamb. He'd been inclined toward the street, where midday traffic and semi-hurried pedestrians passed on their ways to and from lunch breaks, or homes to market, or some such destinations and usual purposes. He didn't respond when Delilah asked, "Are you okay, Dr. I?"

But Joseph's shriek jarred him from his sudden paralysis. He whirled around, in the same motion slamming the door so hard the oldest stack of newspapers buckled and collapsed. Joseph fell back and slid down on top of them, his shaking hands pressed against his ears. This was the first time Constance had seen him cry.

"They're gone," he whispered, as she knelt in front of him and stroked his hair.

This wasn't a time to search for those elusive perfect words, and Constance knew it. Through tears of her own, she simply said, "I know, Joseph. I know." When she put her arms around him, he buried his face in her hair.

Not a minute later, as if another button was pressed on some powerful remote, Joseph's crying stopped as he raised his head. The dim hallway was silent. Constance turned to follow his watery gaze toward the far end of the hall. From the slightly open basement door, a tiny "mew" was followed into the wedge of light by Joseph's beloved Rifka.

Chapter 25

A long time ago, when he would look up from the dark street to the lighted window, Joseph could sometimes catch a glimpse of her. He would stand outside her building on humid summer nights, in pouring spring rain and winter snow squalls, wondering. Wishing. Imagining what it would be like to be on the other side of *those* walls.

Joseph hadn't taken one of those late night walks in more than eight years, but he still thought of them often.

***

He was able to see her only when she would pass in front of the living room window to the bookcase or, more often, to the stereo. He could see the books, but he knew there was a stereo there because he could sometimes hear the music. When the temperature was at least sixty degrees, that window was usually open. There had been Broadway tunes and jazz. He'd heard Janice Joplin a few times and Billie Holiday. Some research had been required to figure out that he'd heard the BeeGees on a couple of occasions and then something else for a while. And along with all that music, the delightful sound of Constance. Her voice often floated down to the spellbound man who was listening.

A curious and eclectic combination, Joseph thought but liked it because Constance did. Even the latest group. He didn't know the name of the band until one summer day when he heard the same music coming from a curious new shop across the street

I. Joseph Kellerman

from his barber. Trimmed and clean-shaven, he went over to Daria's Head Zone to find out what Constance had been listening to all those nights and was transported to another world as he walked through the beaded strands that hung in the doorway.

He'd never seen anything like it. Every color of the rainbow on tie-dyed t-shirts, pants and skirts. Cartoons of dancing bears. Hemp and silver jewelry hanging from metal racks suspended from the ceiling. Sculptural pipes. Incense and other strange smells. The store was overwhelming and, he thought, rather breathtaking. Does Constance come to this place, he wondered while wandering around the shop in a daze.

The next time Joseph stood below that third floor apartment window, he heard *Sugar Magnolia* and *Box of Rain*. He knew the songs by then, because he'd purchased six bootleg Grateful Dead albums from Daria. She had led him into a back room with black lights and beanbag chairs, offered him a hit, which he declined, then sold him the tapes — under the table, she said — and a whole bunch of other stuff he hadn't asked for and didn't need. Guilt, thy name be Joseph Kellerman's wallet too. But he listened to the music a lot, because Constance did.

And he watched her dance. She twirled towards that window every minute or so, her braid swinging.

"Rapunzel, Rapunzel, let down your hair," he whispered. "Save me."

Joseph retreated further into the shadows and leaned against a dumpster. Around and around she glided. Each moment he could see her face, Constance was smiling.

After that night, every time Joseph listened to those same songs during the darkest hours, alone in his own apartment, he would see Constance dancing and smiling there in *his* living room. And he danced and smiled with her. Once. When he accidentally caught a glimpse of his lone reflection in the window that faced the courtyard, Joseph stopped.

"Loser," he scoffed, followed by a brief but hateful conversation between the man in the room and the one in the glass. Then he pulled the shade.

When Constance moved to the house several blocks from her former apartment, Joseph had more windows to watch, though he had to be more cautious. There was a lot more traffic on that street, even at those late hours, and people in the surrounding homes seemed unusually active at night. Lights were on in every one of those houses each time Joseph went for one of his walks. He couldn't help but turn his head and look in as he passed. But he stopped at only one.

On Constance's street, loud parties with boisterous revelers often spilled out onto the sidewalk. From time to time, louder arguments occasionally found their way to the sidewalk as well. While most people ignored the stranger standing in the shadows, Joseph once in while received a guarded stare from someone in a passing car or a neighbor coming home from a late shift. He tried his best not to appear suspicious, lest someone report him or, much worse, she find out he'd been there. He would give a two-finger wave, gesture with his cigarette, and make a face that hopefully conveyed, "The wife won't let me smoke in the house."

When Joseph was able to remain unnoticed and watch, he sometimes saw her in the kitchen. The kitchen was behind the dining room, and the dining room window was in the front of the house, to the left of the door. Standing on the street about fifteen feet away, Joseph was tall enough to see into the lower part of that window, through the open doorway on the far wall to the kitchen sink, where Constance sometimes stood with her back to him. Joseph enjoyed staring at her long hair. Staring and imagining.

He walks up behind her and slips his arms around her waist. Her reflection in the kitchen window smiles back at him.

"Jo-s-e-e-e-ph," she groans, leaning her head against his chest. "I'm trying to wash these dishes."

"Oh, I s-e-e-e."
"Joseph. You're bothering me."
"Good. I like bothering you." He draws her hair to the side and kisses her neck.
"Yes, well, you're still bothering me," she says, then points to the next spot.
He kisses below her ear. "Mm, you taste so good." He closes his eyes and buries his face in her silky down.

So much like Mama's. Joseph ached to touch her hair, the way Papa used to.

***

Sometimes Joseph watched the living room window, which was to the right of the front door. He tried to focus on only Constance. He didn't want to see anyone else in that house. Anyone else *with her.*

When there was activity in the living room, Joseph stood on the sidewalk, in line with the front door, where no one sitting on the couch could see him. Constance often sat in the rocking chair in the corner. He was able to see her profile as she rocked, listening to the music with her eyes closed. There'd been a lot of classical since she had moved. Symphony music, waltzes.

The upstairs windows belonged to what looked like a study to the left and a bedroom to the right. The room on the left was not of much interest to Joseph, because it was never Constance who was in there. He ignored that window, lit or not.

The bedroom was most often dark when Joseph stood outside. On a few occasions, a small light somewhere in the room was turned on. Joseph would duck into the alley between Constance's house and the one next door when, each of those times, he saw her appear in that dimly illuminated window. He would lean around the side of the building and look up. Joseph couldn't see the expression on Constance's face at those moments, but he could tell she stared straight out, not down. What was she seeing? He would follow the direction of her gaze with his own, but there was nothing.

What Joseph didn't realize was that, a couple miles away and directly in line with Constance's eyes, there was 4991 Hopewell Street. The lonely prince's tower.

Chapter 26

Around and around we glide, big circles across the floor. The rest of the world could disappear and I wouldn't notice. You're breathtaking—your tall, masculine body in a black tuxedo. I feel weightless in your arms, floating on the music. How I love to dance with you.

Constance was sitting at her desk. She had been staring at the far wall, deep in thought for several minutes. The painted couple had come to life before her eyes, and she had taken the other woman's place.

Shaking her head a little, Constance forced herself back to reality. "And what's this one?" she asked Maggie.

"*Kunstlerleben,* by Strauss? It's the *Artist's Life Waltz.*" Maggie was kneeling at the side of the desk, her head on folded arms while she listened to the tinny music coming from the old cassette player on top of the appointment book.

"Beautiful," said Constance. She liked the song and loved the name.

Unlike most Fridays between five-something and six o'clock, today there wasn't much conversation between the two women in the front room. They were both much too absorbed in the music and their private but similar daydreams.

On the other side of the wall, there was a woman in the yellow chair. She drew a piece of tissue out of the box and dabbed at her eyes, while Dr. Kellerman listened. But the woman wasn't making a sound. When, a minute or so later, she began speaking again, the man behind the desk appeared to be paying attention to her, but he wasn't. He was still much too absorbed in his daydream, not all that different than those of the two women in the waiting room.

Constance Fairhart and Maggie Carlisle were both disappointed when the hour hand reached six. Oddly enough, but not nearly as odd as it would have been just a couple of months ago, there was no muffled buzzing and the door to the back office remained closed. Things out of the ordinary were becoming less surprising to Constance.

She hadn't used the hole in the wall during Lucille McBride's last four sessions, because Maggie had been arriving as much as three quarters of an hour before her own appointments for a month. But Constance didn't need to see into the back office to know that, lately, Lucille hadn't been crying as hard or as long as she had on Fridays between five and six o'clock for years. Constance had become accustomed to hearing sobbing and snorting through the wall, even when she wasn't seeing the source of the sounds. But not anymore. Lucille's face at the end of her hour had, as of late, been additional evidence that something had changed.

The music ended at 6:04. At 6:08, Constance was still waiting for the buzzer, and she'd begun to worry. *This* somewhat peculiar occurrence could have meant something disturbing. She hoped he wasn't —

Of course not! Constance was mad at herself for thinking such a thing. Again! Dr. Kellerman hadn't done anything remotely like that in *years*. Not since Linda Payne. You should know better, she scolded herself. Let it go, once and for all.

If only present circumstances and attorney Mark Dunst would allow her to.

Constance picked up one of her Conned Cookies, a name she'd made up herself, and took a bite. Ew, do they always taste like this? She forced herself to finish chewing, and put what was left of the cookie back on top of all the others she hadn't been able to give away since Wednesday.

**

At ten past six, the door between front and back offices reopened, and Lucille emerged with dry eyes and a calm expression. She closed the door much like anyone would, with a regular clack. There was a marked difference in her walk too, slow and easy with her purse at her side in a swinging hand. Her back to the two women at the front desk, Lucille stopped in the middle of the room. After a moment of staring at the next door, she looked over her shoulder and stared some more.

"Going home?" Constance asked. She knew there was exaggerated curiosity all over her own face, just as it was on Maggie's.

Though there had never been any talk between Constance and Maggie, or Constance to anyone but Dr. Kellerman, about Lucille McBride, Lucille's transformation would have been obvious to anyone who might have seen her week after week at six p.m.

"No, I don't think I'll go home yet," she said. "There's a dress I've been meaning to try on. It's very low cut." Constance detected an almost naughty glint in the one hazel eye she could see, just before Lucille tossed her scarlet-haired but no longer semi-beehived head. She continued to the door, sashaying and swinging her pleated plaid skirt like a runway model.

"You enjoy yourself," said Constance.

"Oh, I certainly will." Lucille began to hum as she closed the door behind her.

Constance and Maggie looked at each other and smiled.

On the other side of the wall, Dr. Kellerman was smiling too. But he was still hearing music.

Chapter 27

Night was the loneliest time for Joseph. He dreaded each moment Constance would say, "See you in the morning." And it was even worse when she said she'd see him on some other morning, when there was a day and a night or two in between. Far too much time to think.

As usual, he sat on the one available cushion of his couch, with a mass of books to his right and five crocheted throws, handmade gifts from one very grateful client, on the left. Joseph scanned the room. What to look at? How to occupy his mind?

Rifka volunteered a solution when she jumped on his lap.

"Hey, sweet girl," he said and stroked her arched back with a big, gentle hand, while scratching her chin with the other. "Are you Papa's pretty girl?" Joseph wrapped his arms around the hefty, purring calico and pulled her to his chest, then nuzzled his cheek against her head.

He would have passed more time that way, but Rifka didn't remain on the same wavelength for long. She voiced her irritation and was off like a small, hairy walrus into the bedroom, leaving Joseph's arms wrapped around nothing.

"Figures," he said as his shoulders sagged.

Joseph would not follow Rifka into that room. He was annoyed with himself for having left the door ajar when he'd gone in there that morning to grab more clothing from the closet, then hastily removed the shirts and pants to a better location. That was the room, in addition to his office between noon and one, he'd set aside for those awful visions. The room with the bed in which

I. Joseph Kellerman

he'd had meaningless sex with Marta and many others before her. The room where, for the first time since his tenth birthday, he'd sat on Papa's knee, then once again watched, felt, heard and tasted his father's murder in all its gruesome detail. No, he would not go back into that room or sit in the yellow chair unless he was ready to deal with memories. Otherwise, they were supposed to stay away. That was the game Joseph played and the one he often lost. Especially over the past six months.

So, as usual, the box of matches was next. He grabbed it off the coffee table, which was buried under several volumes of collected stamps — a gift willed to him by a client who'd last seen Dr. Kellerman and, a day later, died at the age of ninety-two — five packages of incense from his one-time shopping spree at Daria's Head Zone, and three manila folders full of notes he'd scribbled years ago, when he still took meaningful notes.

Back when Linda Payne was a new client.

Joseph counted the forty-four remaining matches three times over, arranging them one by one in the same direction, switching directions with each count. That accomplished, he picked up a book and guessed the page he'd open to. Got it right once out of twenty-five attempts. Better than last night and the dozens before that. After nine minutes spent trying to whistle through his thumbs and another eight humming four times through some tune he couldn't remember the name of or words to, Joseph was at a loss. Knee bouncing, then two knees, add tapping fingers. Nights were *so long*.

He leaned his head back and looked up at that old piece of cardboard push-pinned to the wall behind him. "I should have called you," he said. Joseph didn't need to mouth the words or whisper. There was no one else who might hear him in the building. "Oh well, it doesn't matter now."

Joseph slapped his legs and stood up as if he were going somewhere, took a few determined steps, then realized he had no idea what he was supposed to be doing. He raised his arms and let them fall in despair.

"Wouldn't it be nice to have a purpose, Joseph? Or sleeping would be acceptable. Better yet, you could be doing what a lot of other guys are doing right this second. Ah yes, Joseph, but they have warm, soft women to do *that* with, too." He laughed, though it didn't feel at all funny. "All *you* have is your damn hand. Sh-h-h-it!"

Along with that last word, Joseph swiped October's junk mail off the counter. He glared at the scattered mess for a long moment, then picked it all up. The next ten minutes were occupied restoring the papers and catalogs to chronological order as much as could be determined, then rubber-banding and filing the bundle behind September's bunch of what should have been trash.

Time for a midnight snack. Dill pickles, herring in wine sauce, and half a loaf of challah. Baked the bread himself. In fact, many of those sleepless, late night and early morning hours had been spent kneading dough, watching it rise, kneading again, watching again, then baking, often observing that final process through the oven window while sitting on the kitchen floor. Strudel and homemade soups were two more of his many specialties.

Joseph had always had a knack for the culinary. That talent ran in the Kellermann family. Or used to. But now there was just Joseph. Only Joseph. And over the years, many of those mouthwatering, nocturnal creations of his had been tossed out the window into the courtyard for the enjoyment of strays and rats. Loneliness had often rendered the dishes and desserts tasteless and unfulfilling. What he really wanted to do was set a pretty table for pretty Constance and cook for her, then eat with her too. A little food, some simple, easy conversation and a lot of just being together.

In years past, Joseph had given her a number of the delights he'd produced during those unoccupied hours of darkness. Once their special talks had stopped happening, the food was something he could share with Constance. A connection, though it was an incredibly poor substitute.

"Oh my gosh, Joseph, this is *so good*," she would say each and every time, expanding her eyes to further demonstrate her sincerity. And every time, she would move to the waiting room bench, pat the cushion and say, "Here, come sit. Have some."

But the doctor would never give himself the chance. He'd reply, "I would, but — " and point to the cuckoo clock or tap his wrist where a watch would be if he wore a watch.

Once alone in his office, "Chicken shit," he would sometimes whisper to his warped reflection in the letter opener. "What do you want, for chrissake? First you want to be with her and then you run away. What is *wrong* with you?"

The rest of the conversation was, of course, very much as usual, until the first client of the day walked in soon thereafter.

***

Except for a space big enough for a placemat, the dining table next to Joseph's over-packed kitchen was covered with books. Psychology books and cookbooks. He'd read each of the former word for word at least twice through, and the case was the same with the latter.

"Maybe you should get rid of that ridiculous shingle and be a chef instead," the man in the yellow chair had told himself, the doctor, during one of his recent noon hours. "You would do less damage that way."

"Ah," said the one behind the desk, "but I'd give them food poisoning. Botulism, *E. coli*. Something would go wrong."

"That would be just like you, wouldn't it."

"Well, it doesn't matter, I'm too old. There's no time for big changes. No time."

"Says who? Surely not Constance."

The doctor shook his head. "No. She'd say — "

"There's always time," said Joseph. "That she would. And she could be right. Why, you might have to stick around another thirty or forty years. People are living a long time these days. Never know how much longer you'll have to sit there and suffer."

"Yes, but maybe ... I don't know."

"What?"

Today, the roles had reversed again. The patient was questioning the doctor.

And the doctor said, "Nothing."

"No, really," said Joseph. He uncrossed his legs and slid forward in the yellow chair. "Come on, now. What were you going to say?"

The image was silent.

"Dr. Kellerman, it's just me here. Or us or ... whatever. Let's be honest."

"I don't know, I'm wondering if maybe I couldn't do a little better. Constance would think so."

Joseph agreed with that also. "She would, indeed. So what do you want to do, then? Tell me how you want it to be. And I don't mean how you wish it could have been. That's then. Water under the bridge, crap under the shoe. This is now."

The one behind the desk gripped the arms of his chair. Answering his own questions was so difficult. He stretched his fingers and thumbs, his palms pressed to the wood.

"Okay," he said. "What I want. I want to lock my brain in a steel box and go have some fun for a while. Maybe one night a week or something, to go out and ... and dance or something. Like other people."

Joseph smirked and slid back. "Dance? Oh, come on."

"What, you don't think I can?"

"Ho no-o-o. I've seen you try, remember? The window?"

"No," said the doctor, "that was *you*."

Joseph again slung one leg over the other. "Well, that doesn't count. I can't do that — " He waggled his hand. "That new stuff. But I'm sure I could remember how to do

I. Joseph Kellerman

the box step. Oh, never mind. Neither one of us will be hitting the clubs."

"So then," said the doctor. The roles had corrected themselves, and he was more in control now. "You don't believe you can be you, with your own past and your own mistakes, and have a life? Oh, Joseph." He shook his head. "You've tried to hide for such a long time. Obviously, it hasn't worked. You're fucking miserable. But you know what, though?"

"Do tell," said the client.

And the doctor told him, "You might loathe Joseph Kellerman, but you haven't given up on him completely. If you had, you would not be sitting there."

"Neither would you," said the man to his image. "You'd be in a box six feet under. Or a trench." He felt a swell of nausea and pushed the invasive vision away. "But I know you, mister. I know you're stronger than you think you are. You *can* make things better."

The doctor nodded. "We both can."

And that had been the end of that. Joseph Kellerman's hour had been almost up, the alarm clock was about to buzz, and there'd been sleeping to fake.

***

Joseph awakened still sitting at the table, his head on his arm, which was on a paper plate soaked with pickle juice and wine sauce. He turned and checked the clock on the stove. 3:25. An hour and five minutes since the last time he'd looked. Longer than usual.

"Four and a half," he calculated aloud. Constance was always there by eight a.m. "And five days," he added. Maggie would be there Friday at six o'clock. Well, before then, but *he* would see her at six. Or shortly thereafter if Lucille ran over, which was fine. Joseph liked Lucille. She sometimes made him want to cry, too. But he never did. At least, not when he was sitting behind that desk.

Shower time.

The upstairs bathroom was the cleanest room in Joseph's building. Spotless, in fact, regardless of the clutter that found its way in there as well. Despite his often unkempt appearance, Joseph had never been a dirty man when it came to personal hygiene. He'd learned that from Mama. Even in that most horrible place he could never speak the name of, he'd tried his best to stay clean. There it had been a losing battle, but he had been meticulous about his private parts and bathroom ever since he'd been given the chance to be.

Joseph detested the dirty habits he did have and hated even more the fact he couldn't seem to give them up. Those cigarettes, for one thing. He wanted to quit. He wanted to ask Constance to stop bringing them. Then he would have no choice. Should he ask? Yes, he decided. Soon. He just needed a little more time. Until then, he would continue brushing his teeth for twenty minutes each night. Besides, it was a great way to pass some minutes. Brush until the gums bled and then some. But a hair trim, if needed, and the mandatory shower came first.

Clothes from another sedentary day gone by were dropped into the hamper. Laundry was another thing Joseph often passed a little nighttime with. He'd had a washer and dryer installed many years ago and managed to keep those same machines going through all those cycles without having to call a repairman. That would require someone coming upstairs. Too personal. Joseph had become quite a proficient handyman out of necessity.

The same piece of clothing never touched his body for more than a day before it was washed, even that pair of khaki shorts. Laundered every night following every day they had been worn. For the past few months, those tired shorts had remained folded and smelling like a dryer sheet in the third

I. Joseph Kellerman

drawer of the bureau he'd long ago moved out of the bedroom and into the living room. And he hadn't been doing laundry quite so often, due to the increased variety in his daily attire. He had thirty of those white cotton undershirts.

***

Hot showers were one of Joseph's few true pleasures. He would stand with his eyes closed and feel the water flow over him, temporarily washing away some of his anxiety. First, however, he had chores to attend to. Scrub up, rinse off, scrub up, rinse off, shampoo and rinse, repeat, scrub up, rinse off. He would read the directions on all bottles and boxes, and follow them to the letter, often twice over and twice as long.

Next came the part he had to take care of in order to relax until the rest of the hot water ran out. Lately, he had been using Maggie Carlisle's image to help things along. But the experience was different with her than any of the women in the Sears catalog. With Maggie, it was film noir romance. Nevertheless, the process took only a few minutes of hot water. Then one more good scrub and rinse before he could just stand there. Sometimes he would sit down in the tub and nod off for a bit, until the water became too tepid for comfort. Joseph Kellerman had a large water heater.

Shower and tooth brushing biathlon finished, he moved on to the challenge of figuring out what to wear for the upcoming day. That decision had been easy for years. But now there were again choices to make. And he figured it was best to keep up appearances throughout the rest of the week. One could never know for sure when someone special might stop by. Just to say hello perhaps? He hoped she would. At any rate, the process of selecting and dressing helped pass a bit more of this loneliest time.

Then something else to eat. Fig bars, cranberry juice, and two slices of ham and cheese rolled into tubes with some spicy mustard squirted into the middles. Constance knew what Joseph liked to eat, although he'd been craving added variety for months. Should he ask? Yes, he decided. He should. Soon.

Ten minutes more were spent tooth brushing again and an additional five flossing, with some music for the dental process. The BeeGees. Joseph had really liked that brotherly trio since he'd first heard the harmony floating out of Constance's window. Found out the name of the group a few days later and bought every album they'd made through 1979.

Joseph returned to the center of the couch and listened to the remaining songs as he watched the purple lava lamp. Those molten wax balls moving together, against one another, flowing, liquid, soft and hot. Joseph crossed his arms, tucking his hands into his armpits, and continued to stare at the dancing blobs. Something about that lamp always turned him on, but there wasn't time to take another proper shower.

He imagined himself dancing with Maggie. They moved like those malleable purple forms, becoming one. And that was enough to get him through until it was time to go downstairs for another long day.

Chapter 28

The building was too quiet and yet too noisy. From the downstairs kitchen, the hum of the refrigerator permeated the entire first floor. The drone and sporadic clanking of the furnace was louder than ever, the incessant ticking of the cuckoo clock deafening. Even breathing was hard on the ears, while the sounds from the other world outside those morbid, dark-paneled walls seemed unusually distant.

Constance wished she could turn down the volume inside and blast those horns and the barking dog, the wind, the voices of people passing on the sidewalk. Even opening the waiting room window for several chilly minutes hadn't done the trick. Instead, she had tried a number of different sounds to drown out those that were making her tense. She'd tried talking to a cat now and then, when one entered the front office, but they'd each quickly moved on to a nap or a litter box in another room. Vacuuming might have worked had the vacuum worked. She'd tried whistling, humming and singing, which had succeeded only in making her more irritable. For the past few days, it had been *Sunrise, Sunset* almost nonstop. Constance couldn't seem to get that annoying song out of her head.

Neither, therefore, could Joseph. For half an hour, he'd been listening to her whistle, hum and sing that same melody, over and over again, though he wasn't on the same floor. Joseph's ears were well-tuned to certain sounds. Today, even the sweet sound of Constance was nearly intolerable, yet he couldn't seem to close his ears. Hands or no.

On Wednesdays between eleven and noon, there hadn't been a client for weeks now. But on this particular Wednesday, the footsteps over Constance's head sounded like concrete blocks being dropped.

They sounded much the same to the pacing doctor. He was relieved when the minute hand on the stove clock approached the end of the hour. Just as the miniature bird would have begun its twelve consecutive cuckoos, Joseph emerged from his apartment, descended the steps that today seemed to shriek with each one of his, passed through the front office with a nod and a cringe for a smile, then tried to disappear.

The click of the door sounded more like a slam to the two people on either side of it.

As Joseph sat down and Constance turned around, they were both thinking the very same thing. Please, say *something* that matters.

***

Since that day almost a month ago, when Joseph had thrown open the front door in a panic and seconds later wept in Constance's arms, he hadn't said a word about it.

Neither had Constance.

Moments after Joseph's crying had suddenly stopped, he'd taken her hands in his as he stood and helped her to her feet. He'd smoothed her blouse over her shoulders and down her arms. Holding her hands for a moment more, he'd said, "I'm sorry," without taking his eyes off the cat at the far end of the hall. He'd wiped away his tears with his shirtsleeve, then walked towards the front room and picked up Rifka, embracing her as he'd returned to his office and closed the door.

A minute before one o'clock, when Constance had tapped, she'd heard a jovial "Come in!" When she had opened the door, there was the doctor, behind his desk, looking more than ready to see his next client.

"Martin is here," Constance had said. "Should I ... send him in?"

Then Joseph had smiled and nodded, and that had been that. But she'd been watching him much more closely since then, even checking in throughout his so-called breaks, as she did on this day.

***

Joseph was holding his unlit cigarette halfway between the armrest and his mouth. He'd pulled the floor lamp back and tilted the shade the other way so he could see better.

Constance thought she saw his lips begin to move.

"They didn't understand," he barely mouthed. "How could they? They weren't there, they couldn't know. And as far as they were concerned, the war was well over. That was a happy time for them.

"Sometimes Mr. Smith would make comments like, 'Isn't this a wonderful place you're in now, Joseph.' Not that he was asking. And 'Joseph, you're so lucky to be here.' Those were the only times he spoke German to me. But he wouldn't let me answer, which was fine. So it was like he was telling me to forget.

"But *I* wasn't the one who'd said anything in the first place. I guess he was hearing things from someone else and probably saying the same to whoever. He didn't want to know. Many people didn't."

Constance saw Joseph shake his head. He put the cigarette to his lips, the lighter to the cigarette, then lit, squinted, exhaled and nodded.

"Yes, that's true, I was an outsider in that neighborhood. I was the German kid, and I didn't bother to correct them. They heard German and thought, okay, German. And that wasn't a popular thing to be." Quick inhale and puff.

"Oh, and I was the dumb kid too. Supposed to be in eighth or ninth grade, but I was in fifth because of the language thing and all those years of schooling I'd missed. Kids beat on me every chance they got. Private school or not, it didn't matter."

Joseph inhaled until his lungs could expand no further, and released the smoke as slowly as he could. He listened for a moment, then "The teachers?" he said. "No, they looked the other way most of the time. But I didn't care."

Another inhale and puff.

"Because the pain felt right, that's why. I knew I deserved it because I was still around to feel it."

Joseph took a final drag on his less than half-smoked cigarette before pressing it out. He put much more muscle into doing so than was necessary, leaving a mashed pile of tobacco and paper in the ashtray.

Most of the time, being in this chair was considerably more difficult than sitting in the one on the other side of the desk. For many of these sessions, Dr. Kellerman had remained behind his desk from noon to one, staring at the useless image in the yellow chair. But neither Joseph had said anything. Neither had wanted to think anything. Many accumulated hours of staring and a huge effort had been required for them to begin in the first place. And it had been an equally great struggle for Dr. Kellerman to one day move from his chair to the yellow one, to become 'just Joseph' and change roles from doctor to client, though they'd been one and the same man between noon and one, everyday for a long time. Where his actual body sat during that hour made a difference though. Made him feel different feelings and sometimes experience different scenes. The chair he was in often affected his attitude.

Thinking she had imagined his lips to be moving, Constance ever so carefully pushed the painting back to the right and resumed her bill paying. Things were tight again this month. Fewer and fewer clients all the time. She would check on Joseph in a little while.

Once again, he looked across the desk.

I. Joseph Kellerman

"Makes no sense," said Joseph to his imagined self. "I was only ten. Yes, I was as tall as some twelve, thirteen year-olds. Maybe older, but still. I worked as hard as I could, but I wasn't strong. Not even at first. And, after a while, I don't know how my legs didn't break like twigs. There were so many reasons I should have died or been killed like most of the others. I was sick, all the time sick and starving and cold, *too*. So *why?* I wish somebody could tell me. It makes no sense. *I* make no sense." Joseph shook his head for the next minute, hearing that last sentence over and over.

The doctor said, "You know one explanation, why sometimes you were spared."

"But there I was, here in the United States of America," the client continued. "It was incredible. And I was given the nicest things. Things I'd never imagined."

"One of them liked you, Joseph."

"Such soft clothes and a shirt for every day of the week, a bed that felt like a cloud, and a blanket with pictures of airplanes on it."

The voice in Joseph's head was trying to drown out the other one. What had once been the task of his subconscious had become a cognizant effort to protect himself from the truth of certain memories. He was trying, but failing.

"He gave you extra food!" the other one shouted. "Hungry, yes, but you weren't as frail as the others! They wasted away, and you didn't!"

"I had a hairbrush and toothbrush of my own!"

"He thought you were pretty, like a girl! He liked to lie with you, Joseph! To touch you! Sometimes he — "

"No! Stop!"

"Why?" asked the doctor. "We've come this far."

Suddenly, breathing was difficult. Joseph felt pain down his legs and up his back, the wood under his hands. "Because, I'm not ... not yet. Please, I can't. *I can't.*"

Dr. Kellerman held up his hands in concession. Some memories would remain in third-person for the time being. A boy observing or a son resting in *Mama's* arms.

Safe for the moment, Joseph continued. "The books, those I liked very much, even though I didn't understand them at first." He looked over at the shelves near the desk. Books crammed sideways above the upright ones. He looked at the stack next to the bookcase. The traumatic amnesia publications and Von Schlossberg texts on top of those. But no thought was given to the little black hole his eyes picked up just above *Transference and Counter-transference in the Doctor/Patient Relationship*. Too many other things to think about.

"And there was so much food," he told the doctor. "So much of everything. What I saw in the Smiths' house was wealth beyond my imagination. And there were people just as affluent and more so all around. But none of those things meant anything to me. I would have given it all back, if only — " He sighed and shook his head. "If only."

Dr. Kellerman nodded but said nothing. He'd said too much already.

"Everyone smiled," said Joseph after a brief silence in his head. "Everyone but me, was how it seemed. There was no way they could comprehend the … annihilation? What's the right word? I don't know, there isn't language for it. But I wasn't going to talk about it. I wanted it to go away, to forget everything I'd tried so hard to believe wasn't real. And everything I thought was my fault."

The word "thought" was something new. Joseph paused when he heard himself think it.

"I pushed the memories away for so long," he continued. "'Don't think about it,' a voice would say. 'Don't remember.' But I would *not* forget my family. I forced myself to see their faces, time after time. There was no one else left who could. But then one day, I woke up and realized I was having trouble seeing Rosa. And

I. Joseph Kellerman

then I couldn't see her at all. Mama went next."

"How did that make you feel?" Joseph heard the doctor ask.

"Guilt was about the only thing I *could* feel. I couldn't cry or laugh. Any emotion was too painful, because it reminded me that I was alive. And they weren't."

"Did you talk with anyone? Tell anyone at all what you'd seen or experienced? How you felt?"

"Of course not. As I said, I felt almost nothing."

"Of course. And what about your new family? What were they like?"

"They were *not* my family. Look, don't misunderstand. I appreciate what they did for me. Letting me live in their house for a while, the things they gave me. All the best things and the best schools. They sent me to a boarding school in Connecticut two years after I arrived. Thought I might fit in better there. Or that's what they said, anyway."

"Did they ever ask about your family?" was Dr. Kellerman's next question. "About your mother at least? After all, she was Mr. Smith's niece."

"Not a word. Which is one reason I said they weren't family. Mr. Smith had never even met Mama. Oh, but there was one time I asked Mrs. Smith if they had any photos of my parents and Rosa. I thought maybe they might have one or two, somehow. But all she said was '*No.*'" Joseph hit the armrest with the side of his hand to punctuate the word. "And I never mentioned them again.

"In fact, there was rarely talk about anything that really mattered. But that's what I preferred. I could say nothing, while they chattered about the weather or money. Even when I'd learned quite a bit of English, and I was a quick study. I learned fast and could speak much like an American. Someone born here, I mean. I tried very hard to and practiced when I was alone. But I, the good actor, pretended I didn't understand, so they spoke to me even less."

Joseph made a "hmf" of a chuckle, but he wasn't laughing.

"But mealtimes were very uncomfortable," he continued. "They hardly said a word to *each other* then, so there wasn't much to preoccupy my mind with. It was so different than home. You know. Home ... before. I was glad to be sent away to school."

Joseph shifted and re-shifted in the chair, listening to the clock ticking on the wall behind him, the metallic clanking and his own breathing, whether he wanted to or not. He glanced at the alarm clock. 2:40. Then he closed his eyes for a few minutes.

During that respite, Constance checked in for the third time that hour. He seemed fine, sleeping again. The painting was straightened.

At that same moment, the man in the yellow chair scarcely perceived a familiar sound. Had he ever heard...? But the vague thought was gone before it was finished.

Joseph opened his eyes. "I was the best student. Read every word of every book I was assigned, and then some. School and books, books and school — they saved me for a long time. From myself. And when I wasn't in class or studying, I worked. I worked in the library, where I could keep reading. Worked for my professors, washing blackboards, passing out exams. Whatever they wanted. I needed to be busy. Hardly slept back then either."

"*Arbeit Macht Frei,*" said the doctor.

"What?"

"Work Makes You Free." Dr. Kellerman translated the death camp sign that had appeared in front of him. He'd had to read it backwards.

Now Joseph read the words for himself. "Guess I'd forgotten that somehow," he said. Then he smirked. "Well, we know *that* isn't true. The sign, I mean."

"So you became quite successful, didn't you, Joseph."

"Technically speaking, I suppose. Von Schlossberg loved telling people I was his proudest accomplishment. But I didn't feel proud at all. I still cannot understand how people looked at me the way they did. I don't know why they thought I was helping anyone."

I. Joseph Kellerman

"You don't think you helped people?" the doctor asked. After all, the man in the yellow chair was a psychiatrist, too.

"People helped themselves. They came here because they were ready to face their problems and get well. Or better, anyway. Some just needed a place to go, a safe place and someone to listen, who wasn't involved. But those that worked through things and moved on, well, I don't think I had much to do with it."

"But you used to *go* to people, also. You reached out."

"Those were studies. I was being busy."

"But you cared about them, Joseph. You can't deny that."

"No, I can't," he conceded. "But —"

His mind went blank at 12:55.

12:56

12:57

As though not by the power of Joseph's imagination, the doctor said, "Well, it's at least half the battle to be ready. But, by the same token, we all need to ask for help once in awhile. To talk to somebody, share things. And by the way, Joseph Kellerman, I for one think you were better than you think we were. Or at least I can be." Sometimes the image confused his personal pronouns, wherever he might be located.

"Do you really think so?" Joseph asked himself.

Then another digit flipped.

***

Constance cleared her calculator the instant she heard the muffled buzz. Today, however, when she entered the back office, silenced the alarm, and turned to face the man she had cared for for over twenty-three years, she was startled to find herself looking straight into open eyes.

Chapter 29

Constance looked at the cuckoo clock for the third time in a minute. "Excuse me for a moment," she said to the client on the bench, seconds before 12:58. She pushed herself back from her desk and stood up as the buzzing began. She took two steps towards the door to her left, but the buzzing stopped. At a loss, Constance returned to her desk and sat there, doing nothing for the next two minutes, until the door to the back office opened and Dr. Kellerman welcomed his one o'clock.

At two o'clock, the doctor wished the departing client a good week and welcomed the next. He did the same at three, four and five. When he opened the door at six after six and stepped into the waiting room before Lucille did the same, Joseph was smiling.

***

"Well, I was pretty shocked," Maggie replied. "Not to mention mad. I mean, I felt like he should have told me right away. But I know why he didn't? And after thinking about it, I'm actually *glad* he didn't? Because if I'd known he knew, I would have been way too ashamed to get past that. We never would have happened."

"Why should *you* feel ashamed?" Dr. Kellerman asked the young woman who was sitting only a couple of feet away from him.

Maggie had been so anxious to continue talking when she went from the waiting room bench to the yellow chair that nothing about the significant change, the rearranged furniture in the next room, had phased her. Neither had the questions.

"Well, I don't," she said. "Or not anymore I don't? But you know how I was raised and all. Not that that's *bad*. No, my parents are awesome. It's just that I felt like I wasn't pure anymore? And on top of that, I'm a hopeless romantic. As *you* well know." Maggie added emphasis to that last statement with a poke. She sat back and told the doctor, "I wanted my first time to be really special."

Joseph stared at the back of his forearm. He could feel the spot.

"Special," he said.

"Yeah, I wanted it to be on my wedding night. I mean, I know lots of people marry people who've been with other people before them, and it's no big deal. To me it *was*, though. That I saved myself, I mean? But I've come a long way since I met Danny. It's like, I used to feel dirty? And like the rape was *my* fault? That I could have maybe stopped him somehow. Brian, I mean."

"You are *not* to blame for *his* violence," Joseph interjected, pointing and looking directly at Maggie.

Constance smiled, teeth and all. This was good to see, parroted words she'd mentioned to him in passing or not. He was involved!

"No, I know," said Maggie. "But, I mean, if I'd known Jeanette had told him? And it figures. I mean, she's been following me around since we were sixteen, and she has just as big a mouth now. And we both met Danny at the same time, when we were in his class together? And they became pretty good friends. I mean, I guess I understand *why* she told him? He said Jeanette really wanted things to work out with him and me, and she thought it would help if he knew. So he wouldn't think I was, you know, cold or something?"

A moment passed with just the soft, white noise of a soaking rain falling on the other side of the covered window. Dr. Kellerman was trying to think of useful words, while Maggie was pausing because she thought she should.

Apparently the doctor didn't have another question or comment yet, so Maggie said, "I should have realized he knew, though. I mean, he didn't even try to kiss me that whole time. He says he just figured that, when the time was right, I'd be ready to talk about it? And get closer if I wanted to? And I am now? And I do? *You* know what I mean."

With the floor lamp behind and off to the side of the yellow chair, Maggie could see the thoughtful expression on Dr. Kellerman's face as he nodded.

Then he narrowed his eyes and said, "So."

So she waited

And he asked, "How do you feel?"

Maggie placed her hand over her heart and gazed at the ceiling.

Dr. Kellerman looked up, too. When he glanced back at her, she was again looking at him, now with a puzzled frown. "How do I feel about what?"

"About everything," said Joseph. "The past, the present, the future. About yourself."

About me, he thought but didn't say. He knew he shouldn't think it either.

And Maggie thought Dr. Kellerman was sounding more like just a man than a psychiatrist. "Well," she said and, after a little more thought, replied, "Optimistic? Hopeful?"

Joseph watched and waited.

So Maggie elaborated, now a pro after all those one-hour monologues. "Obviously, the past doesn't just like, disappear? But we can learn from it? And I've realized I *have* learned to live with it, and I'm moving on with my life. I mean, that's what we have to do, right? That or give up."

Still nothing more from the mouth of the man, but he was listening.

"You know," said Maggie, "in a way, I think I'm a much stronger person now. Not that I'm *glad* it happened? I mean, if I

I. Joseph Kellerman

had my choice. But now I can maybe help other people who went through what I did. Or even help with different things, because maybe I'm a more sensitive person now? More aware? I don't know. But also? When I think about what happened to me? I look around and feel like, hey, much worse has happened to a lot of people. Shit, look at the Holocaust. Makes my experience seem *pret*-ty insignificant."

Constance was startled by the example.

As was Joseph, but he managed a response. "It is significant," he said, staring through his left sleeve. "It happened to *you*."

"Oh, I know what you mean." Maggie was enjoying this bit of two-way conversation. "It's like, when it's you? I mean yourself? Whatever hurts you is a big deal. But I also think I have to have perspective, right? At least I still have a lot of life ahead of me." She leaned forward and knocked on the arm of the doctor's chair, then added, "And I'm *going* to make the best of it." Maggie smiled, satisfied with how she felt and what she heard herself say.

So was Constance.

This time, Friday from six to seven-something in the evening, Joseph Kellerman was very much present inside the back office at 4991 Hopewell Street. He was by no means at the place where Maggie Carlisle was, but he now had a smidgen of hope that someday maybe he could be. If there was enough time. After all, he still had a long way to go.

Chapter 30

Bill sees you first. I turn my head to follow his gaze, across the crowded banquet hall towards the entrance.

You're a vision in white satin. The material drapes easily over the curves of your body, against your smooth, cream-colored skin. I watch you as you stand in the doorway, searching. You see me, and your face lights up.

We meet in the middle of the room.

"You're gorgeous," I say.

I extend my elbow, then lead you back to the bar.

Dr. Kellerman's fantasies were as real to him as the recent events his favorite client was describing. Both scenes had started out nearly identical, the differences being the leading man and the color of the dress. Not to mention the point of view.

"So then we hung out for a while and had some wine," Maggie continued. "Well, I sort of stood there, holding the glass. You know *me*, I'm more of a fruit smoothie with protein powder kind of girl. But, anyway, we hung out for a while around the bar? And all these people kept talking to us? But we were kind of in a different place. He like, kept one hand on me the *whole time*. And I could feel his body near mine? Like, right behind me? It was so amazing, I could hardly pay attention to what anyone was saying."

The words gushed from the young woman in the yellow chair, and *Kunstlerleben* faded into Dr. Kellerman's ears, though he had no idea where he'd heard the song or what it was called. Not that he was wondering.

I can't wait a moment longer. Another man's eyes are still looking your way. Bill has developed a crush on my girl.
I reach out, and your fingers weave into my mine. I take you to the dance floor and lift your hand, my palm to yours. I place my other hand on your waist and draw you to me.
"You're incredible," I whisper, my lips to your ear.

"He was such a gentleman," said Maggie. "You know, we'd never danced together before? I didn't know what I was supposed to do with my other hand! Like, put it on his chest or his shoulder or *what*. Man, did I have the jitters. But once he put his arms around me? The way people normally slow dance? I felt so relaxed, like I was exactly where I was supposed to be."

Maggie scratched beneath her right ear, then touched a finger to the inner corner of her left eye to remove a speck of something that wasn't there. She still felt a little uncomfortable with the doctor, even after all these weeks. Actually, she'd been considering discontinuing these sessions. The things Maggie now thought about day and night she could talk about with Jeanette, any time she wanted. And for free.

"Dr. Kellerman, let me know if this is totally grossing you out?"

Joseph smiled. He was engrossed in his own world. Maggie's words had been getting through, but certain things had been modified and twisted between her mouth and his mind. Somewhere along the line, infatuation and longing had become something more.

Around and around we glide, big circles across the floor. The whole world could disappear and neither of us would notice. I feel so happy, so alive, as we float together on the music. How I love to dance with you.

"Well, anyway," said Maggie, but she and Constance were the only ones who heard the words.

The scene in Joseph's mind veered off from the one he'd been listening to. As he and Maggie moved in circles, she became someone else and he felt different. The man in the back office of 4991 Hopewell Street was part of the visions, but no longer in control.

"Will you marry me, Mama?"

You lead me around the room, while Papa dances with Rosa. Rosa laughs as he swings her off the floor.

And you say, "But I'm already married, sweetheart. Someday, though, you'll find a special lady who will have eyes for only you."

"Will she dance with me like this?"

"Oh yes. But it will be different in a wonderful way."

"Different how?"

You smile at me, but not like you usually do. Maybe because I just turned six.

"You'll know when it happens," *you tell me.* "You'll be a man then, like your Papa."

Yes, that's how I want to be. Just like Papa.

"I love you, Mama."

"I love you too, sweetheart."

"Dancing with him was sort of like how I imagine making love will be," said Maggie, who felt herself blush. But what the heck, she thought, Dr. Kellerman won't laugh, he's a psychiatrist. So she told him, "It's like, I've always thought about it as so much more than, you know, the actual, um … consummation? Like it's a union of two spirits? And like, communicating with your bodies? *You* know what I mean. And it's kind of like, when you're dancing? If you open yourself to the music and go with it, you feel so free. Like you're not even in your own body. And it was so cool being able to get to that place *with* someone? It was like there was nobody in the room but us. Oh, man, I've never been so happy."

When Maggie cleared the romantic image from her mind, she saw tranquility on the doctor's face.

Papa and Rosa dance out the open door, laughing, and we're alone. We move in silence, just being together. I feel safe and close my eyes.

I feel your body near mine.

Joseph felt an exhilarating sensation and opened his eyes. The face of the young woman he was dancing with came back into focus. She had been Maggie. And then she'd been Mama. But now she was someone else. She looked like Maggie in some ways and just like Mama, but this was a woman he knew much differently and more intimately than either one. Joseph was flustered.

Kunstlerleben faded out.

"Dr. Kellerman?" Maggie repeated and reached to touch his hand. He had closed and opened his eyes, then looked surprised, like he'd been groped from behind. "Did I say something weird?"

"Uh, no. No! Not at all. I was just ... it was a perfect evening. That you had."

Then droning and tick ... tick ... clank, tick ... tick.

"Well!" said Maggie, halting mid-shrug. Another second ticked by, and she exhaled and relaxed her shoulders. "Guess that's it for me today. It's a little early, but I have some stuff to do? And I want to practice tonight."

Joseph was distracted but said, "Okay. Well. This was good! Thank you."

"Yeah, no problem."

Doctor and client stood up at the same time.

"Oh hey, Dr. Kellerman, I meant to tell you, there are still some tickets left for the New Year's Eve concert? I mean, if you'd like to go?"

A flat "Oh" was Joseph's response. He had nothing more to

say to that. All of a sudden, he couldn't think at all.

"The doors open at eight-thirty," Maggie told him. "So there'd be plenty of time to go to dinner or whatever. And then after? There'll be champagne and dancing and all that good stuff. It would be really great if *you* were there, too." Maggie patted the doctor's arm. "I have a feeling it's going to be a very special night."

Maggie gave Dr. Kellerman a glance and a smile, sure he knew what she meant.

Joseph opened his mouth but still couldn't produce a sound. I'm ready now, was what he was thinking. I wasn't before, but now I am. It's too late for some things. Too late a long time ago. But now there's you. So let down your hair, my Rapunzel, and let me in.

No, I mean, let me *out!*

He followed Maggie and reached around her to open the door. That energy she had once spoken of now made perfect sense.

Joseph stopped there, inches inside his office, and watched. After exchanging casual pleasantries with her friend in the front room, Maggie left the door to the hall wide open behind her.

Still sitting at her desk, Constance turned her head. She knew he was standing there. "Joseph?" she said.

But the door clicked shut.

Chapter 31

"Drooling *hags*," Bernie sneered. He could feel the blood pumping to his face. "They were standin' there in the lunch room, gawkin' at 'im, like ... like he was some kinda freakin god. They were like, 'Oh, he's s-o-o-o sw-e-e-e-t.' And then they were sayin' stuff like, 'And he's not all macho, like other guys with big muscles.' Yeah, right, all they want is to jump his bones. *Whores.* They stand there at their registers, all drippy sweet. 'Thank you, sir. Have a nice day, sir.' *Bullshitters.* They're just thinkin' about how big every guy's dick is."

Bernie looked down and winced. He felt so inadequate. And he hated women for making him feel that way. It was *their* fault. And he hated men also. *They* gave him so much to live up to. Bernie Babbish felt like he didn't fit in or belong on either side of the gender gap. Didn't belong, period.

"That's what Mother's always thinkin' about," he told the doctor. "I see 'er lookin'. Every freakin guy that walks by, she's lookin'. But she sure ain't gonna get any, that ugly hound." Little feet and fingers were tapping double-time, as he furrowed his brow as much as it could be furrowed. Bernie forced a fart. Ah, but how much better it felt to be a man.

As the rant continued, Bernie's hot air faded from Dr. Kellerman's ears, though he was sitting much closer to this particular patient — there was no calling Bernie Babbish a client anymore — than he ever had in all those twelve hundred some-odd Tuesdays. Instead of flatulence and foul language, Joseph was hearing that waltz again, and he smiled. The timing was horribly inappropriate, considering what was going on in the real world in the back office of 4991 Hopewell Street, but only Constance noticed his expression. During these doctor-client sessions, she could now see the right side of Joseph's face through that little hole in the wall. When he was alone in there, Dr. Kellerman's usual chair was empty, and Constance could no longer see the yellow one.

Just before the last two numbers flipped to 00, the music and harmony were squelched when the furious man blasted back into Dr. Kellerman's consciousness. Tight fists pounded the arms of the yellow chair. "That bitch! I should chop her oozing head off and dropkick it off the freakin Tobin Bridge!"

Almost as much to his assistant's surprise as his patient's, Dr. Kellerman leaned out of his chair and took firm hold of those two flailing wrists. Constance's left eye was glued to the wall.

"Mr. Babbish! Sir!" Joseph's voice moderated as he said, "Bernie. Hey, look at me. *Look.* At me."

The confused child in a grown man's puny body was so shocked by the touch of those strong hands and the sound of that steady, self-assured voice that he immediately sat up, still and quiet, and gaped at the giant who'd taken hold of him.

I ... I *am* lookin' at you, he was thinking.

"Bernie, I understand why you're so angry. Any time you need to get it out, you come see me, okay? I'll be here, and we'll talk. And there's no charge, so don't worry about the money."

Dr. Kellerman let go, but Bernie remained in suspended animation for several seconds. Then he lowered his arms and turned to look behind him at the ticking thing he hadn't had reason to look at for many years. "Oh no," he said, "*it's past my hour.* I gotta go."

Shell-shocked, the patient rose from his chair and toddled to the door. With hands clasped, clutching some of his pink oxford, a subdued Bernice Babbish bid good evening to Constance Fairhart "ma'am" as he made his escape. The closer he got to the next door, the more steadily he moved.

I. Joseph Kellerman

"See you next week?" Constance asked the back of his matted, curly-haired head as Bernie disappeared into the hall.

"Might have to work or something" was what she thought she heard, just before a resounding clunk.

Now standing in the front room together, the doctor and his assistant looked from the window to each other and shook their heads.

Chapter 32

"I remember when she was just a tiny little thing," said Joseph as he leaned towards the window. His feet were planted a few feet from the wall.

Constance had been sitting at her desk, watching him stand there for more than a minute, and her mind had wandered to a place it hadn't been in many years. When he put his hands in his pant pockets like that, the fabric pulled tighter across the back.

Oh, *stop.* She realized what she had been looking at and thinking about. But the internal wings continued flapping.

For a moment, Constance thought she hadn't heard what Joseph said. Then it sunk in, and she asked, "When who was?"

"Delilah," he said, still leaning.

Constance got up and went to see what Joseph was seeing. Their cheeks were no more than two inches apart, as he bent closer to the glass.

The young woman he was speaking of was standing on the sidewalk, looking cold in a cropped, red leather jacket and talking about something serious, it appeared, to her brother. He sat on the steps next door, arms on his knees, his wrists and head hanging as he stared at the concrete between his feet.

Constance turned, leaned against the wall, and studied Joseph's eyes as they looked intently through double panes to the scene beyond. His irises were as solid a brown as she'd ever seen, even in the sunlight.

He said, "She used to have those — " then swiveled his index fingers at the sides of his head.

"Pigtails," said Constance.

Joseph laughed without making a sound. "Yes, and yellow ribbons," he added.

"Yes! Yes, that's right!"

"And those elastic things with the big bobbles," he said.

Constance smiled. "Yes."

Joseph turned away from the window, walked over and sat on the waiting room bench, his long legs outstretched and crossed at the ankles, hands once more in his pockets.

Constance went back to her desk and sat on the front edge of it, facing him.

Looking at where'd he'd been, he said, "I used to bring her flowers sometimes. Little wildflowers from the park. Dandelions mostly. She'd stick them in her hair and say, 'Thanks, Dr. I.'" Again he bounced with muted chuckles.

Constance was loving this. She crossed her arms, tilted her head to the side, and watched and listened some more.

"I saw Delilah when she first came home from the hospital," said Joseph. "A bundle in a pink blanket. After that, I'd see her every once in a while, when her mama would take her in the carriage or sit with her out there. And then she started playing by herself. She *always* had that doll."

"Gretchen," said Constance.

Joseph said, "Gretel." Then he looked at her for the first time since he'd followed the eleven o'clock into the waiting room at 12:04. "You do know where she got it, don't you?"

Constance shook her head.

"Me," said Joseph.

"*You?*" She hadn't meant that to sound the way it did.

But he nodded proudly and averted his eyes. "*I* gave that to her. Well, I gave it to her mama to give to her. Delilah was only six, seven months old at the time. Never thought she'd like that silly thing so much. I didn't see it for years, and then, all of a sudden, there was Delilah on the steps, cradling that doll like it was real."

"Well, no wonder she's so sweet on you!"

"Oh, no, no, I'm sure she doesn't know it was from me. And don't *you* go telling her, Miss Fairhart." Joseph glanced up and brandished one of those index fingers.

Constance smiled and shook her head, but he'd already looked away again.

"She eventually lost interest in that doll," he said. "Oh, and the, uh — " He tapped his forehead a few times. "What were those things she used to play with?"

"Things?"

He waggled his hand. "Those little crisscross things. With the little red ball."

"Jacks?"

"Yes, that's it, jacks."

Joseph was quiet as he remembered watching from his office window. Little Delilah sitting hurdle-style on the sidewalk, tossing, swiping and catching as she carried on an intense conversation with her doll and their invisible friends, oblivious to the occasional passerby who stepped on them. So often Joseph had wanted to go out there, to sit on the sidewalk and join her. Or just listen to *her* pretend.

He now enjoyed that same scene from the waiting room bench. "She was a wonderful child. Never tried to be older than her years, you know. She didn't have to."

He licked his lips, then scraped them with his teeth, as the braided rug materialized. Then he looked up at a tiny mole below the left corner of smiling pink lips. "I remember the day I came back from the clinic and saw her with an orange-headed boy. They were sitting at opposite ends of the step, pressed against the rails like they couldn't get far enough apart." Joseph pushed a puff of air out his nose. "I was sure those two would get married someday."

"Actually, she is getting married," said Constance.

I. Joseph Kellerman

Joseph's eyebrows shot up. "Is that right! Huh. M-y-y gosh, imagine that. To that same boy?"

Constance repressed a laugh. "No, I don't think so. His dreadlocks are black."

"His what?"

"His hair."

"Ah. Well, I must congratulate her. You know, I haven't spoken to Delilah in ... well, not since, um." Joseph looked puzzled.

"My last vacation," Constance reminded him.

"Right," he said soberly, then slapped his leg. "Well, that's wonderful, our Delilah's getting married. Have you met the young man? Is he a good fellow, I hope?"

"He seems lovely. And head over heels for her."

"Well, good, good, she deserves it. And he best take excellent care of her, or *I'll* have something to say about it."

Joseph slid his feet back and bent his legs. He bobbed his knees in and out a few times, then got up and returned to the window. Walked right up to it this time and said, "So I guess we might see some children out there again in not too many years."

What Joseph didn't see was the mixture of sympathy and sadness on Constance's face when she said, "Perhaps." She didn't want to tell him Delilah and her fiancé would be moving to Cincinnati in the spring.

The next words out of Joseph's mouth, as he turned around and sat against the windowsill, dealt Constance a very pleasant blow. "How's your little niece, by the way?"

"My —? You mean, Lori?"

"Yes. I think. The one who sings *Edelweiss?*"

"Yes, Lori! My, you have an incredible memory, Joseph."

Lori hadn't been to 4991 Hopewell Street in more than twenty years.

Joseph shrugged. "For some things, maybe."

"Oh, well, she's doing wonderfully," said Constance. "But now she's singing that to her little boy."

"No, she isn't old enough to have a son. *Is* she?"

"Joseph, she's old enough to have *three* kids. The twins are in first grade, Joey's two and a half."

"Joey?"

Constance smiled and nodded. Lori's husband's middle name was Joseph.

"Oh my, where's the time gone, Constance? Seems like it was ... eons ago that you brought her here. She took your hairbrush out of your purse and pretended it was a microphone. Remember that?"

"Sure do. You clapped and requested an encore. And was she ever smitten with you!"

"Really?"

"Oh, yes. She used to ask me, 'Aunt Contents'—that's how she used to say it—'Aunt Contents, when can we go see the man with big ears?'" Constance slapped her hands over her mouth, but the corners of her smile snuck out.

Joseph tugged on his earlobe as his smile melted away. "You only brought her that once," he said. "I thought maybe I scared her."

"Joseph, why would you think such a thing!"

"I don't know, I'm not very good with kids."

"Now, that isn't true at all." Constance had always noticed how much more at ease Joseph seemed to be with children the few times there had been any around. They had taken to him so quickly. And he didn't even have to try. She said, "I've seen you, Joseph. You're a natural. You would have been an excellent — "

Oh my God, thought Constance. What did I almost *say*?

Joseph nodded as he heard himself finish her sentence in his head. His expression dampened further.

He now looked much like he had for years.

"But I thought I told you," she said, trying desperately to make amends. "My brother, Lori's dad, he got a better job in Seattle, and the family moved out there. That's the *only* reason she didn't come back."

And that was true, although Constance had never mentioned it to Joseph. She hadn't thought he cared.

Now he perked back up a little. He didn't smile but said, "You used to look after the children while I was with a client. With the parent, I mean. I'd hear all that giggling going on out here. But I don't know who was louder, you or the kids."

Constance performed a guilty as charged look, which came off more like a naughty adolescent who thought it was funny. "Sorry," she said.

"And you should be. Such a distraction." The imp shook his head with a most disapproving frown. He wasn't sure, but he thought he felt his eyes twinkle ever so slightly.

They did, and Constance noticed.

"Well," she said, "I think these walls used to be thinner." Then there was a stretch of ticking and the pat of little feet, as she watched Joseph watch Rifka waddle out of the kitchen and across the room to the corner hutch, which wasn't quite closed. The cat inserted a paw and disappeared, and Constance said, "But thank you for asking about Lori."

More ticking and some refrigerator humming, as two people tried as hard as they could to come up with more words.

Finally, Joseph pushed himself off the sill and took the three steps to his office door. He put his hand on the knob, and that's when something came to him. He said, "I *do* care, you know."

Doctor and assistant had been together for so long, he could sometimes slowly read her mind. But Constance didn't have a chance to reply before Joseph had closed the door behind him.

Not that she had any idea what she might have said.

Chapter 33

Joseph's head and neck were the only parts of him in the front office when he asked, "Miss Fairhart, do you have a moment?"

"Absolutely, Dr. I. Joseph Kellerman, sir." Constance straightened the papers she had been reading, tapping them on her desk. She placed them back in Orla Heffel's file, set the manila folder in front of her, and aligned it just so. She folded her hands and looked up, as the rest of her boss emerged from his office. "What may I do for you?"

Once again, this was the time he was supposed to be sitting and maybe sleeping in the yellow chair. Constance was very glad about whatever was happening to Joseph, because he seemed more relaxed and even more outgoing these days. A bit like the man she used to know a long time ago. But better.

"Well, I was wondering," he said.

Constance maintained her eager expression while Joseph raised his chin, grabbed the tie and the slip knot at his throat, and shook. He yanked on each of his cuffs, added "In your opinion," then closed his mouth again.

Constance leaned forward, as if that might help extract the rest of his sentence, but Joseph still stood there, silent. Sometimes it was like pulling teeth. She said, "In my opinion."

And he clasped his hands and shook the question out. "What should someone wear to a concert?"

"A concert," she echoed.

"Yes, mm-hmm. A musical ... concert."

Constance was afraid to get excited. She forced herself to

I. Joseph Kellerman

sound casual. "That depends what kind of concert we're talking about." Then she decided not to make this any harder on him than it clearly already was. She said, "But if it were a holiday show at the Symphony perchance? Well, I'm sure some people dress up. I'd expect most would."

Maggie had also asked Constance if she and her "man" would like to come to the New Year's Eve performance. Not that Constance had told Dr. Kellerman. The occasion was part of her other life. And though Maggie was a client, her invitation to an event that would take place outside the office nullified the connection. Maggie had later told Constance she'd asked the doctor if he'd like to buy a ticket, too, but that he hadn't said yes or no.

Constance had then explained to Maggie that Dr. Kellerman was not a night person, that he didn't go out much, so she shouldn't be surprised if he didn't attend. Constance had known without a doubt that he wouldn't go of his own accord. And she certainly wasn't going to pressure him. But it was Constance herself who was now amazed and delighted to learn she might have been wrong.

With one hand on a hip and the other stroking his shaven chin, Joseph paced and frowned, as if pondering a difficult theory. "So a suit then. Or maybe a tuxedo."

Constance smiled at the waltzing couple. "I'd go for the tux," she said, then got a hold of herself and told the walking man, "But a suit would be fine. Or a sports jacket even, although I don't think there's a dress code." Constance pondered that statement for a moment, then tilted her head the other way. "But, then again, I haven't actually been to a concert like this before. I haven't been to any show, period, in ages."

"A sports jacket," said Joseph, nodding as he frowned and stroked harder.

Constance recalled the young Dr. Kellerman. "I thought you looked great with that goatee," she said. "Ever considered growing one again?"

All movement stopped as he looked at her. "Really? Do you think I should?"

"Definitely. A man with a goatee. Especially a man with a goatee *wearing a tux: very* sophisticated."

Joseph smiled, too. Then he spent the next ten minutes upstairs.

***

"Excuse me, Dr. Kellerman?"

"Come in, come in." He gestured towards the yellow chair with his left hand. In his right there was a pen. There was an open manila folder on his lap.

Constance said, "I just wanted to let you know," then lost her train of thought when she realized the brightness of the room. The dusty blinds on his office window were, for the first time in more years than she could figure at that instant, raised. They were as high as they could go, and Bonsai and Wadofur were perched sidelong on the sill. "Uh, that your four o'clock, Mr. Ladd, called. He's working late tonight, so he asked if he might reschedule for next Wednesday. But all of your regular slots are full, actually, so I was thinking later one evening or maybe — "

"What about noon? Could he make it then?"

"Noon?" said Constance. "Oh. Well, I could ask."

Dr. Kellerman usually replied with "Whatever you think is best."

"Sounds great," he said. "Oh, and Miss Fairhart?"

"Yes?"

"I do have another question, if you don't mind."

"Of course. I mean, no." She sat down, nearly on top of Rifka, who hissed and oozed onto the floor. Constance said, "Oo! Ask away."

"Well, in your opinion, where — "

"In my opinion," Joseph's assistant interrupted, leaning forward.

I. Joseph Kellerman

"Yes, um, where might one take a lady to dinner before such a concert? Being formally dressed."

Although hours had passed since he had first broached the subject with Constance, Joseph hadn't stopped thinking about it since Maggie's invitation had been presented to him a week ago.

And Constance hadn't stopped thinking about it since Joseph had mentioned the concert this morning. So this was to her also a natural continuation of their earlier conversation. At the same time, she was still digesting the idea that, for the first time in almost five years, he was even *talking* about leaving the building. She was positive she understood why he was being indirect; he wasn't sure if he could go through with it. She would try her best not to pull too hard.

Joseph waited while Constance smoothed her wrinkle-free skirt from waist to knees.

She sat back and crossed her legs. "Well," she said, "that depends on what kind of food *this* lady prefers. Seafood perhaps?" She gave him a knowing glance. Seafood was her favorite. Joseph knew that.

What Joseph did not know was that Constance had been invited to the concert.

Imagine, she now thought, two special friends spending an evening together after all these years! He was understandably shy about it, but they had been together for so long, they could read each other's minds like newspaper headlines. She felt giddy.

"Seafood," he repeated. "No. No, I think she's allergic to fish. Or maybe it's just shellfish. I think she mentioned that. Actually, I believe she prefers Chinese, uh ... you know." Snapping fingers, hand waggling, then he pointed at his silent assistant and said, "Cuisine."

What was he talking about? Constance had told him quite a few times in the past that she didn't like Chinese food, that the monosodium glutamate gave her headaches. And they had eaten fish-n-chips and fried shrimp and even sometimes clams on numerous evenings while discussing clients and professional topics. They'd kept the delivery boy from Atlantic Seafood Emporium quite busy and probably funded a year's worth of his college education with all those generous tips. Yes, it had been a very long time, but certainly Joseph hadn't completely forgotten. He remembered so many *other* details. Constance was confused, not to mention concerned.

There he sat, clean-shaven and clean-cut in a long-sleeved shirt, an awful tie and navy chinos. The light from the uncovered window illuminated the dust, the chairs, the desk, the stacks and all the other stuff, and those beautiful eyes of his, now with a different expression than any Constance remembered ever having seen on the face of this man she'd cared for for over twenty-three years. And talking as though going to dinner and a show with *some woman* would be just another evening on the town as usual? She should have been overjoyed for him. She wanted to be. But she wasn't.

Proceed with caution warned the voice inside Constance. Something isn't right.

She'd stood up and taken two measured steps towards the door before turning back halfway and responding to Joseph's original question. "I'll have to give it some thought," she told him. "I don't eat out all that often."

"That'll be fine. Thank you very much, Miss Fairhart."

She nodded while glaring at a little dark hole in the wall. Then she went back to her desk to sit and think about all of this.

***

"God forbid anyone ever ask how *Lucille* is doing," said the woman of that name, with a scowl on her somewhat less angular face. She pounded her chest as she added, "How *I'm* feeling for a change."

Dr. Kellerman winced, but Lucille felt only what was in her

heart. And a sharp poke from her cross.

Joseph was watching the woman who for years had sat in that yellow chair, weeping with deep despair and frustration. On Fridays between five and six o'clock, she'd allowed those sequestered feelings to flow freely in his presence. Over the past few months, the tears had given way to new emotions. Lucille McBride was far from a Bernice "Bernie" Babbish, but she was angry now and there was hope.

"And all those years of what should have been my childhood, spent taking care of my mother's other children *and* my mother and father. If my mother wasn't out ... screwing around with other men, she was getting drunk. And Father? Oh, well, he'd come home, inhale the dinner I had prepared for him, then saw logs in front of the television. Not even a word of thanks. *Ever.* 'He works very hard for this family,' my mother would always say. She'd yell those words if I dared ask if I might go to a friend's house or, heaven forbid, spend some time alone for a change. How could I be so selfish? That's what she'd always ask *me.*"

Lucille had shredded another piece of Kleenex, most of which was now confetti on her lap.

Dr. Kellerman was holding his chin, one finger in front of his mouth, his elbow propped in his other hand. He was thinking about what Lucille was telling him. A childhood lost was something he could relate to. And he was allowing himself to do so.

"I was the one who was always fine," Lucille continued. "Gotta look fine, act fine, *be* fine. Lucille's just f-i-i-ine."

Joseph could relate to that as well.

"But did anyone even ask?" she said. "Did anyone ever give any thought to how *my* day had been?"

Dr. Kellerman said, "Well —"

But Lucille nearly shouted, "Of course not! And now I take care of five children of my own and a husband! Well, what ... about ... Lucille? It's damn well time I take care of *me.*" She dabbed at her nostrils with the last bit of tissue in her hand.

What happened next brought a genuine smile to Lucille McBride's face, as well as that of the woman who was watching through the hole in the wall. Lucille reached out and shook Joseph Kellerman's extended hand.

* * *

"Sometimes I wonder if maybe they've got it right," said Lucille. "Thinking about themselves first all the time, putting their needs and their desires before anyone else's." She wasn't feeling angry at the moment and looked at Dr. Kellerman with the question as much in her eyes as in her words. This time she waited for his reply.

"Sounds to me," he said, "like you've described people — parents and a husband — who put themselves first, middle *and* last. Forget about anyone else." Joseph wasn't feeling like a doctor at all. This was more like talking with a friend.

His friend, Lucille, said, "But they must be doing *something* right, don't you think? They aren't the ones sitting in this office."

"Maybe they should," said Joseph, smiling with one side of his mouth. "Well, someone's office."

Lucille flapped her hand at him. "I think yours is just fine, Dr. Kellerman. Oh, I hate that word. No, you and Constance are the *best.*"

Joseph didn't know how to reply to that, so he changed course a bit. "Maybe it's a happy medium we need to find. Somewhere between they, he or she, and me, me, me."

"Hmm," said Lucille.

Joseph closed her file. "We all need to feel safe," he continued. "We all need to be taken care of sometimes. Sometimes we need a lot." He nodded and added, "And that's okay."

For the first time in four years, two months and one week, a dry-eyed Lucille McBride watched and listened to the man who had so patiently sat in this room with her, letting her vent her feelings all those Friday afternoons, without saying much of anything.

He rubbed his left hand with his right as he said, "Perhaps if one allows himself to be ... *vulnerable* and ask for what one *needs* ... and *wants*, then he —" Joseph gave up the effort with a heavy sigh, stopped rubbing and sat there, doing and staring at nothing.

"Dr. Kellerman? Are you all right?"

Joseph was silent for a moment more, then replied as he looked over to the window and the street beyond. "Mm-hmm," he said.

I will be.

Chapter 34

Joseph followed Lucille to the door. "Miss Fairhart, may I see you for another moment?" he asked, then "Hello, Miss Carlisle," he said in a deep, gentle tone that was meant to convey something like "You're more than a client."

Constance walked towards the doorway and the man standing in it, as Maggie politely returned the doctor's smile and gave her attention back to Lucille, who had stopped to chat on her way to the hall.

Constance said, "Certainly, Dr. Kellerman," and brushed past into his office. He closed the door and followed his assistant, wringing his hands. Without hesitation, she sat in the doctor's chair, while Joseph balanced on the edge of the yellow one.

"I'd like to ask for a favor," he said. "If you wouldn't mind, I would be grateful."

Mind? I'm thrilled! She told him, "Anything, Joseph. What do you need? Or want."

"Well." He cleared his throat and snuffled. "I, uh, I tried on an old suit of mine earlier. Still fits, actually." He sucked in his stomach.

"*Does* it?" said Constance. "That's great!"

"Yes," he agreed without breathing, and they nodded for a bit. Then Joseph let his belly out. "So, here!" he said as his hand ejected from his pant pocket, holding a prescription. "I took down the measurements." He leaned over and pointed at the information, then looked up at her and waited.

Constance straightened and pinched the edge of the paper.

I. Joseph Kellerman

"Oka-a-ay. And?"

"Yes, and so I was wondering, do you think you might rent a tuxedo?"

"Me?" she said.

Joseph clarified, "For me, I mean," then bit his lip. He and Constance were both still holding the paper, their fingertips touching.

"Oh, absolutely! Not a problem at all," she told him, and Joseph let go. "Unless ... or, that is, I could go with you, and you could try some on."

He jiggled his head. "Oh no, no, your selection will be fine."

"Well, all right then," said Constance, beaming with pride. He was doing so well! "I'll take care of this first thing tomorrow."

A smile appeared on Joseph's face too, but his was from embarrassment.

They stood and walked to the door, he nearly stepping on her heels. Constance didn't see him almost touch the small of her back as he reached around her. She was looking at his measurements, but thinking other happy thoughts.

There was no reason for her to be worried, after all. Or jealous. Joseph had been alone long enough. He was talking only about dinner and a show, but who knows? If this woman, whoever she was, was the reason he was going out in the first place, she must be someone very special.

Yes, Constance decided. I *am* happy for him.

"Oh, and Miss Fairhart?"

"Yes, Joseph?" She turned and they were practically nose to chest.

He had opened the door a crack, but now closed it again. "One last thing," he said, flinching. "Would you mind terribly ... or could you possibly find out for me what kind of food Maggie prefers?"

What! The voice in Constance's head screamed, but her jaw locked. She had no idea how to respond. She barely nodded, while slowly leaving the room. Her mind was racing.

Oh my, this was not good. No, this was much worse than bad. All the time she had spent watching through that little hole in the wall on Fridays between six and seven for the past five months, and she'd neither seen nor heard anything that indicated something like *this*. How had she missed it? Joseph was about to ask Maggie Carlisle for a *date*? *What was he thinking!*

What he was thinking was a breath of fresh air, some uplifting, uninhibited conversation and a lot of being open and free. Just like Maggie.

"See you in a bit," said Joseph Kellerman's inspiration, touching Constance's arm as she walked past into the back office.

When Constance turned around, she caught a fleeting glimpse of Joseph just before he closed the door. He was smiling, but not at her. A great day had suddenly turned into a terrible one.

At that moment, Constance could not have cared less about that nagging attorney Dunst and all of his aggravating calls about Linda Payne, and what that whole situation might cost Joseph. If she didn't stop *this* from happening, if she didn't protect Joseph from himself this time perhaps more than any other, she feared the very worst. The same thing she'd had good reason to fear numerous times during all those years she had somehow managed to prevent him from bleeding to death.

Constance could only imagine how Joseph would feel when Maggie would react to his inappropriate advances. She sensed that, in this case, he was thinking more along the lines of courtship and romance than blatant sex — a sudden hunch — but that was neither here nor there. Constance knew the response would not be pleasant. Maggie had trusted him with her most private feelings and fantasies. And she'd spoken much more about Danny than anyone or anything else. Maggie would be shocked and probably disgusted when Dr. Kellerman made his revealing move.

Poor Joseph. To at long last reach out to someone and be turned down flat, to put it mildly. Then how would he feel?

Embarrassed, ashamed. Guilty. Constance was certain the blinds would once again prevent the sunlight from entering his office. And he would surely retreat to the corner behind that oversized desk. But that was nothing compared to what Constance feared most. How much could one man endure before he'd lose himself?

Just like Linda Payne.

Just like Mom.

***

Constance was sick with nerves as she pressed the side of her face to the wall. She was sure she knew what he was thinking as Maggie described her first and very passionate kiss with Danny. The smile in Joseph's eyes, eyes that stared at the scene Maggie was painting with her words, now revealed its meaning to Constance. She knew he wasn't imagining Maggie with Danny.

Breathing only when necessary, Constance continued to watch. She could see enough of Joseph's expression to know she had better think of something, *do* something, soon. She jumped when Wadofur rubbed against the back of her leg.

***

Constance knocked like a woodpecker as she opened the door. "Dr. Kellerman!" The urgency was in her voice as well.

He had put his hands on the arms of his chair, his elbows raised. He'd leaned toward Maggie, who had just stopped mid-sentence on the word "love."

"Miss Fairhart!"

Joseph jumped to his feet. Constance *never* interrupted a session. And now, of all times, she had barged right in! He'd been caught in the most wonderful daydream.

Not to mention in the midst of changing positions. His left leg had fallen asleep.

"I'm so sorry," said Constance, "but I thought you'd want to know right away that I heard a cat, and, I don't know, it sounded more like a scream, and it came from upstairs, so I thought — " She'd run out of breath and things to say at the same time. Constance felt guiltier than ever, but this was necessary.

The question was, would it be *enough*?

Joseph ran his eyes around the room. Bonsai was on the window sill, Rifka on the green velour pillow. With his hand an inch or so off Maggie's shoulder, he said, "Please excuse me, Miss Carlisle, I'll be right back. Don't go." With that, he rushed into the front office and up the stairs, two and three at a time.

Constance heard the door open and close, then began her appeal. "Maggie, dear, *please*."

"Hey, what's wrong? You don't *look* so good?"

Constance grabbed the lumpy canvas bag and Maggie's closest hand, then back-stepped towards the open door, pulling the young woman out of the yellow chair. "It's all right, dear, everything's going to be fine. You've done so well, and it's been such a pleasure getting to know you."

Maggie didn't know what she was supposed to be doing. She just kept walking with the very uptight woman who had turned and was now holding her arm, still babbling.

"You're such a strong and vivacious person, and you've got your whole wonderful life ahead and so much to look forward to. And Danny, well, he sounds lovely. I'm sure you're going to be fine."

Maggie found herself standing by the door to the hall. She said, "But — "

And Constance blurted out, "Maggie, I'm begging you, please, let this be the end of it. You don't need this anymore, you've got so many people who care about you."

"Yes, but — "

"But here!" said Constance as she hurried to her desk. She grabbed a pen and piece of paper. "Here's my home number. If you ever want to talk or just need another friend. Anything at all.

Or you can phone me here, but please."

Constance glanced up at the door to Joseph's apartment. She could hear him clumping around, looking for Wadofur. He would find his beloved cat at any moment, safe and sound in the bedroom closet amongst the clothing and shoes and whatever else was in there.

This was taking far too long.

Maggie said, "I don't — "

And, scribbling again, Constance told her, "Please don't be angry. Not with Joseph. It's *my* fault, I should have seen this coming and done something a long time ago."

Long before you ever came here, thought Constance as she threw the pen onto her desk and turned back.

"I don't understand," said Maggie. "Is there something I can do to help you? I'll do anything. I mean, you've done so much for — "

This time, Constance cut her off without speaking. She closed her eyes and shook her head as she put her hand on Maggie's arm. "It's far too much to explain right now. I will, though. Soon, but not here. Joseph is too emotional. He's ... confused."

As was Maggie. She cocked her head and frowned.

"He's been through so much," Constance explained. "You can't even imagine. I've tried for years to protect him from any more pain. But, this time, though, I was so afraid of what might happen."

"Wow," said Maggie.

And Constance said, "I'm not a professional, and I don't know what else to do. But please don't say anything to Joseph. If you see him, just, I don't know, thank him. Lie if you have to."

"Lie?"

"Oh, Maggie, you're such a kindhearted and caring, *sensitive* woman. So please." Constance let go of the arm to take the paper from her other hand, in order to open the door. She turned the knob, pulled and said, "For his sake?"

Staring at the phone number that had just been shoved in her face, Maggie thought about all of this for another few seconds. She didn't know any of the details, but, she decided, her friend's confusing words were enough. So she pinched the paper, which was instantly released, and stepped into the doorway.

"Okay," she told Constance, "but I still expect to see you at the show. *Both of you.*" Maggie smiled, then closed the door behind her.

But she paused by the sconce.

Oops. In her tizzy, Constance had written her phone number on the back of a prescription. Man, Dr. Kellerman's handwriting was awful. Looked more like "44L36WX36L151/2" than ... well, whatever medication. Should I give this back, Maggie wondered.

Constance was listening intently. What was Maggie waiting for? Leave already! Then she heard the muffled footsteps *she'd* been waiting for. A door opened and clunked, something squeaked, and Constance released a heavy and much-needed sigh. As she began to take a normal breath, however, her body once again went stiff. She raised her heels and turned to look up to the landing. Straight into the eyes of the man she had tried much too hard to protect for over twenty-three years.

Time seemed to come to screechless halt. No ticking, no humming, no droning or clanking. Not the pat of feline feet or passing cars. As though the rest of the world and all walls and doors had disappeared, and both of them noticed.

Constance opened her mouth, but Joseph ended their silence. "She isn't coming back," he said. His voice was calm, subdued, almost monotone.

Constance felt her head move, right to left to right to left, as if her body were no longer under her control. All she could see were those haunting eyes, staring into her. She felt exposed. "I'm sorry," she said, "but ... I don't know what to say."

That was something Constance Fairhart had never before

said to Joseph Kellerman.

"Just say, 'You're welcome,'" he told her, then turned around and disappeared.

Chapter 35

"How are you?" she asked.

Joseph lifted his head from the seatback, but didn't open his eyes. He'd been sitting between a mound of books and a pile of throws, trying to figure out what to do next. The matches had been counted and arranged, one grouchy calico cuddled against her will, the day's junk mail read and organized. But the mind had a will of its own and had wandered off against Joseph's, and that's when he heard the voice. This time, the voice didn't sound like his. It was soft, concerned and kind. Still, he resisted. He wasn't sure if he could bear to see her right now. He felt too ashamed.

But again, "How are you?"

"No," Joseph told himself. "This is *not* the time." He barely raised his eyelids, but barely was enough.

"It's all right," said the woman standing on the opposite side of the coffee table. "This doesn't have to wait until Monday at noon."

The man on the couch was incredulous. He closed his eyes as tightly as he could and shook his heavy head. "*Es ist alles nicht echt,*" he insisted, then grit his teeth and looked again. The vision remained, even clearer than before. "*Mama?*"

There was no reply from the statuesque woman with the aquiline nose and a mole on her right cheek. She just looked at him with those blue eyes. Yes, the eyes and the hair, they were indeed very similar. But the rest? Well, quite different, in fact.

For the first time in a little over twenty-three and a half years, Joseph was seeing Anna Kellermann's face. And for twenty-two years before he met Constance Fairhart, he'd seen no face at all.

Now Joseph conceded with a nod. He did want to tell her something. So she settled on the floor and waited through two false starts. The third time he opened his mouth and took a breath, he said, "Thank you for being with me when I needed you. I couldn't have made it otherwise. Even though —" Joseph didn't want to admit it, but he knew he had to. He rested his head back again and surrendered. "Even though I know you weren't really there. Not after the train to ... that place."

"Josef."

"Yes, okay, okay, I'll say it! I'll say it." He picked up a book, mumbled, "Seventy-two," opened it to page ninety-eight, then set the book down on the pile of throws. He inhaled, blew out the air and said, "You were gone before that. After Rosa didn't come back, you got weaker by the day. And the work was too much. You tried not to show it, but I knew."

Joseph replayed this confession several times through. His words didn't match the evidence engraved in his head. The new soundtrack didn't go with the familiar scene, but he knew it was the scene that still was wrong. Two years and now one missing face. So he concentrated instead on the truth. He couldn't visualize it, but he knew what had happened.

He said, "One day, when I came back from the factory, you weren't there. So I asked, 'Where's Mama?' and Papa said, 'She went to a place where she can laugh and dance, like she used to.'" Joseph felt pressure building beneath his eyes. He blinked hard. "And I didn't ask anything more. I could think of you the way you were before, how your hair used to sparkle and your beautiful smile. That's how I needed to see you, even though I knew. And I've known all along, I suppose. It's just that I became so used to imagining you with me that it seemed like you really *were*."

Joseph felt the bricks begin to fall from his shoulders as he was speaking. From a slump, he bounced into a resolved hunch at the edge of his seat, elbows on his parted knees and hands in motion as he continued intently. "There was that nice woman. Layla. No, Lila! Lila. I don't remember what she looked like, but she and her husband and their daughter, Ellie, they lived in that room with us, for what? A year? Yes, and then Lila lost her husband. And then our Rosa was gone. Then you."

Joseph's hands went limp, as his tears fought their way to the surface. He wiped them away and said, "Lila was very good to me, very kind. Ellie also. And sometimes I pretended they were ... well, not who they really were. Not that I ... I mean, that day, when I turned ten, I know that wasn't you and Rosa."

"No," Anna agreed. "It wasn't."

"No, but the stories and all that, now *that* was real. We'd always done that. Some things I remember so vividly, it's like I'm there, while here is somewhere else. But it's true. Sometimes, or much of the time, when I remember, I don't know what happened when. Or it seems like things that happened years before something else I remember are connected, one after the other. I don't know anymore how it all went. Now, I do know there was another train before that one, when we had to leave our house. And we were crammed in, and we couldn't sit. I was so afraid, but you said, 'It's all right, Josef, I'm here.' And you sang to me and made me feel safe."

When Joseph stopped talking, Anna Kellerman said, "But?"

"But that day, on my tenth birthday, it was just me and Papa. And Lila and Ellie were there, and I was pretending it was how it used to be. That the four of us were still together. Oh, but no one could *ever* take your place. Or Rosa's. I just wanted so desperately to believe you were there. God, how I missed you."

"I was there, Josef. I always have been, because I'm part of *you*. As Papa and Rosa are."

This time, the man who once had been the youngest Kellermann allowed the tears to overflow onto his cheeks. "Yes," he whispered. "Good. Because I still might need you."

"Yes," said Anna, "but *she's* here for you, too. In the way you need most. All you have to do is let her in. Talk to her, Josef. You have to."

"But it's difficult, Mama. I feel so many things."

"I know, sweetheart. I know. But I know you can do it, because I know what you're made of. *And who.* You remember that."

Joseph nodded. "Always," he promised, staring, photographing with his eyes. He was so afraid to lose her again.

"It's okay," Anna told her son when he decided it was. "Go on, now. Talk to *her.*"

Joseph studied his mother's exquisite face for another long moment, then lowered himself to the floor, sliding his back down the front of the couch. In slow, precise movements, he cleared the coffee table, stacking the books, boxes of incense and matches to his right. To his left, he stacked the three manila folders in chronological order, with Payne on top. Then he looked at the ceiling. "This isn't how it's supposed to be," he began.

"With you and me?"

Joseph dropped his eyes. The image had changed. He said, "*Of course not, Maggie,*" and she vanished.

Joseph looked around the room. "I mean this. Any of it. My life is not how it's supposed to be."

"Tell me how it *is* supposed to be."

Joseph heard the very familiar voice but couldn't bring himself to see her again. Not just yet. But he was glad she was there.

"I want to know," she said. And, of course, she meant it.

Sleet began pelting the dark windows, as Joseph thought about what he wanted to say. Intermittent plinks rapidly multiplied into a full-blown assault on the glass, creating quite a din. He raised his voice when he told the woman on the other side of the coffee table, "I'm the son of two incredible human beings. They were so full of life, it was contagious. People were drawn to them both. I remember there were always visitors. They'd come to talk with Mama or hear Papa's stories or listen to him just … prattle on about anything. Oh, they'd l-a-a-augh. No matter how bad things got, my parents had faith and hope. And Rosa, what a fighter she was. But *me?*" Joseph grabbed his shirt with both hands, as if he were about to pick himself up and throw himself against a wall. "I'm their blood, but look what I've done! I've ruined everything! And I've wasted so much *time.*"

Now he looked at her. He wanted her to agree, to say, "I know, Joseph. I know." But she didn't. She closed and opened her eyes, and said nothing. She was not being critical, just listening.

The sleet had already subsided.

Joseph let go of his shirt. "I should be home right now."

Then he saw it and smiled a little. Such a cozy room.

"There's a Christmas tree over there," he said, pointing. Almost nine years had passed, but still he remembered.

Joseph's mind moved him from cold, wet shadows, through the glowing window to the right of the front door, into the house.

I walk to the fireplace and set the menorah on the mantle, amongst our family pictures, then turn to look around the room. It's so much nicer from inside. So much warmer.

Joseph frowned as his own living room came back into focus. He closed his eyes. He saw the other room again and said, "My little girl would have hair like her mother's. She and Mama would be sitting together in the rocking chair, and my son — " Joseph pushed himself up onto the couch and put his arm around his child. "My son would be on my knee, and I'd be telling a story. Or by now I guess you'd think you were too old to be sitting on your papa's knee, wouldn't you? But that's all right, both you kids could be bigger than I am and you could still sit on my knees and listen to stories. Can you just see it, Mama?"

Joseph opened his eyes and felt silly. He continued to no one but himself.

"Mama would be sitting there, smiling at me and laughing. *My* wife. I should have been with her for more than twenty years now.

I. Joseph Kellerman

More than *twenty years*."

Suddenly stressed, Joseph raised one shoulder then the other, stretching his neck, and squeezed and released his hands. He scanned piles, boxes, bags, baskets, racks, rows and furniture, searching for a distraction, unsure if he wanted to go on. This unscheduled session was becoming too demanding, but he couldn't stop or control the emotional roller coaster.

"To share my life with someone," he said. "To lie next to the same woman every night. The one person who would know me better than I know myself, who'd love me despite everything. My faults, my disgusting habits, all the horrible mistakes. She'd put her arms around me and tell me that everything will be okay, that she's right here with me. And I would always do the same for her. And we'd dance together in our room." Joseph looked up and saw the dimly lit window.

He sat back, his arms loose, palms-up on the cushion, and experienced a scene he now knew as well as all the others. He could hear the music, that lovely waltz.

This time, though, the scene continued beyond *Kunstlerleben*. Thanks to the words of Maggie Carlisle, Joseph had developed a most wonderful fantasy. In the beginning, it had been almost a duplicate of hers. But as the weeks since Friday, July second, had passed into almost five months, the fantasy had become entirely his own. He could see and feel and hear and taste it so completely.

I hold your hand in the air, while your other hand rests on my chest. But we're no longer moving. The music has ended, and the only sound is our breath. There's no need for words.

I pull you closer. You're trembling slightly, even after all these years.

I stare past your face, towards the floor, but I'm looking at nothing. Feeling everything. I lower my head, brushing my cheek against yours. I feel you release my hand, then two hands on my chest. My heart is pounding.

I hold your hips. Turning my head, I draw my lips against your cheek as my fingertips trail up your side, your shoulder and neck, down your jaw to your chin. I turn your face towards mine. For an instant our lips are barely touching. I taste your breath.

With one hand on your face, the other under your hair, I kiss you, hard but gentle. And kiss you and kiss you, as you kiss me. I feel your arms around me. And your hands, they're moving on my back. I run my open mouth up your jaw to your ear.

"Joseph," you whisper and raise your chin. I kiss your neck. My lips are wet from yours. You taste so good.

You kiss my ear. You know that's my special spot.

With the last bit of strength in my passion-weakened limbs, I reach down and lift you, carry you to the bed, and set you on your feet beside it.

You kick off your shoes and kneel on the bed. I hold your waist as you unbutton my shirt, push it off my shoulders and down my arms. I unbutton my cuffs and let my shirt fall to the floor. You run your hands down my stomach. I want to tear off my clothes, but this is too special to rush.

Still standing, I rest my knees against the bed and close my eyes. I touch your wrists as you unbutton my pants. I inhale through my nose.

I open my eyes and look into yours, then lean in for another kiss. You smile and lean away. You're teasing, and I smile, too.

You rest your hands on my hips as I unbutton your blouse. I push it off your shoulders. You drop your arms, and the blouse falls to the bed. I reach around you, unzip your skirt, unhook your bra, run my hands up under your hair. And you unzip me.

Seconds later, there's scattered clothing but not a shred of fabric between us. With one arm supporting your waist and the other myself, I lay you down. My body says, "Now!" but my mind says, "Slowly." I run my fingers down your face, over your mouth. You are so beautiful. I'm in awe of you, even after all these years. Especially after all these years. I know every inch of you. Your skin,

I. Joseph Kellerman

the fine lines at the corners of your eyes, your sweet lips. But every time is still like the first time.

I run the back of my hand down your neck, along the edge of your breast, down your side, then slip my hand beneath you. I kiss you again, passionately, as our bodies entwine. I feel that familiar wave of ecstasy as I melt into you.

Joseph felt no pain down his legs or up his back. There was no wood under his hands, only her soft, comfortable body. The experience was almost too much. It was *so real.*

"*That* is how it's supposed to be," he said after several minutes of nothing but breathing. "That's how it's *supposed* to be."

As if a truck came slamming into Joseph Kellerman's second floor apartment, so did the rush of anger hit him head on. He grabbed a book, stood up and hurled it at the wall. "That's what *I* want!" The tears came again in full force, and he barely managed to whisper, "That's what I've always wanted."

Joseph cried harder than he ever had. He cried as hard as he could, until his eyes went dry. Doubled over between books and throws, his throbbing head in his hands, he felt her arms close around him. Now, since the hallway, Joseph knew what those arms were like. But, this time, they didn't feel like Mama's.

There were no flipping digits and time wasn't important, but minutes later he sat up and was ready to continue.

"I don't know why I couldn't do it. I should have been brave like Papa, and kept my chin up. And if I'd had even a touch of Rosa's spunk. Now, though, looking back at myself, I feel ... I feel hideous. I mean, I know I was just a boy." Again a rush of anger, and he shouted, "A little boy! And that's all I wanted to *be*!" Joseph threw another book. "I didn't want to be ten when I was eight, or fourteen when I was ten. I wanted to play, not work. I wanted to cry, not keep my chin up. I wanted to be that boy on his papa's knee, listening to fairy tales just for fun. So why has it taken me all this time to say it? To admit it? All the guilt was the innocence of a child. How could I not have forgiven myself a long time ago?"

His own image appeared on the opposite side of the coffee table. "Do you want an answer?" the other Joseph asked.

"No! No, just ... don't."

The imagined one put up his hand and kept his mouth shut.

"Maybe if I'd forgiven myself for what I thought I did," said the man on the couch, "and maybe if I'd forgiven myself for wanting to live, and I did want to. Even after all of them were gone, *I* wanted to live. Did you hear me?"

The other Joseph nodded.

Then the real one said, "But maybe if I had forgiven myself, maybe I wouldn't have hurt the others. Maybe I wouldn't have done things I don't know if I can ever forgive myself for. I doubt anyone else would."

The image wasn't optimistic, either, but the man was thinking about trying to find out.

Joseph reached down and lifted the three manila folders full of notes back onto the coffee table and laid them out in front of him. Dianne, Kim, Linda. He could send them letters maybe.

Maybe even Miss Von Schlossberg.

Or maybe not.

"But what was done to my family was not my fault," said Joseph. "And it wasn't God's fault. Not for any of it. Oh, I don't know what I believe. But I'm angry, though. I'm *so angry.*" He felt the rage again. "I hate them!" he screamed and clenched his fists. "*Murderers.*"

There was a restful pause as Joseph watched Bonzai and Wadofur race through the room and out the hatch.

"So many hearts were broken," he said once the flap had stopped flapping. Then he raised a finger. "Hearts, but not spirits. Many who survived, they were determined to live again, and they did. Many of them lived well and found happiness, while still remembering. But I wasn't able to do that. I was weak."

I. Joseph Kellerman

Not a sound from the image. He didn't quite agree with that last statement, but Joseph would talk about it another time. But maybe not with himself.

"So many times I've asked myself, 'Joseph, what's wrong with you? Why can't you snap out of it and bust out of this cell you keep yourself in?' *I'm* the one who's been in the witch's tower, you know."

"I see," said the other.

Joseph said, "I tried to save myself, but I couldn't. This hasn't been a life. It's as though I've been watching myself from the window, and the other part of me was out there, going through the motions, feeling nothing. Or trying not to. And the whole time wanting. Wanting *so* much. Wanting what I could have had."

He looked across the coffee table, but all he got was "Mm-hmmm."

"All the answers I used to have for all those people, but I had none for myself. And I suppose I still don't. But you know what?"

"What, Joseph?"

"Do you know how tired I am? I'm so tired of this."

"Tired," said the other.

"Oh, shut up, already. I can't do this any more. I won't. Not in here." Joseph touched his forehead. "I need people," he said. "I need *her*."

"Yes, I know. And I know you know it can't be like we wish. Not with her, anyway."

Both Josephs knew who they were talking about.

"I know that," said the one on the couch. "But that's all right. It has to be." He nodded for a bit, then said, "I can still love her, though, can't I? And maybe I can make things better."

"Yes, Joseph. She *is* right, you know."

Now both of them nodded. Yes, Constance was right. There was always hope.

Chapter 36

Constance had no idea what to expect after Maggie Carlisle left the yellow chair and 4991 Hopewell Street for the last time. And months would pass before she would know how much, if anything, Joseph had heard of that last conversation.

He'd heard most of it.

At the time, however, Constance could only wait, worry, and wonder what each hour and day would bring. But that's what she was used to doing.

What would happen now to the man she had been with for over twenty-three years? She didn't learn all the answers at once, but it didn't take long for her to feel sure she did not have to fear the worst.

But there *were* changes.

Within days, Joseph had a five o'clock shadow that soon turned into a mustache and a salt-and-pepper goatee he often stroked while deep in thought. Which he often was. He traded the loafers that rubbed his ankles for those comfortable old Birkenstocks. Constance told him she was going to repair the buckles and would have no arguments to the contrary. And she strictly forbid him to wear undershirts with nothing over them when seeing clients. Instead, she picked up some colorful t-shirts with various Bostonian attractions pictured on them. Joseph hadn't asked her to, of course, but he'd always loved her taste in just about everything.

Except maybe that Grateful Dead stuff. He decided he'd never really liked that music very much. And he didn't like the name at all.

Constance also strongly suggested he throw away those khaki shorts. That he wouldn't do, Joseph told her, but he did get rid of a few threadbare undershirts. Which was the first time he'd thrown away anything but calendar pages, empty packs of cigarettes, used tissue and cat litter in a very long time.

And about those cigarettes. Constance went through all overstuffed drawers and boxes on the first floor, and filled and emptied the wastebasket three times over with every carton, pack, unused and half-smoked cigarette she could find.

"If you want them," she said with hands on her hips, "you're going to have to go out and get them yourself."

"Hmf!" was the reaction she got.

Joseph made a lot of faces and plenty of childish remarks, including some jabs about her cookies, during the process of being made over by Constance Fairhart. But he enjoyed it immensely.

The alterations in Dr. Kellerman had their influence on his clients as well, but not all responded the same way.

Although the doctor's attentiveness was quite uncomfortable for a while, Bernie Babbish decided to put up with Doc's occasional outbursts and continue his weekly visits to the yellow chair. And it was not uncommon for Bernie to call or show up at odd hours. Sometimes he felt so angry. He'd even recently said so.

Orla Heffel, on the other hand, canceled several consecutive appointments, then stopped calling altogether. She'd said Dr. Kellerman wasn't "so good no more" and didn't appreciate how he'd been interrupting her. She'd also said there was something in the air in that office that was aggravating her asthma and had no choice but to find a new place to hang out once a week, a place with a freakin sofuh, at that. After all, she was addicted to therapy too.

Dr. Kellerman asked Constance if she would call Miss Heffel and refer her to a good clinic. Orla really needed help.

As far as her unspoken thing with Bornio whasisname, Orla offered no explanation to anyone why she stopped showing up at room thirty-four of Bobbie Dee's. But the old man in the room below knew exactly where Orla was on Wednesdays at midnight like clockwork, and now the people in fourteen instead were cleaning bits of plaster and white dust off their rug and television when all the commotion overhead finally ended. Just in time, every time, for the movie on Channel 4.

Lucille McBride continued to arrive at 4991 Hopewell Street, twenty minutes before her scheduled Friday afternoons at five. She looked forward to her visits with Constance and just as much to her hour or so in the yellow chair. She was feeling better about herself these days and more so all the time. And now her husband's appointments were Saturdays at ten a.m. Constance had assured the McBrides that she and the doctor were happy to accommodate Richard's very busy schedule.

A few weeks following his initial appointment, Mr. McBride was joined by his wife when his own private hour or so with the doctor was through. Richard remained in the yellow chair, while Lucille occupied that which had once served a certain cellist when she had given a solo performance inside that same building. The McBrides' relationship benefited immensely from their shared hours, as well as their individual ones in both the front office and the back.

Most of Dr. Kellerman's clients responded well to his increased lucidity, interest and interaction. Many made notable progress.

Dr. Kellerman continued to see people in his office every weekday and some weekends. These days, however, he didn't need a name penned on each and every line of every face-covered calendar page and a corresponding body in the yellow chair from one hour to the next to preoccupy his mind when he didn't want to think about or be alone with himself. He had, at long last, begun to make peace with I. Joseph Kellerman. And he'd also begun to incorporate Joseph, the man, into Dr. Kellerman's sessions with his clients. That was as much of a help to him as it was to them.

Joseph and Constance once again took advantage of some

I. Joseph Kellerman

unscheduled hours and evenings to sit in the back office and have private conversations about professional matters, even a few that had some personal implications. If one were to have peeked through that little hole in the wall during those particular hours, there would have been an equal chance that the profile seen would have been a man's or woman's. Constance had been the one to reinitiate those talks, but Joseph hadn't protested, not even in jest. As time went on, Joseph and Constance were more like friends than employer and employee.

"I used to be decent at all this," said Dr. Kellerman during one of his midday breaks. "Wasn't I?"

Constance nodded. "And you will be again," she assured him. "Even better than before." She would try her best to be certain of that.

Joseph picked up his ham sandwich, but raised it only halfway to his mouth before setting it back on the plate in his lap. "Constance?"

"Hmm?"

"Tell me the truth."

"Of course."

"Do you think it's too late?" he asked, looking his confidante straight in the eyes.

"Not at all," she replied. "There's still plenty of time, Joseph."

Just checking, he thought. That's what I expected you'd say.

Chapter 37

"May I help you?" Constance asked. She didn't know the man in the beige trench coat, who was standing in front of her desk.

"*You're* Miss Fairhart?"

"That's me!" she replied with her usual, friendly smile.

"Well, it's nice to meet you in the flesh." He winked with an unbalanced grin.

"I'm sorry, I don't —"

"Mark Dunst, attorney at law, at your mercy." He offered his hand, which Constance graciously shook.

Uh-oh was what she was thinking.

"Don't worry," he said. "My bark's a little worse than my bite."

"Oh, well ... good."

"Yeah, you know, I was going to call again but figured, ah, what the hell. This isn't *that* far out of my way."

Constance's left eye started twitching. "I wish I could help you," she told the attorney. "I really do, but ... well, to be honest, I can't for the life of me figure out what I did with that file. It's completely *my* fault, though, the doctor had nothing to do with it."

"Yes, well, I have news for the doctor. So where is the mystery man, anyway?"

"I'm afraid he's with a client," said Constance, "but I'd be glad to give him a message."

The attorney thought something was funny. "Connie, can we talk privately for a moment?"

"Of course, Mr. Dunst. There's no one here but me. The doctor's with a—"

"Client," they both said. Then he chuckled again. "Yes, I know. But, please, call me Mark."

Constance sat there, straight-faced.

"Anyhow, this is about Linda Payne. Now, I'm not at liberty to be giving out information, except to say that our good Dr. Kellerman is off the hook."

"Oh!" Constance smiled and stood up. "How? I mean, I never thought he was on the hook in the first place. There would've been no reason to think so."

"Well, I guess I *could* give you the basics," Mark Dunst said. "After all, I've been harassing you for what? Five, six months."

"Seven," she corrected him. "But that's quite all right, you were doing your job."

Although, not very well, she thought. He'd let her get away with all of those feeble excuses. The file may have gotten stuck in someone else's. Things are in such disarray, we're remodeling the office. We've just returned from vacation, so why don't you let me take your number again, and I'll get back to you. Like he enjoyed hearing himself say, "This is attorney Mark Dunst," much more than he cared about the case.

"Yeah, well, you've always been unreasonably cordial," he said. "And you're even sweeter in person."

Constance wasn't flattered. She was very curious, though. "I assure you, Mr. Dunst, anything you tell me will be held in the strictest confidence," she said en route to the other side of her desk and the attorney, drawing him away from the hole in the wall. He had a rather loud voice.

"Well, as it turns out, our Miss Payne had been sampling shrinks all over the city for years. An hour here, two hours there. 'Bout fifteen months ago, she found one who fulfilled her needs, if you know what I mean." He winked again.

Maybe it was a tic, Constance hoped.

"So anyway, that horny bastard's secretary, his daughter, she catches him in the act, right there in his office." Dunst grinned and shook his head. "So she threatens to tattle if Daddy doesn't stop treating his patient. Well, seems as though Daddy took the threat seriously and cut our Miss Payne right off. Sex, meds, the whole thing."

"Oh my," said Constance.

"Yeah, I could tell the first time I called the office; she knew something, all right. Tried to put me off at first, but I turned up the heat and melted her down. The old guilt trip, you know. 'That poor Miss Payne,' I said, 'Nobody and nothin' to turn to but a bottle of pills.' And then, whadduh you know, went fishing for trout and caught me a salmon."

"Excuse me?" said Constance.

"Yeah, I stopped in one day, and, lucky for me, the doctor was out. So I had Daddy's little girl all to myself. Although she's far from little. But, anyhow, we chatted a bit, and then I say, 'Yeah, you know, you've gotta wonder what poor Miss Payne's life would have been like if she'd gotten the treatment she really needed.' And then, man, it was like I couldn't have shut the broad up if I'd wanted to. Starts telling me how Daddy kept Payne company on the couch."

The attorney thought that was funny, too. "Amazing the guy could still manage at his age," he said. "But the daughter, she was probably as desperate as her old man. I mean, she was the one watching, right? Or I should say spying on him. The whole thing's unreal."

The wheels in Constance's head were spinning with increasing speed. She knew she could pry this guy's unscrupulous mouth open even wider. But did she want to? She didn't really have to think about it.

"So, anyhow," he said, "turns out this Von Schlossenberger had quite an impact on Miss Payne. Guess she figured he was in love with her. Even the daughter says she would have been much better off sticking with Dr. Kellerman. Says *he's* as honorable as they come. Her words exactly. So it seems Miss Payne had been thinking about coming back here for some real therapy after the big brush-off. B-u-u-u-t it appears she chose Door Number Two instead."

Constance said, "Do you mean Von *Schlossberg*?"

"Stay with me here, Connie. Have I lost you?"

"No. No, I've got it."

Constance glanced at the clock Joseph had fixed at her third request in a recent twelve-hour period. The cuckoo was about to call six times, and, soon after, the client would leave the back office. These days, the doctor would probably follow. But his assistant didn't want *that* to happen while *this* guy was here. She said, "I do appreciate your stopping by, sir. I'm sorry I couldn't have helped clear this up sooner, but you *are* good at your work."

"Yeah, well." Attorney Mark Dunst sniffed and did a head-cock shrug with a one-eighty-degree eye roll to the ceiling. "Hey, tell the good doctor we'll be in touch. We'll still be wanting a depo."

Constance figured as much. But she would deal with that later. Somehow.

"Thank you for coming by, Mr. Dunst." He opened his mouth, and she said, "*Mark*. And best of luck to you."

Constance had guided him towards the hall as she'd spoken those words. Just after the final one cleared her mouth, the door to the front office was closed behind him.

Another tiny piece of the obscure puzzle of Joseph Kellerman's life had come together for the one trying to solve it. But Constance had long known who'd created that little hole in the wall. That part had been simple. Though she still didn't know even close to all of the details, she did understand the basic plot. And that's all that Constance Fairhart really needed to know.

She watched the stuffed suit in the trench coat strut past the front office window. "Hi, hon'!" she heard him say, then Delilah's voice as she responded with an energetic "Oh, *please*!" And, knowing her, most likely the finger.

Chapter 38

Constance walked slower than usual down the hall as she tried to settle her nerves. She hadn't realized just how excited, nor how tense she was. Not until climbing those same six steps she had climbed countless times over the past twenty-three years, eight months and twenty-four days. But this time was different. She was not about to go into that room to sit behind the desk.

Constance put her hand on the knob, but turned instead to the light and took out her compact. Should I have worn a brighter shade? She examined her rose-colored lips from multiple angles. Constance rarely wore makeup, but she thought it made her look more sophisticated, which is how she wanted to be on this particular evening. Yes, she decided, the occasion called for something more outgoing. Unfortunately, though, a quick search of Mom's old needlepoint purse for the Fire Coral produced only a pen and little spiral notebook, a wallet, two tickets, mints, and the other pair of earrings Constance had agonized over while getting ready. She now made the swap from Mother-of-pearl to gold-plated for the third time in as many hours.

The compact replaced and purse popped closed, Constance tucked a wisp of hair behind her ear, then unbuttoned her coat and adjusted and smoothed her new off-white dress. White had seemed inappropriate somehow.

Oh, but I should have worn the green, Constance thought. Off-white was still too obvious. She began considering the possibility of running home to make the switch. Or maybe hailing a cab.

But before she'd arrived at a final decision on this most recent

I. Joseph Kellerman

dilemma, seven muffled cuckoos came from the next room. No, there was no time left for big changes or stalling any longer. So Constance gathered her wits and opened the door. Once inside, however, she didn't know what to do with herself. If only she could dust a bit, de-fuzz some cushions. Balance the books? Maybe the litter box in the downstairs kitchen needed tending to.

Constance stood there holding her breath, the purse, her stomach. She could feel her heart beating. That all too familiar room seemed completely foreign. So much like the day of Joseph's first and only phone call, but now with a lot more stuff in it. She had felt way back then much the way she did now. Uncertain but hopeful.

Would he change his mind? Lose his nerve? The what-ifs began streaming through her head, but it was not a minute more before Constance found out for sure. Years of waiting and wondering were finally over.

The door at the top of the stairs opened, and a scuffed black shoe and the bottom of a black pant leg emerged onto the landing. Constance stared at Joseph's feet, as he descended the squeaky steps. To her, this was happening in slow motion, and it felt the same to him. In fact, the movement had been virtually undetectable for a very long time.

One might have said, had one perhaps been watching through a well-placed hole in the wall, that the look on Constance's face was like that of a mother admiring her grown son, thinking, my, what a fine man my boy has become. But it wasn't that simple. There was much more showing through the eyes of Constance Fairhart. And not even she could have transferred the feelings into words that would have satisfied her.

Joseph Kellerman's eyes were likewise speaking volumes. His emotions would have been far more difficult to read than hers, had anyone but Constance been privy to the scene. But no one else was there, and she needed no explanation. Neither of them said a thing.

Joseph was full of nervous excitement and a substantial amount of anxiety, yet he'd been the one to broach the subject directly, to ask Constance if she would accompany him to dinner and the show. She'd said yes before he had finished the question. And, lucky for him, she already had two tickets. By the time he'd made up his mind, the concert was sold out.

Looking and even feeling dignified in his rented tux and long black coat, Joseph approached his companion and extended his elbow. Constance wrapped her hand around his arm, and he pressed her hand to his side.

It was time to go.

On their way out of the room, Joseph and Constance both glanced at the painting that hung near the door to the hall. The same painting that had occupied that spot for more than twenty-three years. The same spot where a photograph of Dr. Wilhelm Ludwig Von Schlossberg had once been, until the day his embittered daughter stormed out of 4991 Hopewell Street and Joseph Kellerman's life, definitely for good for each of them.

Constance had often sat at her desk and stared across the room, daydreaming, *The Dance* directly in front of her since April 17, 1970. That had turned out to be a much better location than the first one she had tried that very same morning, on her second full day as Dr. Kellerman's assistant. Joseph had passed between Constance and that painting at least once a day on most days for more than twenty-three years, and he had always taken notice of both.

Now the sound of two sets of footsteps moved down the hallway, one in front of the other. Even empty, that dim, dark-paneled corridor wasn't fit for side by side.

Constance felt a light touch on the small of her back and wildly flapping wings in her stomach, as Joseph reached around her. The brass knob was turned and the heavy door opened after only a slight hesitation.

I. Joseph Kellerman

Seconds later, "Hi, Constance!" would have been heard through the waiting room window had anyone been left inside. Constance waved back at the woman in the turquoise apron and winter coat, who was standing alone on the stoop of the row house next door.

Then, "Hi, Dr. Kellerman!" Delilah's mother had needed a moment more to match his smiling face to the name on the shingle next to a windowless gray door that looked exactly like her own. She'd long ago stopped wondering what the I. stood for.

Constance, on the other hand, had stopped wondering two days ago.

***

On December 29, 1993, Joseph Kellerman and Constance Fairhart, as had once again become usual, sat together in the back office. This time, however, they were not discussing anyone but themselves.

"I have to ask," she said after considering the question for most of a minute. "Why now? I mean, what is it that's changed?"

Joseph was slow to respond. He looked at her with thoughtful eyes as he stroked his goatee. Constance didn't even lean forward in the creaky chair.

"Actually, I've been working on it for many years," he said. "And now I'm ready to start from the beginning and do it right."

Constance remained silent. The way he was squinting, she could tell he had more to say.

"But why now? Well, when I figure that out ... *if* I do, you will most definitely be the next to know. Or if you happen to figure it out first, please do fill me in."

"Perhaps we can figure it out together," Constance suggested. "If you'd like to." She waited again, but he didn't say yes or no, or nod or shake his head. He just looked at her in a peculiar way, as if *he* were waiting for something. They both waited together, then she raised an invisible megaphone and said, "Planet earth to

Joseph."

"Isaac."

There was a palpable pause.

"I'm sorry?"

The man in the yellow chair smiled a little. "The I," he said. "It's Isaac."

Constance didn't try to think of a response.

He said, "But I'd rather you still call me Joseph."

And that was enough for her.

***

Two nights later, Delilah's mother watched her neighbor and his ... well, she watched the doctor and Constance disappear down Hopewell Street and around the corner.

If someone had been left behind in the room where Joseph Kellerman's devoted companion had waited longer than anyone else, it would have taken no time at all to notice a significant change. That is, if that person had seen the room before December 25, 1993. As of Christmas Day, there was a much more cheerful scene on the wall behind Contance Fairhart's desk. "Soulmates," read the engraved plate on the bottom of the painting. The artist: Tobias Edwards, III. In this, his most recent piece, Toby had painted a three-quarter view of the ageless woman's face, her yellow hair in a loose French braid that hung down over the front of her shoulder. She was seated on a backless wooden bench, leaning against the man she loved. But only Toby and Constance could see the painted man's face; he sat with his back to the viewer, his arm around the front of Constance's waist. It was a simple piece, really, but one she would never tire of looking at. The painting brought so many good feelings to her heart.

When Toby Edwards had created *Soulmates,* he'd seen only one man in his mind. And he always would. Constance, however, would always see two. Toby knew that. He had known that for a very long time, ever since he'd confessed his feelings and Constance had reciprocated in kind. She loved them both, Toby and Joseph, and that was understood and accepted by the one she had shared her other life with for nearly twenty-two years. After all, there were different kinds of love, and Constance Fairhart had plenty to give. Which was one of the many reasons they both loved *her*.

Shame on you! The voice inside Constance had scolded her when she'd hung that special new painting behind her desk, this time with Joseph's blessing. Or, rather, at his insistence; although he hadn't watched the exchange. She'd felt a twinge of guilt when the deed was done, but that had nothing whatsoever to do with finally removing that angry-looking, poor excuse for art from the wall. And it had nothing to do with what she had done with Marta Von Schlossberg's painting afterwards, when it joined nearly three hundred unread newspapers bound for the city dump. No, that twinge of guilt was for what she had done next. Constance had positioned the second beautiful painting her other companion of more than twenty years had created just for her, slightly lower than she'd once tried to hang *The Dance* in that same location. So it was no accident that the little hole in the wall remained hidden behind the bottom, right-hand corner of a picture frame.

On the night of New Years Eve, had someone inside 4991 Hopewell Street gone from front office to back, the scene in there would also have looked a bit different to the knowing eye. More normal, one might have said. Except for a sleeping lump named Rifka, the dingy yellow armchair that had served many troubled souls for so many years, now sat empty after another day's service. There was a small, empty space on the oversized desk as well. The space that had most often been occupied by the alarm clock Joseph had approvingly watched Constance drop into the wastebasket on December fourteenth. In the center of that same desk was a stack of paper, the doctor's notes for his new project, tentatively entitled, *The Psychoanalysis of a Fairy Tale: One man's true story,* a cathartic reflection and confession not necessarily intended for publication. The street lamp shining through a gauzy curtain was the only light in the room; the floor lamp in the far corner had been turned off several hours earlier. And little Bonsai and fuzzy Wadofur sat on the sill, waiting for their beloved to come home.

But no one was there to see any of that. For the first time in almost five years, not even Joseph Kellerman was left behind inside 4991 Hopewell Street.

***

Later that same night, just after toasting the new year with a touch of their champagne glasses and then a very light, very quick kiss between two dear friends, *The Dance* really did come to life for both of them. Just like it was supposed to.

And I. Joseph Kellerman and Constance Fairhart lived happier ever after.

About the Author

BORN and raised in Rhode Island, Debra Lauman is a 1990 graduate of the University of New Hampshire, with a degree in Environmental Conservation. An avid backpacker, she often comes up with the ideas for her stories while trekking. Much of **_I. Joseph Kellerman_** was written during a 2,200-mile thru-hike of the Appalachian Trail. Debra is currently working on her next novel while hiking the trails near her home in central Arizona, where she lives with her husband, Steve.

To read Debra's Appalachian Trail journal and learn more about the author, her work and her upcoming adventures, visit her website at www.debralauman.com.